THE HAMLET TRAP

THE HAMLET TRAP

Kate Wilhelm

ST. MARTIN'S PRESS NEW YORK

THE HAMLET TRAP. Copyright © 1987 by Kate Wilhelm. All rights reserved. Printed in the United States of America. No part of this book may be used or reproduced in any manner whatsoever without written permission except in the case of brief quotations embodied in critical articles or reviews. For information, address St. Martin's Press, 175 Fifth Avenue, New York, N.Y. 10010.

Design by John Fontana

Library of Congress Cataloging-in-Publication Data

Wilhelm, Kate.
  The Hamlet trap.

  I. Title.
PS3573.I434H36 1987   813'.54   87–16368
ISBN 0–312–94000–9

First Edition

10 9 8 7 6 5 4 3 2 1

THE HAMLET TRAP

ONE

Roman Cavanaugh closed his eyes and turned his head away when he saw Ginnie sailing down Pioneer Street on her ten-speed. The next time he looked, she had crossed Main safely and was slowing down for Lithia Way. He took the breath he had not dared attempt and walked around the theater to the stage door. He was smiling slightly, but his fear had been real and heart-stopping. Ginnie was his only living relative and he sometimes thought that if anyone loved another person more than he loved Ginnie, he would die of it.

He seldom saw the theater anymore, unless he was showing it off. It was perfect—from the brass hinges and copper spittoons to the cherubs on the ceiling, from the acres of scarlet velvet drapes everywhere to the twenty-foot-diameter cut- and stained-glass chandelier in the lobby. Perfect. He had resisted the temptation to rename it after himself and stuck to the original: Harley's Theater.

"Morning, Ro," William called out from the stage where he was examining one of the traps. William Tessler, in his sixties, Ro's age, had been the technician so long that people said when the builders started excavating they had uncovered him and he'd refused to go away. Ro waved to him and headed toward his office. William had looked at him with candor when Ro said his niece was going to work with Harriet, the set designer. Is she good? William had asked. Ro had assured him that Ginnie was very good and he had nodded. So why're you telling me this? his nod had implied. Ro had asked him how he felt about working under a twenty-four-year-old girl.

"If she's good, what else is there to bother with?"

William was not a designer, but he could put together anything Ginnie said she wanted, from the Eiffel Tower to a swarmy dungeon to a surreal black-and-white dreamscape. It was as if they had been built to work together. Now, with Harriet retired, Ginnie was the only set designer they had, and this team simply got better every year. This was Ginnie's fifth season.

In his office Ro heard Ginnie enter and yell to William and Spotty, the watchman, who would be leaving along about now. You always knew when Ginnie had arrived. Ro's smile was broader as he started coffee before approaching his messy desk.

Ginnie stuck her head in, as he knew she would, and greeted him. "Hear from Wonder Boy yet?"

"He called from Bend last night. He'll get in this afternoon. Underestimated how long the drive would take. No one from back East believes the distances out here."

"Got a cup of coffee?"

"Come on in," he said in mock resignation. "And, Ginnie, stop calling him Wonder Boy. You'll forget and say it in front of him. And please don't swear like a sailor, at least until he gets to know you."

"Sure," she said, taking the coffee cup from him. "Thanks. In fact, I quit cussing. Haven't you noticed?"

"When?"

"Couple of weeks ago. You know, I started it when I realized I'd never grow t——" She looked at the ceiling and said primly, "One

2

day it occurred to me that I probably would never become a voluptuous woman and no one would believe I was grown up, so I decided to use language to make the point."

"And you gave it up?"

"Right. I decided what the h———. I decided I didn't give a f———. I decided I didn't care."

Laughing, he poured himself more coffee. Ginnie was rangy, with dark curly hair that she kept too short. She wore sweatshirts, blue jeans, and crazy T-shirts and sneakers. Today her shirt had a smoking dragon on it. Ginnie had lived with him after her mother died, then she had gone away to school and at twenty-four had returned, two years into her master's program. She didn't give a shit about the degree, she had said cheerfully then. She had hung on for the experience of designing sets and now she was ready to go to work for Harriet. She had shown him her portfolio and half a dozen models, and he had hired her.

He had been anxious and watchful in the beginning. When she hung around the theater before, as a kid, she had been coltish, childlike, obviously sexually immature, in no real danger. She was still too young, but with a difference: She was now independent. The first smooth-talking, handsome actor who came down the pike and saw a good thing in her because of who she was, who her uncle was, would twist her like wet spaghetti, he had thought, and he had been wrong. She treated them all with affection, like pets. Now he felt sympathetic amusement for the fresh young actors just out of school who came along and got a crush on her, and many of them did, whether or not she had developed a womanly figure.

"Has Wonder Boy picked out the winner yet?" She asked when she finished her coffee and was leaving his office.

"Ginnie, please. No, he hasn't."

"Well, sh———oot," she said, and winked at him. "How can I start thinking about the set when I don't know what for?"

"There'll be time, plenty of time. Now get. I've got work to do."

Ginnie wandered backstage greeting various people who were arriving: Anna Kaminsky, grumbling about the way the actors mistreated their costumes, as if she had nothing better to do than take up this seam, let out that one . . . And clean them. Always, clean them. She was leaving Monday for a vacation in Phoenix. Eric Hendrickson arrived, his brow more furrowed than usual. "Henry Dahl is sick," he said in a tone of disbelief, incredulity. How dare Henry Dahl get sick now! he was actually saying. Two more shows to go! He'd pump him full of penicillin personally. . . . Gary Boynton had to see William right now—he had found such a deal on redwood one-by-eights! Jessica Myers slouched her way toward props, her eyes distant and dreamy. Jessica had a new friend, her third this year. They were planning a long trip, starting Sunday night. . . .

Bobby Philpott and Brenda Gearhart arrived together and flushed when Ginnie raised an eyebrow at them. Bobby was lights; Brenda, sound.

"When I go take that workshop on laser lighting," Bobby said diffidently, "we thought Brenda might look in on some new sound techniques."

"Her technique looks pretty sound to me as it is," Ginnie said. Brenda blushed even more.

Could there be such a thing as a simultaneous manic depression? she wondered. Everyone always got manic at the end of the run, and it was always coupled with a depression amid the talk of vacations and trips and new affairs and whatever.

One show tonight, she mused, two on Saturday, and a matinee on Sunday that would finish the season with the last performance of *Harvey*. Finis. End of season. Already the theater felt different, as if a presentiment of loneliness had invaded it. Ginnie had been gone much of the summer and would not be leaving again until after the new season was well launched. She knew her Uncle Ro was grooming her to take over for him one day; he had asked her to sit in on the selection process for the next season, be in on the precasting decisions, budgets, everything. She was not certain she was ready for those responsibilities yet.

She glimpsed Kirby Schultz conferring with Eric. Kirby was the director who was leaving to make his fortune in television. She wished him well and thought it was just silly of Uncle Ro to be furious with him. Even if Uncle Ro was right and Kirby ended up hating it, he had to try, she had decided months ago, and tended to side with Kirby every time the subject came up.

"They're sloppy," Kirby was saying to Eric when she got within earshot. "I timed it on Wednesday and they're running nine minutes longer than they were a month ago. Timing's everything in a play like *Dracula*, everything. Take them through the second act, that's where it bogs down."

Eric nodded silently. Poor Eric, she thought, passing them, waving. He had been so certain he would get Kirby's job.

"Not creative enough," Uncle Ro had said when she questioned him about it. "A director's got to be as creative as the writer or he's nothing. Eric's a great stage manager, a great prompter, a great one to get the most out of actors at rehearsals, after a director's told him what he wants."

At ten she left the theater, where she really had nothing to do at this time. She rode her bike slowly through town toward the university, where she was to meet Peter and go with him to inspect a house that was a possibility for Wonder Boy and his companion. She grinned, remembering the expression on her uncle's face when she called his find by that name. But it was his fault, she reasoned; he had praised the new director too fulsomely not to evoke some reaction.

Harry Rosen waved at her from his car, on his way to his insurance office, she guessed. She liked Ashland. Everyone she saw who was a resident, not a tourist, smiled at her, waved, spoke, somehow greeted her. She liked that. All her life until she had come here she had lived in one big city after another, one apartment after another, always a stranger among strangers. Here people made her feel welcome and even useful. At least one time each year they asked her to come to the high school to talk to the art students; the Cascade Gallery had invited her to have a show twice now, with her models on display for a week to ten days at a time; if there was an art show, they asked her to be on the jury; she had spoken at the

5

university several times. . . . It was good to belong, to have a community. A town of fifteen thousand was just right.

"Hey, Ginnie! Over here!"

She braked, spinning out her bike on gravel in the driveway of the university-staff parking lot. Peter Ellis covered his face with both hands. He peeked through his fingers.

"Good God!" he said. "Do you always stop like that?"

"Is there another way? No one told me it, if there is."

"Chain the bike and let's go. I have to be back by one. Time to see the house and have lunch. Okay?"

She nodded and very quickly joined him at his car. Peter was six feet tall and fair; he moved as if his joints had not been firmly linked. He was an archaeologist at the university. He had been here for a year working on his Ph.D. dissertation, which he hoped to finish by spring. This quarter was his last here. Then, back to U.C.L.A., dig in and finish the paperwork, he said.

"Tell me something about the house," Ginnie said as he started the car and backed out. "How'd it happen to turn up at this time?"

"Warner and Greta Furness tried to rent it out during the summer, but no luck. They said no actors and no students, and that didn't leave much, I guess. They want a year's lease. They're at Harvard for a year. Yesterday I heard about it and thought of you and your new director and here we go."

Peter was easy to be with, not demanding, and not theater. He seldom even came to the theater to pick her up, or to meet people there. He did not expect her to be any more comfortable with his university friends than he was with her theater friends. In a way, that tended to isolate them when they saw each other, and that, she knew, would not work if things ever started to get more serious. They would have to make some adjustments then, but for now it was fine. They hiked together and looked for good spots for him to dig, went to the coast or the high desert now and again. Sometimes he made dinner for her and sometimes she did it.

The house he took her to was on Alison, up a steep hill, about midway between the university and the theater, half a mile from each. The hill was not as steep as the one that led to her house on

6

West Park Street. Much of Ashland was built on the mountainside, some of the streets so precipitous that she refused to drive on them at all.

"It's beautiful," she said, standing in the driveway. The house had two stories and looked expensive, with carefully sculpted grounds, immaculate paint.

"They'll make a deal. They don't want it empty all winter. Let's go on in."

It was a three-bedroom house, richly furnished, carefully maintained. She nodded. If Wonder Boy didn't like it, let him find his own house.

"Take the key," Peter said. "Show it to them and if they want it, they can get in touch with Warner. Otherwise, just give it back to me sometime. Here's the name and number." He handed her a slip of paper.

"Okay. So I'm a broker or something. Where for lunch? I'm starved."

"You're always starved."

Ginnie had never been able to ride her bicycle all the way up her own hill. But she was getting higher each time, she thought grimly, when she had to get off and walk the rest of the distance that afternoon. Her legs throbbed. At her own house she nodded with satisfaction. It was perfect for her. The yard was messy with uncut grass, dandelions, overgrown bushes, last year's leaves turning a rich brown where they had collected in dips and along the walk, against the foundation of the house. She had dug up the backyard and had sown wildflowers, two pounds of seeds, at twenty-eight dollars a pound. The back was a kaleidoscope of color nine months of the year. She intended to have the front dug in the spring, plant it to wildflowers also.

Her uncle had looked at her with incomprehension when she told him she intended to buy a house. She had the insurance money, she had said firmly, and that was what it was going to go for, her own house.

Inside, she looked at her belongings with the same satisfaction she had felt surveying her yard. Everything in it was hers, things she had chosen herself. It was bright with color—she loved color, none of that neutral, good-taste, decorator stuff for her. The rug in her living room was red, the couch deep forest-green, one chair yellow. A Cherokee wall hanging was red and orange and yellow and blue. . . . There were plants in red and blue ceramic pots. She had caught the startled expression on the faces of visitors now and then, but most people liked it after that first surprise. The colors were carefully chosen, nothing clashed with anything else. She used colors the way they were used in tropical climates, in Indonesia, or Malaysia. It all worked.

She called her uncle and learned that Gray Wilmot and Laura Steubins were due at the theater by four. They had checked into a motel already and were cleaning up, relaxing.

Although she had intended to change her clothes, she forgot, and when she arrived at the theater to meet Wonder Boy, she was still in the jeans and T-shirt she had worn all day. She joined the throng in Ro's office.

William was there, and Eric, Kirby, Anna, Brenda, Bobby . . . most of the actors who had been put through an extra rehearsal for *Dracula*. Everyone wanted to meet the new director. Ro saw her and called, "That's Ginnie. Meet Gray and Laura."

She could not see Laura for the people between them, but Gray was tall enough to spot.

"Hi!" she yelled, and he nodded. Grim, she thought. Probably dead tired from the long drive, and now a mob scene, just what he needed. She ducked to get a glimpse of Laura and grinned at her. Even tireder than he was, apparently.

"Ginnie's located a house you might want to rent," Ro was saying, his voice carrying over the other voices in the office. "Whenever you want to see it, she'll take you."

"Maybe we should do it now," Laura said. "I'd like a nap before dinner. It's been a long day."

He didn't like that, Ginnie thought, watching Gray's expression tighten. And she doesn't like theater people. Like Peter.

"That makes good sense," Ro said heartily. "Ginnie can drop you off at your motel after you see the house. And I'll pick you up at six-thirty for dinner. Okay?"

They made their way through their welcome committee, and she led them out the back to her car. When she opened the door, they both got in the backseat without speaking. She walked around to the driver's side and got in, and realized that they thought she was a gofer, Ro's secretary, or a stagehand or something. She thought cheerfully, well, fuck you, too, Wonder Boy.

TWO

They had met at a party given by one of Laura's friends. He had looked over the group and withdrawn to a chair near the front window. There were fifteen or sixteen people in the room, all familiar to Laura, some of them friends, most merely acquaintances. Eventually she had found herself in the chair opposite his and they had nodded at each other silently. The music was too loud and the room reeked of pot and spilled wine.

"Having a good time?" he asked with an edge to his voice.

She shrugged. "Typical *Harvey* party."

"Where can you get something to eat at this time of night?" he asked abruptly. "Something not pink, not to go on crackers, not cheese."

She ended up going with him to an all-night restaurant, and she learned about him during the next few hours as they talked and drank coffee. He had had to make the choice, he said, take this part-time job, or hang on in New York hoping for a chance to break in.

And in New York, he had added, only he had known he was not just another green pea in a field of peas. He could live on what he made, he had said, and she understood this to mean that perhaps he would be able to pay rent and eat, but perhaps not. There was no screaming demand for new theatrical directors, he said.

"Or anyone else," she said. She had been lucky to get her job with Marianne's new advertising agency and she had it only because she and Marianne had been friends for a long time.

When they parted early in the morning, she knew that something had started. That was in October. Just before Thanksgiving she saw his first play. It was not very good, but the reviews blamed the actors, not him. He had done more than anyone had expected, one reviewer had written, considering what he had to work with.

He was angry and defiant and determined. And he was badly hurt. He made his cast work overtime in rehearsal for the next performance, and by the time the run ended he was exhausted. By Christmas they were living together in her apartment.

She knew from the beginning that he was trying desperately to get a job with any theater, anywhere. He sent résumés, reviews, pictures, wrote long letters, followed up every lead. At times he was jubilant with the possibility of this or that working out; then, when it didn't, he was so low in depression that she was afraid for him.

In March, a very lovely sophomore was in his next production, *Pygmalion*. Watching the rehearsals, Laura wondered how he could not fall in love with the women he worked with. When she mentioned it later, his expression was blank. Then he said, "You look at a marble sculpture and see only the beauty of the finished work, right? How do you think the artist feels about the marble? It's nothing but raw material. That's what the actors are, raw material, and the finished play is the work of art, the raw material forgotten, not important."

She prayed that he truly believed that. She made an effort to still the quiver of jealousy that had presented itself to her as fear.

When he moved in, Marianne had asked, "Whose idea is it?"

She had not been able to answer honestly. She really did not

11

know. When Marianne asked, "Do you love him?" her answer had been immediate and sure. Yes, she loved him and would do whatever it took to keep him.

In September his break came. As soon as she opened the door to their apartment, she knew something good had happened finally. Roses were on the table, the air was fragrant, but it was more than that. The heaviness was gone; it was not like walking into a pressure chamber. Gray yelled from the kitchen and charged into the living room, swept her up, whirled her around, kissing her. "I got it! I got the Ashland job! Ro Cavanaugh was in the audience when *Pygmalion* opened! He loved it!"

At dinner she listened to his excited voice and tried not to think what the words actually meant. Something was ending. After less than a year, something was ending. Gray was thirty-one, two years younger than she was. He was handsome in a classical way, lean and hard of body, thick dark hair, deep blue eyes. He could get a job modeling, she had said once, and he had reacted furiously.

"I don't have to be there until November first," he said, swirling wine in his glass harder and harder. "Six weeks to get everything wrapped up here. We'll drive and use a rented trailer for the stuff we can't sell. It'll take five or six days. A vacation along the way, a little sightseeing." The wine splashed out of his glass and they both laughed.

She finally said, "What about my job? You're assuming I'll go too?"

He nodded. "I was assuming you'd go."

His exuberance had vanished; now he was dark and withdrawn, overwary. Sell what stuff? she thought. He had nothing to sell. He meant for her to sell her furnishings, undo the life she had been building for five years.

"I told them we'd be there a few days early, to catch the last performance or two of this season," he said.

Slowly she nodded. They both knew she would go. Ashland, she thought. Ash land. An image of burned rubble formed in her mind, ashes blowing in the wind, ashes in her mouth, bitter and sharp.

They planned their trip, made changes, planned alternate routes, and they had a garage sale, then another one, and then gave away what they could not sell and would not take. The weeks evaporated too fast, leaving a final frenzy of activity, including a visit to her parents to say good-bye. Her father had said in the beginning that his daughter was welcome in his house anytime, and his daughter and her husband were welcome, but there was one extra bedroom and no unmarried couple could share it. The visit was for one day, uncomfortable for everyone.

Connecticut, Pennsylvania, Ohio, Kansas . . . finally the great Rocky Mountain range, and then the high plateau country. They had stopped at the Craters of the Moon in Idaho, had spent a few hours in the plains of Idaho, crossed the Snake River into Oregon, and were on a road virtually without traffic, with high-desert sagebrush and an occasional juniper tree the only visible life. "What a wasteland," Gray had said, and gone back to his reading.

A few days before they left home, he had received a carton of manuscripts. His first job, he had told her, was to judge a play-writing contest. The winning play would be his first production. Those he found totally hopeless he marked with a red N and put aside. Most of the manuscripts were ending up in the reject box. He read while she drove.

Ash land, she kept thinking. They passed more lava fields; the mountains were stark and wind-carved, outcroppings were black volcanic material, foreboding, almost evil.

"Listen," Gray said. He read from the manuscript; "'Daughter, you must not go out with that no-good Stanley. You know you will end up pregnant and what will your father say?'"

"That's pretty direct," Laura said, laughing. "Are they all like that?"

"No, ma'am, this is one of the better ones." They both laughed.

How easily he picked up whatever accent he heard. He sounded just like the Kansan who had commented on a restaurant with those words. "You could be an actor," she had told him once.

He had nodded. "But they have no power, no control. It's the director who decides what kind of reality will be created on the stage. A good director makes the actors believe in that reality, and they make the audience accept it. But before anything can happen, the director has to step into another world, live in it, know it's real. A good director and a good writer share that world in a way no one else can understand, or enter. The writer sees his world, hears his people, but all he can produce are marks on paper, signs pointing to symbols. The director does magic, moves those symbols through another dimension and creates life with them. The actors are tools, only tools, like models, made to be used. I won't be used," he had finished flatly.

Sometimes it frightened her very much when the thought came unbidden that maybe he was not as good a director as he thought. It frightened her even more when she came to realize that in his world some people were tools to be used, and others were the users of those tools, and she knew that she and Gray were in separate categories.

When she glanced at him again, he was reading another play, this time moving his lips, saying the lines under his breath—a good one finally.

That night she heard her first coyote crying in the distance, lonely, wild, unknowable. She felt a spasm of terror. And that night she roused to see a crack of light from around the bathroom door, dozed, awakened again, then came wide awake when she realized he had been in there for hours.

"Gray?" She called a second time. The light went out and he returned to the bedroom.

"Restless," he said, getting into bed.

In the morning she found the play that had interested him folded in half, pages dog-eared, penciled notes in the margins. She would read it while he drove, she thought, but she put it aside, forgot it.

"You were all over the bed last night," Gray said at breakfast. "Dreams?"

She shook her head, lying. There had been dreams—nightmares, actually; already the details had blurred, only the feeling of terror persisted. She knew that in her dreams wild dogs had fought over her bones, that she had cried out over and over and no one had come.

And she could not tell him. She could not say to him, "I can't go with you to ash land because I'll die there."

THREE

What perverse or even malign spirit overcame Ginnie she could not have said, but she yielded to it without a struggle and adopted a guide-extraordinaire attitude. "Over there is Lithia Park," she said brightly. "Very pretty. You can walk two miles, maybe three. Great madrone trees, ponderosa pines, beautiful flowers. It leads into the Elizabethan Theater grounds. The Oregon Shakespearean Festival is what brings people here, of course. The Harley simply capitalizes on the overflow. Ninety-three percent attendance each season. Not bad for a town of fifteen thousand. Of course, the university has forty-five hundred students. I don't think they count them in the census. So, twenty thousand. Medford is up the road about twelve miles and that's another forty thousand, and people are scattered all through the valley. It's the Rogue River valley, by the way, wonderful white-water rafting. They've had it on television sports any number of times."

On and on she prattled. When she glanced at them in the rearview mirror, Gray was staring stonily out his side window, Laura gazing just as intently out the other one.

"This is the steep way up to the house," she said, shifting down. "There's another way up that isn't bad at all. I'll take you back that way. And here it is. The view's pretty nice during the day, but at night it's spectacular!" Ginnie parked in the driveway, jumped out, and opened the back door before either Gray or Laura had a chance to.

"Why don't I just give you the key and let you roam by yourselves," she said brightly. "You'll have things to discuss about the house. I'll wait here."

She watched them enter and then turned her attention to the view. It was spectacular day or night, just as the view was from her own house. The mountain dropped down to the valley floor, where the main part of town was, then there was a relatively flat area four or five miles wide, then foothills that rolled exactly the way Delaware countryside did, and beyond that, more mountains. Behind her the mountain continued upward, heavily forested, deep green summer and winter, with firs, pines, spruces, madrones—conifers and broad-leaf evergreens of a rain forest merging with trees of a drier climate. Everything was here together. It was nearly chanterelle time, she thought; she and Peter were going on a great mushroom hunt after a good soaking rain. Any day now it would rain, the start of the new season, but this day was brilliantly clear, the sky gloriously blue, with idealized clouds, the kind that children draw, glowing marshmallow clouds. There would be another breathtaking sunset later.

Inside the house, Gray watched Laura examine the rooms. Too expensive, they both had said on entering, but he wasn't sure. Maybe the owners were desperate to have it occupied during the winter. He would call. And meanwhile he didn't give a damn about room size, or furnishings, or even the view. It was okay, good enough, if they could afford it.

"You going to tell me what's bugging you?" he asked abruptly.

"Nothing." She stiffened with the words in a way that meant: Don't push, not right now, anyway.

He understood her signals, maybe even better than she did. He did not push. He knew part of the problem: as he had become more and more excited and eager, she had become more anxious and withdrawn. What he had seen as the opportunity to meet colleagues, she had seen as the threat of an overwhelming mob. Already he was categorizing the people he had met, and she probably didn't remember a single name, except for Roman Cavanaugh. He understood, but felt impatient with her sudden insecurity. This was his world in a way that the University of Connecticut had never been. Here he would be in charge, in control, not a part-time flunky serving at the whim of a jackass who had tenure. Laura had gone into the kitchen to check on cookware: apparently they would have to buy nothing, it was all in the house, except for linens, and they had packed hers in the trailer. Gray gazed out the window at the view across the valley, and wanted only to get on with it, to start his new job.

Laura returned carrying a notebook. They would have to get the electricity turned on, and the phone, find out about garbage collection. . . . "It's really a nice house," she said uncertainly. It was, but it felt like someone else's house. Wall-to-wall carpeting, soft beige plush, fine furniture, not quite antique, but not Grand Rapids either. A fully equipped kitchen, even a microwave, laundry room equipped . . . The problem was that she kept expecting the owners to enter momentarily and demand an explanation. Gray had walked to the front of the room and was looking out at the street, the driveway. She looked past him and saw the girl who had brought them here. The wind had started to blow, molding her jeans to her long legs, her hair against her cheeks. She glanced from her to Gray and thought clearly, of course, never an actress with her lovely face and body, but someone like that, someone loose-bodied and not beautiful and somehow free.

"Ready?" he asked, turning back to her.

She nodded. She couldn't tell if he had even been looking at the girl in the driveway, but if not now, later, another day. She did not try to rationalize her certainty. It came fully developed bearing its own load of acceptance and dread and inevitability.

Ginnie had the door open for them when they got back to her car. Her cheeks were bright from the wind, her hair tumbled every which way. When she started to drive, she asked, "Do you ski? Mount Ashland is wonderful for skiing, everything from cross-country to beginners' slopes to high-speed downhill."

Neither of them skied. "The wind made me think of it," Ginnie said. "There's been snow up in the mountains already, and the wind smells like warmed-over snow. We hardly ever get any down here, but sometimes you can smell it."

Laura glanced at Gray. He shrugged, paying little attention to their guide, evidently not interested in her or her strange observations about weather.

Ginnie took them down the less-steep way and then on to their motel. She gave Gray the slip of paper with the phone number of Warner Furness and offered her services as chauffeur, guide, whatever they needed in the coming week or so until they got settled in. Gray thanked her politely and distantly; Laura forced a smile, and she left them alone.

"What do you think?" Ro asked her over the phone that night.

"You mean Gray and Laura?"

"You know that's what I mean. He didn't like the production, thought it was too draggy."

"Well, so does Kirby," she pointed out.

"Yeah, I know. Anyway, what do you think?"

"Too soon. Ask me in a couple of weeks. Has he told you the contest winner yet?"

There was a pause, then Ro said, "It's one called *The Climber.* Have you read it?"

"Nope. Didn't read any of them. Do you have a copy?"

"Just the file copy in the office. Juanita will run off some Xeroxes tomorrow. You want to read it in the office?"

She hesitated. Peter had asked her to go to Silver Lake with him over the weekend to a dig that had attracted students from the entire Northwest over the summer. Now that there were only professionals at the site, he was interested. She made up her mind suddenly. "I'll drop in tomorrow and read through it. You don't like it?"

"I don't know," he said peevishly. "It's just not the one I would have picked, I guess. Anyway, read it and tell me what you think. See you tomorrow, honey."

She called Peter and was a little surprised at how disappointed he sounded.

"I've been trying to get you off to myself for weeks," he said, "and you keep dodging. Did Ro know ahead of time that you were considering going away?"

"I'm not sure. Why? What does that mean?"

"I bet he did."

"Come back in time for the party, okay? Between eight and nine?"

He said he would try and she knew he would make it. That was the only condition she had imposed, if she had gone at all, that they be back in time for the big party at the end of the season. Had she mentioned it to Uncle Ro? She thought not, but could not be certain, and even if she had, so what? Uncle Ro was not trying to run her life, she thought emphatically. If anything, he ignored her private life as if it didn't even exist.

If he asked if she was sleeping with Peter, would she tell him? she wondered. Probably. But she knew he would not ask any more than she would question him about his private life.

"Got a cup of coffee?" she called at his office door the next morning. It was raining and she felt smug about not being out camping at Silver Lake. The last time she and Peter had camped out in the rain, both sleeping bags had been soaked and he had caught a cold. She shrugged out of a poncho and held it at arm's length to drip in the hall, not on the office carpet.

"Hang it up somewhere," Ro said, "and come on in. Come on. Such a mooch. Don't you buy any coffee of your own?"

"Hell no. How was dinner with Wonder Boy and the Lady of the Lake?"

He looked pained. "They were both pretty tired. They've taken the house and plan to move in today and he's going to take the trailer to Medford and turn it in and be back here in time for the matinee. Ginnie—" He paused and turned back to the coffee machine, looked at it instead of her. "Why'd you call her that?"

Ginnie had regretted the words as soon as she uttered them. She had not thought of Laura in any particular way since leaving her and Gray at the motel, had not thought about any title or nickname for her. The words had formed themselves in the shadows of the cave of her mind. "I don't know," she said slowly. "I won't do it again."

He nodded. "She's just tired from packing and the long drive, shy with so many strangers all at once. She'll be all right. And so will he."

Ginnie sipped the coffee and knew why those particular words had come tumbling out. Laura had a doomed expression, a sad, aware, and doomed look.

"Well, here's the play," Ro said, handing her a folder. "Take it over there and read through it. Juanita's coming in at ten to pick it up."

His office was twenty feet long, only about ten feet wide. At one end was a mammoth desk, always messy with piles of papers, stacks of manuscripts, letters, a fifteen-inch-tall bronze clown, some pretty paperweights, things no one had touched in years, Ginnie felt certain. His secretary, Juanita Margolis, was forbidden to move anything there, but Ro could shuffle through things and come out with whatever it was he sought practically instantly. Everything else in the office was meticulously neat, as were his apartment, his person, his car, the rest of the theater. Only his desk was a rat's nest.

In the middle of the office, exactly in the way of traffic, there was a round table where Ro often ate lunch. He had not cooked a meal

21

for himself in twenty-five years, except for toast once in a while. There were bookshelves, a neat liquor cabinet that opened to make a bar. At the far end there were comfortable overstuffed chairs covered in green leather and a matching couch. A redwood coffee table with a burl top, six feet by three, several inches thick, made the couch impossible to get to without great determination. There were windows on the outside wall, but Ginnie never had seen them open, or with the red velvet drapes drawn apart. It was always now in Ro's office, never day or night, or any time in particular, just now. It was not quite soundproof, but almost. She could faintly hear the noise of the crew onstage, getting set up for the matinee: *Pal Joey*.

She sat in one of the leather-covered chairs, put her feet on the coffee table, switched on a lamp, and opened the folder. The play had been written on a computer, printed in terrible purple dot matrix. She groaned. "I bet it won't reproduce at all," she called.

He sighed. "We'll see."

She knew what would happen. Juanita would end up retyping the whole damn thing and getting her own copy Xeroxed. Poor Juanita. She wondered what she would give up for Ro. Her arm. Her cats. Her mother. Whatever he demanded. She started to read.

When she finished she looked up to find him regarding her, frowning. "It's a piece of . . . Uncle Ro, it's awful."

He let out a long breath. "I was hoping it was just me, out of touch or something."

"There must have been something better than this. Do you have the other submissions handy?"

"He read them all. He was pretty emphatic about this being his choice."

She dropped the manuscript on the coffee table and stood up. If Gray stuck to it, he would have this one. It was in his contract that he was to judge the contest. "What a stupid thing to agree to ahead of time anyway," she said. "You should rewrite the contest rules. If there's nothing worth producing, nothing gets produced."

"Meanwhile the horse is long gone."

"Who wrote the goddamn thing? Maybe we could send him a mail bomb or something."

"Her. Sunshine. That's all, just Sunshine."

"Yeah, it would be. Boy, what a mess! Think we can talk him out of it?"

"We'll let it ride over the weekend and meet Monday. You, Eric, William, Juanita, Gray, and me. Ten Monday morning. "I'll hand out copies tonight or tomorrow. Don't let on that you've read it until then, Ginnie. I don't want any trouble over the weekend. God, I wish I could ask Kirby to come Monday."

She agreed that he could not do that. Kirby was out as of Sunday; this was not his fight. She went to the door. "He must see something in it that we missed. I'll give it another good read over the weekend."

"As I will, I assure you. Thanks, Ginnie. Just thanks."

She grinned at him. "Wonder Boy just might shake things up around here more than you counted on, Uncle Ro." When he had decided on Gray as Kirby's replacement, he had said the group needed new blood, needed a good shake-up. She thought that probably that was exactly what they were going to get.

FOUR

All the rest of Saturday Ginnie worked in the shop, a large quonset hut where the sets were constructed and stored. It always smelled of paint and newly sawed wood. She was making decisions with William, labeling items to be stored, making notes in her notebook to go in her file. Keep the bay window intact; break down the soda fountain from *Bus Stop*; return the jukebox to the collector who had donated it for the season. . . . The quonset-hut shop was a jumble of scenery, removed from the stage, brought out from backstage as each show finished now, each piece demanding a separate decision. Keep this flat, it can be painted a couple more times. That sofa has had it. Tear it down, keep the frame. It was hard work, and dirty work. The wonderful fireplace from *Dracula*—it worked on a revolve. When the secret panel opened, the whole thing turned to reveal the loathsome crypt of the monster. . . . Tear it down.

She made notes. William made notes; Gary Boynton, the shop

foreman, made notes, all different, not interchangeable. On Monday the actual work would begin; hoists would lift pieces to the overhead storage areas, the crew would attack other pieces with hammers, crowbars. . . .

The crew began to bring in scenery from *Pal Joey* and Ginnie moved out of the way. Her hands were grimy, her face was dirty, her hair gritty.

"Hi," Gray Wilmot called at the door. "William around?"

William appeared from the rear of the shop. "Afternoon, Mr. Wilmot."

"Please," he said. "Gray. Just wanted to tell you that was a terrific set for *Pal Joey*. Really effective."

"Thanks, but you should be telling Ginnie, not me."

"I thought Ro said you did them."

"Nope. He said I build. Ginnie designs. I just do what I'm told."

Gary Boynton's voice bellowed nearby. "Dammit, Mikey, don't drop it!"

"Better move a bit," William said, and stepped out of the way; Gray followed. Now he could see Ginnie.

"I didn't realize that was your work," he said with a touch of stiffness. "They're both really good. I'm looking forward to working with you. See you later."

He left, and William turned to look at Ginnie when she chuckled. "You baiting him, girl?"

"Now, William, don't be a nag. I've about had it for the day. How about you?" He nodded and she patted his arm. "Give Shannon a kiss for me. See you tomorrow." Shannon was his semi-invalid wife whose heart condition grew steadily worse.

The rain had almost stopped; now it was a patter of isolated showers from stranded clouds that looked lonely in the clearing sky. The air smelled of rain and earth mold and forests and wood smoke. By next month Ashland would smell like a giant wood stove. There was a bite in the air signaling a frost soon, if not this night, then the next, or within a week, probably. Autumn had arrived.

She walked home without haste, stopped to chat a minute with Jarrel Walsh, who owned one of the best restaurants in town, then stopped again to speak with Dancy Corman, who worked in the bookstore that she passed every day. A clump of people stood near the Elizabethan Theater parking lot, actors and Marguerite Demarie, the costumer. Their season was ending, just as the Harley's was, and tomorrow night the party would wend from backstage to backstage as all the theater people in town celebrated another good season. For the diehards, there was Ro's apartment to wrap it all up with a catered breakfast at dawn. She waved; they waved back.

This was what Peter didn't understand, she thought, climbing her hill, hardly feeling the strain in her legs. He thought when she said they were like a family that it was simply show-biz jargon and it wasn't. Any of them could get together at any time and be deep in conversation within seconds and care about the conversation. Right now everyone would be interested in the new director, what he was like, what his routine would be, how he treated actors, stagehands—everything about him, because it could affect any one of them. The actors moved from one theater to the other, stagehands worked both, as did the construction crews. What happened at Harley's echoed through the Shakespeare bunch, the Angus Bowman bunch, all of them. Every rumor made the entire circuit with startling speed.

Peter had tried to convince her that it was just like that at the university, at corporations, everywhere. She didn't believe it. In theater, she had said, every single day you're laying it on the line again, risking everything again. You can't get a reputation and coast on it, not for long. No tenure, no security, no tomorrow; only this show, this run, this performance.

Peter was thirty, and she knew that Gray Wilmot was thirty-one, but he seemed ancient compared to Peter. Theater people all seemed old compared to other people, old and forever young and gullible at the same time. "You can't expect much from a relationship with another theater person," Brenda, the sound technician, had said once over lunch. "You'll be working Toledo while he's in Las Vegas. But you can't expect *anything* from someone from the real world. As soon as they've seen the show once, it's 'What else is new, honey?'"

26

The only reference her uncle had made to Peter had been oblique. "It's good to know someone from outside now and then, just to remind us what that's like."

She walked up to her door and turned the key in the lock and realized that she was brooding about Peter because this was his last term at school; he would be leaving, and he liked things finished, settled. He didn't like quitting with things undone. Okay, she told herself, so she would have to make a decision, but not right now, not tonight, or tomorrow. All she wanted right now was a shower and food. God, she thought, she was starving.

Everything backstage had been cleared away to make room for tables and chairs, for a twenty-foot buffet. A five-piece band played, and when they took a break, someone put on tapes. Upstage was cleared for dancing. On the buffet there were turkey and ham, shrimp creole, avocados stuffed with crab, chicken breasts in a hot Mexican sauce, potato salad, carrot salad, hearts of palm, mushrooms vinaigrette . . . There were liquor and champagne and red and white wines, and silver urns of coffee.

Ginnie danced until she was soaked through and through. Laura danced with Ro, then William, then with whomever came along and asked. She was a good dancer. Gray did not dance. Peter arrived at ten and Ginnie danced even more with him. One of the actresses, Amanda White, propositioned one of the actors and they left together. Kirby got drunk and wept and declared that he had changed his mind, he did not want to go to Hollywood; he would cancel his contract. Peter and Laura danced a waltz and everyone made room for them and watched and applauded when they were done. Then Ro made a speech and introduced Eric, who handed out awards. There was an award for the most original ad-lib, for the longest pause for a forgotten line, for the cleverest save the night that Eric forgot his promptbook, for the most athletic entrance or exit. . . .

The Shakespearean crowd arrived; some of the Harley people left, and after that it was impossible to tell them apart. Then it was two in the morning and Ro made a signal to the band. The leader stepped forward with an acoustic guitar; Bobby dimmed the lights and turned a spot on Ginnie. She had protested vehemently against this, but Ro had insisted and finally had agreed to make it a duet with her. Another spot found him. Ginnie's singing voice was too soft for a performer, but there was no sound now except her voice and the plaintive guitar. She sang.

"The party's over/ it's time to call it a day . . ." Ro walked to her and they finished the song together; the spots went out, leaving inky blackness for a heartbeat, then the lights came on full and everyone applauded madly and many began to weep. The party was over. The season was over.

Laura was standing near Peter, both suddenly subdued. This was Gray's world, she was thinking, this was what he had been looking for, hungry for, and she would never be part of it. And Peter was thinking that Ro would never let Ginnie go again. Ginnie came up to them, flushed and sweaty.

"Corny, huh? Ro's idea. I told him it was corny."

"It was perfect," Peter said. "The perfect way to end a party. Do you have your car?"

"No. I thought you'd be driving and no point in a parade. Now?"

He nodded and Laura looked away, embarrassed by the sudden sexual tension that seemed to radiate from him. She watched them leave; it took a long time for them to get free of all the people who wanted a last hug, a last word with Ginnie. Gray came to her then.

"Ro said a small group will go to his apartment for a while. You up for that?"

"Do you want to?"

"Yeah. I think so."

She nodded, but what she ached to do was go to their house with him, go to bed with him, make love for hours with him. She felt a rush of jealousy when she thought of Ginnie and Peter, and it was followed swiftly by a feeling of pity for him.

The caterers were starting to clean up and she heard the refrain in her mind: The party's over.

FIVE

At the party, Ro had handed Ginnie a copy of the play—retyped by Juanita, as she had predicted. She had reread it that morning after Peter left, and it was even worse than she had remembered. When she got to Ro's office at ten, the others were already there, and she could tell that it was going to be a stormy meeting. Eric was scowling deeper than usual. He had a permanent frown that was meaningless, but when it deepened this much, so that the lines looked incised with ink, people walked warily. William looked sad, hung over, and he was not a drinker. He looked tired, though, probably stayed as long as the continuation of the party at Ro's house had gone on. Juanita, Ro's secretary, had a carefully held neutral expression, and that in itself was alarming. She was slim, in her late forties, with black hair and very dark eyes; she was so intelligent that people often took whatever problem they had to her, fully expecting her to have answers, no matter if it was physics homework for the college students who worked as stagehands, or a lighting problem, or something to do with costumes—whatever. She was wasted here, Ginnie sometimes thought, but Juanita was not about to go anywhere else. Ginnie suspected that she and Ro had been lovers, and were no longer, although Juanita still loved him. Ro looked exactly the same as always. Late nights, parties, long hours, nothing marked his face. Age was catching up to him so gradually that people who had not seen him in years always felt a jolt of surprise that he was unchanged.

Gray was wearing a sweater and jeans and he seemed completely at ease. It was the first time Ginnie thought he did look at ease.

They all had coffee and arranged themselves in the comfortable furniture around the redwood coffee table. Ginnie did not put her feet up on it.

"There are about three things I want us to get to this morning," Ro started. "General procedural stuff. A schedule. And the contest winner. Want to start with that?"

"A couple of questions," Gray said. "The rules don't say how the winner is to be notified. Do you do that, or am I supposed to? The copy I have doesn't even have a name, you know, just a number. I want to get together with the writer about some revisions."

"We go by number so no one can cry bias," Ro said. "I've got the list. But, Gray, I think we have a problem with the one you chose. What do you think, Eric?"

"It's rotten," he said brusquely. "Amateurish, badly written, juvenile in every way."

Gray flushed and looked from Eric to William.

"I agree," William said.

Gray looked at Ginnie; she shrugged and nodded.

"It's unanimous," Ro said then. "Juanita and I also agree that it's a bad play. Did you read all of them?"

"I read them," Gray said in a hard voice. "I didn't realize that the contest was to be judged by a committee that included builders and secretaries. Why did you have me read them if that's how the winner was going to be chosen?"

Ro regarded him for a long moment; no one else moved. "You're to judge," he finally said. There was no trace of cordiality in his voice. "The contest states that the winner will be notified by phone, a check sent by the first of November. It also states that we have the right to produce it. Not that we're bound to do it."

"It can be interpreted either way. The winner could sue."

"Listen, Gray, and listen carefully. This isn't something I'm likely to say to anyone more than once. This theater is mine. I made it what it is, and by God, I'll preserve what I have here. Contest rules be damned. I don't know what you see in that play. I've been wrong before. I could be wrong this time. We'll see. But, Gray, there isn't a play or a playwright I wouldn't yank if I thought it would harm this theater, these people." He paused, then added, "There isn't a contract I wouldn't break if I had to to keep safe the things I consider important. Do you understand me?"

Gray was very pale, his eyes fierce and unwavering. "And I will do anything I have to to preseve what's important to me, and that's my own integrity. We have a contract, Mr. Cavanaugh, but I would quit, walk out in a second, if I thought I couldn't preserve my independence as a director."

Slowly Ro nodded. "That's fair enough. Why don't you tell us what you see in that play."

Gray opened an envelope and pulled out the folded and written-on manuscript. He turned to a page near the end and read: "'As you rise, on what live and writhing matter does your foot fall?'" He read well, in a descending tone, and when he finished the line, he waited for a long beat, then folded the play again. "That one line redeems the play," he said. "It turns it into tragedy of the first rank. Until that line Evan has been a besotted, lovesick fool worthy of no consideration, much less sympathy. But all at once, through one brief question, he is revealed as a tragic figure. Because he knows. It becomes tragedy when the victim knows his fate is destruction and he can't turn away from it. When the rabbit falls to the fox, or the steer to the hammer, the dove to the eagle, we experience a lot of different emotions, but not the sense of tragedy. For that there has to be human awareness."

There was a long silence. Ro reached for the coffeepot and poured himself more coffee before he spoke. "That's one line of an hour-long play. I personally think you're reading more into that play than the writer put there, but we agreed that you're the judge. One thing, Gray: I want to see your promptbooks."

Ginnie thought Gray was going to walk out then, but with a visible effort he remained in his chair and nodded. "That's your right," he said evenly.

"Let's get on with the rest of the agenda," Ro said, and they talked about the fall schedule, when and how the other plays would be chosen, the meetings they would have to discuss the rest of the repertoire. "So twice a week we get together and by December we have our lineup," Ro finally said. "Anyone—anything else?"

Now Gray stood up. He looked at Juanita, then at William. "I'm very sorry," he said in a strained voice. "It came as a real surprise to find opposition like that. I reacted very badly and I apologize."

William nodded, ready to get on with the business of theater, but Juanita's eyes were cool, her manner extremely proper and polite. "Of course," she murmured. "Excuse me."

Ro stood up. "Ginnie, want to mooch some lunch?"

"Sorry. I'm going mushrooming. Why don't you come with us? Be good for you to get out in the open air."

"In the woods?" He looked aghast. "Anyway, the woods are full of pot farms and booby traps."

"Those shitheads," Ginnie said with a sniff. "We'll avoid all suspicious clearings, and tonight it's chanterelle omelet! Goddamn, I wish they'd leave the fucking time alone! Just remembered daylight saving time is dead. Gotta run."

In half a minute she had done what none of them had been able to do through the past two hours, Ro realized, watching her with great love as she ran from the office. William was grinning, shaking his head; Eric's scowl was hardly noticeable; Gray looked bewildered and much younger; even Juanita had loosened up with a suspicion of a smile at the corners of her mouth. Incongruence, he thought, rising. Ginnie was a model of incongruence, trying to act grown-up by using bad language, dressing like a teenager in ratty jeans and sneakers, moving like a hyper boy, streaking this way and that. He turned to Juanita. "Do you want to have some lunch with me?"

"Muchrooms!" Ginnie said with satisfaction, surveying a mesh bag that was bulging with the red-gold harvest. She and Peter were resting, their backs against a venerable pine tree, their legs outstretched. The woods were deep here, with little undergrowth; the ground was spongy, the silence profound.

"So tell me the story of the play," Peter said lazily.

She had recounted the tense meeting. She took a deep breath and started. "This guy, Evan, is a climber, mountain climber, can't resist the highest peaks, all that stuff. Right? So one day he finds a woman wandering in the woods and he takes her home with him. Bingo, trouble. His wife doesn't like the strange woman. No one likes her except Evan, and he falls for her. She comes out of nowhere, no past, nothing. Suddenly she's there in his life. Things go to hell with the marriage. He's some kind of middle-management mugwump in a corporation. His boss comes and meets the strange woman. Evan gets dumped, of course. Final act shows the wife lying facedown on a bed in their home. Her hand relaxes and a pill bottle falls to the floor. Evan is climbing the highest peak yet and stands on the top, then jumps. And the strange woman is seated at a café table with the boss, laughing, drinking champagne. Curtain down."

"Whew," Peter said. "It doesn't sound so bad."

"Who is that mysterious woman? Why does the wife take the pills? Why does Evan take a jump? Sunshine just says this is how it is, folks." She sighed.

"It's surprising to me that Ro backed down," Peter said after a moment.

"You don't understand him. He's convinced that Gray is really good. He'd hire the devil himself if he was good and fire him if he wasn't. Gray's on the spot with this one. Uncle Ro admires anyone willing to fight, but he'll give him the bum's rush if he thinks he'll hurt the theater."

Peter touched her arm, then pointed off to the side. She squinted and finally saw the creature he was showing her, a chipmunk.

"Golden ground squirrel," he whispered.

The animal was studying them as intently as they were examining it. It craned its neck, reared up high on its haunches, and then with a flicker was gone. Golden, buff, sable, white . . . She automatically sketched it, painted it in her mind, fixing it permanently in her memory.

"We'd better head out," Peter said reluctantly then. They both got up, brushed themselves, and started the long hike back to his car.

Peter had been amazed at her ignorance about the woods, the mountains, the geology of the area, and he had started to teach her. He had instructed her in what she had to carry in her daypack: a space blanket—such thin Mylar that it had virtually no weight, but might save her life if she got lost and the temperature plummeted. A poncho, nearly as light, a wool sweater or sweatshirt, matches and a candle, toilet paper . . . She had protested that she didn't want to camp out, just walk in the woods, but he had been firm. Most people who get lost planned no more than a stroll in the woods, he had said. She was used to the daypack now and hardly gave it a thought. It was usually packed and ready to snatch up without adding anything except a piece of cheese or fresh fruit. She kept raisins, nuts, chocolate in it.

She watched Peter's strong back and legs as he led the way. Superficially he and Gray were very alike, she realized. The difference came from within them. Peter carried peacefulness and Gray's burden was tension; and that made them so different that few people would even notice the similarities in build. Oh, she corrected herself, casual observers might mistake one for the other, but no one who had been with either of them for more than a minute.

But how much liking made up for a lack of love? she wondered.

There seemed no end to the amount of liking she felt for Peter, and there was even love mixed with it, but it wasn't the right sort of love, she was afraid. When she thought these things, she always had to admit that she wasn't even sure of that. Since she was not certain what it was that others called love, she was not certain how it differed from what she felt for him. Or if it did. She knew that thinking about falling in love, marriage, a real commitment to anyone made her anxious, fearful, and she understood that least of all.

At the car Peter rummaged in a bag and brought out two sandwiches, handed her one.

"Why didn't you tell me you had food?" she demanded. "I ate everything I had and I'm still starving!"

"You're always starving." They ate before he started the drive back. They had a narrow log road to follow out of the woods and wanted to be done with it before dark, but Peter seemed unhurried, relaxed. Now he said, "You have your busiest time coming up, don't you?"

She nodded, her mouth full.

"Will you save some time for me? I want to be with you as much as you can stand these next weeks. I feel as if my time is running out. If I can't get my message over soon . . ."

Solemnly she nodded, but she knew there would not be many free hours after the next week or so. As soon as the plays were chosen for the new season, she would have her work—preliminary sketches for the sets, finished drawings, models, detailed drawings for William to work with, overseeing the lighting, meetings, meetings . . .

Peter studied her face, then he kissed her lightly and turned on the ignition. "You can finish eating while I drive. I'll cook the mushrooms when we get back. Do you realize that you hiked about eight miles today? I expect that any second now you'll start feeling it."

Six

Her real name, Sunshine said, was Elinor Shumaker, but she had changed it in the sixties, seventies, sometime. She was a shapeless woman of thirty-five in a long plaid skirt with a petticoat showing, hiking boots, a padded jacket over a sweater over a man's plaid shirt. Her eyes were gentle and vague, pale blue, her hair vaguely blond. She carried a large quilted shopping bag with rope handles; it bulged and clunked when she put it down, rattled and clinked when she picked it up.

Laura glanced at Gray. What were they supposed to do with her? Sunshine had called from the bus station half an hour ago; she had arrived, she said, and hung up.

"Do you want some coffee or something?" Gray asked, taking the shopping bag from her.

"I don't drink coffee," she said softly. "Caffeine's really bad for you, you know?"

36

"Uh, yeah, I guess so. Look, Sunshine, do you have any place to go? Why are you here? I told you we'd mail the check."

She smiled gently. "I thought it'd be neat to watch a play going into production, might even try out for a part or something, you know? I'll find a room or something. And you said we have to rewrite it and I thought I should be here for that, you know?"

"We'd better call Ro, or Ginnie," Laura said, her voice grim. "We're strangers here, too," she said to the woman. "We don't have a clue about where to tell you to look for a place to stay."

"I'll get by," Sunshine said, not moving.

"I'll give Ro a call," Gray said in desperation. He left Laura with Sunshine and made the call; in a few minutes Juanita appeared.

"So you're Sunshine," she said without surprise. "Well, come along. There's an apartment building where they take in actors all the time, by the week, month, year, whatever you want. How much can you afford to pay?"

Sunshine smiled at her. "Hundred a month, I guess. More if I have to. But no smokers or drinkers." She turned back to Gray and Laura. "Will we be working in your office or something? I don't have a typewriter, you know?"

"We'll work something out," he said. Sunshine left with Juanita, still smiling, her bag clinking and rattling.

Silently Laura and Gray returned to her car. She got behind the wheel. When they were both settled she said, "She is not to set one foot in our house! You know?"

"Christ," he muttered. "Holy Christ! She's stoned out of her skull."

Laura started to drive. Tightly she asked, "Gray, what exactly am I supposed to do here? You're busy and you'll be busier, but what is there for me to do?" There were no jobs in Ashland, she had learned already.

"Can't you just relax for a few months?"

"Doing what? There's nothing here! Don't you understand? I'm in someone else's house with nothing to do and no one to talk to and nowhere to go."

"We've been here less than a week, for Christ sake! What do you expect?" He said, more quietly, "Look, Ginnie's having Ro, the two of us, and her friend from the university for dinner tomorrow night. Peter can introduce you to a whole new set of people, not theater people."

That was the problem, she admitted to herself. When they first met, he had moved into her circle of friends effortlessly. Over the year she had dropped most of them, but it had been gradual, and there were a few she had kept to the end in Connecticut. He had not moved into the university theater group the way he was doing here. He had known that was a stopgap, temporary, and he had not cared to make the effort then. And she had been busy. There had never been quite enough time there, but when she gazed into the future here, the next months anyway, all she could see was herself alone in a stranger's lovely house where there was nothing for her to do.

She jerked the car when she shifted gears climbing their steep hill. "Goddamn it!" She glanced at Gray; he was looking out his window and seemed very distant, too far to reach.

"Ignore the mess," Ginnie called out when they arrived at her house the next night. "Just step over anything, or kick it out of the way."

She had yelled for them to come on in, and now as they stood in the foyer, she appeared, wiping her hands on a towel. "I sent Peter out for some whipping cream, and Uncle Ro's late. He's always late for dinner at my house. He hates the preliminaries, all that cheese and stuff. Hang up your things in the closet behind you. My hands are sticky." She backed her way into the living room, leading them. "Come on out to the kitchen, okay? I'm up to my elbows in pie crust."

The house was all up and down. Stairs led up to the kitchen, which was large with many cabinets, a handsome oak table with six chairs. Other stairs led to other areas. It seemed too big a house for a single person. On the table in the kitchen there was a blue ceramic platter with Brie and wheat crackers, grapes, and prosciutto, paper-thin, rolled and held with toothpicks. White wine was in a cooler, red wine in a decanter.

"Please help yourselves," Ginnie said, waving to the table. "I have to get this goddamn crust in one piece in the pie pan. . . ." She worked at the counter, muttering under her breath. After a moment, she drew back and surveyed her effort. "To hell with it," she said. "That's why I decided to send Peter for whipping cream. It can hide a multitude of sins."

Ro and Peter arrived almost together and she moved the platter and wine to the living room. Dinner was late.

When it was finally ready, Ginnie brought a casserole to the table and said in awe, "My God, look at it! It's gorgeous!"

It was salmon with shrimp and crab stuffing, and it was beautiful.

"Haven't you made it before?" Laura asked.

"Nope. I always try things out on company. Oh, salad." She jumped up to get the salad from the refrigerator.

"I'm too chicken to experiment like that," Laura said. "What happens is that I try everything out the week of the dinner party, and by the time we have it a second time, I'm bored with it."

"I guess I figure why should I suffer alone if something doesn't work." She looked at her uncle. "William said that Sunshine was in the costumes today. Anna will take her head off for her."

Ro looked unhappy. "I know. We straightened that out. She was just trying on stuff, she said, smiling like an angel. I marched her around the theater, showing her what's off limits, where she's allowed to go. She wanted to go below and see the trapdoor mechanism. Her words."

Gray shrugged helplessly. "Darned if I know what to do with her."

Ro said, very quietly, "Me too."

And that, Ginnie thought, was known as allowing enough rope. "We'll work on the play this week, maybe into next week," Gray said. "And then I'll tell her to go back home until late January."

"What trapdoor?" Peter asked suddenly.

"A lot of theaters used to have a single trapdoor on stage," Ginnie said. "They called it the Macbeth Trap, for Banquo's ghost to make his appearance and disappearance."

Ro snorted. "Where'd you hear that? It's the Hamlet Trap. That's where they bury Ophelia."

Ginnie flushed. "I don't believe you. It's the Macbeth Trap. Everything I've ever read about it says that."

"Well, honey, I think you read the wrong things." Ro's voice was easy, he was relaxed, enjoying the evening, the home-cooked meal. Neither he nor anyone else was prepared for the flash of anger that made Ginnie's voice shake when she abruptly left the table.

"Would it ever occur to you that maybe you could be wrong? Why is it always the other person?"

Gray reached for the wine and poured more for himself and for Peter, who was watching Ginnie with a frown. "I've seen it both ways," Gray said. "What I told Sunshine was that there's been a plague of spiders below stage and we had to call in exterminators who used some kind of spray on them. She doesn't go places that have been sprayed."

Ginnie came back with small plates for pie and started to clear the table. "Now you see the magic of whipped cream," she said, but her voice was strained.

As soon as they were all finished, Peter said, "Maybe you'd like to see the house? Would you mind, Ginnie? It's such a great house," he added to Laura. "And her models are terrific."

"Let me," Ro said, and took Gray and Laura off for a tour.

Peter held Ginnie in his arms. "What happened? Are you all right?"

She nodded. "It's . . . I don't know what came over me. It's okay now. Sorry."

Together they filled the dishwasher and prepared the coffee tray. Then the others returned to the kitchen, talking about the models of stage sets that Ginnie had done.

"They're wonderful, just wonderful," Laura said. "What a shame they aren't on permanent display somewhere."

Ro nodded emphatically. "In the lobby. I keep saying we should set up a showcase in the lobby."

Ginnie laughed and shook her head. "Come on. Let's have coffee."

"Gray, how do you feel about musicals, operettas, even opera?" Ro asked suddenly.

Ginnie stopped and looked at Gray, waiting. He nodded, puzzled by the question.

"You see, Ginnie and I tried to talk Kirby into something last year that he really balked at. Never saw him come on so stubborn, but there it was. We had to give it up. What we wanted was *The Threepenny Opera*. Kirby turned it down flat, and if the director says no, you'd better back off or you'll have a mess on your hands."

Gray's eyes had narrowed. "It's a major production. Do you have the singers, the musicians?"

"Some of the best."

Ginnie began to sing in a husky voice: " 'And the shark he has his teeth and/There they are for all to see./ And Macheath he has his knife but/ No one knows where it may be—' "

She broke off and laughed. "It has wonderful music!"

She could tell by Gray's attitude that he was hearing the Kurt Weill music in his head. She put the cream on the tray and Peter picked it up to take to the living room. That was when the party ended, Laura later thought, when Gray nodded, and then again, with enthusiasm, and the three of them, Ro, Ginnie, and Gray, forgot Laura and Peter for the next two hours.

They were talking animatedly about the pros and cons of updating it rather than making it a period piece when Peter motioned to Laura and asked, "Did you see Romeo and Juliet in the workroom?"

Laura was certain that none of the others even noticed when she and Peter left.

"Do you know *The Threepenny Opera*?" Peter asked in the workroom.

She shook her head. "I know the song Ginnie sang, or at least it was familiar when she sang it. I couldn't have come up with it by myself."

"Me too. Here's Romeo." He took a tiny doll from a shelf and placed it in one of the sets. It was in scale. "And there's Juliet, hiding as usual." He put her in a different set. Each model set was about fifteen inches high, about that deep, and a little wider. Laura thought one set was for A *Doll's House*; she didn't know the other one. They were not labeled.

"Two different worlds," she said faintly. "They'll never get together that way, will they?"

He moved Romeo to Juliet's world. "How strange to think of all those worlds existing side by side, each one playing out its little drama, none of the people even aware of the other worlds, other people."

Shelves filled one whole wall; the sets were side by side from floor to ceiling, pigeonhole worlds, each cut off from the others, invisible to the others. Laura shivered and drew her sweater closer about her. Romeo and Juliet were together for the present, but she knew what the future held for them.

"It must be fun to make worlds, play with dolls, and call it work," she said.

He nodded. "Speaking of work, Ginnie says you're looking for a job. There's a man at the university, Dr. Lockell, who's looking for a research assistant for a book he's doing. It's his life's work and he's been at it for years and God knows if he'll ever finish it, but he does want an assistant."

"In what field? I've never done anything just like that."

"Paleontology. But it doesn't matter if you know the subject. Believe me, he knows it. He's out to prove his theory in the face of opposition from the establishment that Indians were in the area thirty thousand years ago. The conventional wisdom is that they came twelve thousand years ago, no earlier. He's been amassing data for forty years. Now he's looking for someone to help sort it, to type his notes, organize his findings. He really doesn't want an expert, just someone able to do organizational work. Would you be interested in talking to him about it?"

She nodded. "You got our house, and now you're finding a job for me. How can I thank you?"

With a wry grin he moved Romeo once more, away from Juliet, out of her world. He looked at the two dolls and said, "Maybe, if they can't get together all that much, they need someone else to talk to, someone who understands about all those separate worlds."

Laura wanted to weep, for both of them.

SEVEN

G innie slumped in a chair in her living room. "It's the damn budget meetings that get me," she groaned. "Gray made Eric fly off the handle by suggesting maybe he wouldn't be able to keep up with all the stage managing, prompting, helping with the directing, and Eric yelled that he could do it, but not with Gray standing over his shoulder all the time. Uncle Ro had to get between them, and then he stirred it all up again by saying he still thinks Sunshine's play should be abandoned, and Sunshine put down a well or something. She's driving everyone crazy." She sighed and accepted the glass Peter held out. It was a rather strong gin and tonic. She drank gratefully.

Peter nodded. Laura had told him that Gray's rewrite of Sunshine's play was driving him, her, and Sunshine all mad. No matter what he did, Sunshine undid it. Her current version would run three hours. Gray had said it would work, and he'd make it work if it killed him. He was up most of the night, night after night with it. As far as she could see, it got no better, just longer.

"Ginnie, is it always like this at this time of the year?" Peter asked.

She shook her head. "Part of it is. This is when they do all the repairs on the theater, painting, cleaning the carpets, plumbing, all that work that gets put off during the season. But the rest of it . . . It's because we have a new director, that makes people nervous; and that woman." She shook her head, drank again. "That helps. Now, let me tell you our program for the year."

He put his finger on her lips. "No more show biz for tonight. Finish your drink, wash your face, and change your clothes. Remember the dinner my department's giving me? It's tonight, one hour from now."

She jumped up. "Oh, damn! I forgot!"

"I know. But I remembered and there's plenty of time."

She looked stricken. "How can you stand it? Why do you put up with me?"

"Because I love you. Now scoot."

There were twelve people at the dinner in Margo's Restaurant, and although Ginnie had met most of them at one time or another, he was certain she did not remember. She charmed them all anew.

"When I was in grade shool," she said late in the evening, "I took my collection of rocks for show-and-tell. Remember show-and-tell? It's how they torture children and get away with it. We had to participate. Anyway, I got up and showed my sorry bunch of junk and talked about the Indian heads I had found and they all laughed. I fought at recess with a boy who was built like an ape over it, won, too. It was years later that I realized they were arrowheads."

She told theater stories only when asked. ". . . so she finished her aria and jumped over the balcony," she said. "The stagehands were there with a trampolinelike thing, a fireman's net or something. Well, she hit it wrong, and up came her feet, then a second time, and even a third time. The audience pretended not to notice."

Finally it was over and Peter and Ginnie walked to his car. He put his arm around her shoulders. "You were swell,' he said.

"What do you mean?" she asked carefully.

"Ah, Ginnie, I've known you for eight months now, in all kinds of moods. Tonight you were an Oscar candidate. Thanks."

"I'm sorry," she said in a low voice. "They're nice people."

"Shh. No more. Let's go home."

Their lovemaking was almost desperate that night. Ginnie was almost desperate, he thought later, when she was asleep. She knew it was ending, he thought, just as he did. And there wasn't a damn thing either of them could do about it. He had seen Ro in the restaurant when they entered and had pretended not to; Ginnie had not seen him. He had hated the man with an intensity that was alarming at that moment. Ro would win, Peter realized, and not have to lift a finger, say a word. There was nothing he, Peter, could offer her that could compete with what Ro could give her. He thought of her model sets, of Romeo and Juliet in separate worlds. It was a long time before he could sleep.

Ginnie prowled the theater. Outside Gray's office door she paused momentarily. He was shouting, "Damn it, Sunshine, what would a real live man say when he brought home a strange woman? Not, 'This is my angel of destruction.' My God, not that!" Ginnie moved on.

William was directing a crew changing a cable from the overhead grid. She watched for a second, moved on. Bobby was in the light box, playing with his new system. She watched the light sweep across the stage floor, moved on. Anna yelled at a deliveryman not to put it there, goddamn it! Eric and Brenda were arguing about something near the call-board; Brenda stormed away, Eric turned and yelled at a painter. Ginnie left the backstage area, made her way through the dim auditorium, using a penlight now and then in places where the stage lights did not reach, and finally sat down in the last row center. She carried her sketchbooks and pencils in her bag. She stared blankly at the stage, ignoring the men working on it, ignoring the lights that changed with incredible speed. Bobby was having a private light show. After a while she brought out a sketchbook, and her hand flew as she did one sketch after another, hardly even looking at what she was doing, only occasionally shining her light on the pages. After a time she got up and moved to the left of the auditorium, sat down and began to sketch again. She moved several more times, barely aware of when she did so, paying little attention to where she was sitting, never staying long in one place.

She was startled suddenly by Sunshine's voice directly behind her. "Is that how you do it, in the dark? I should have guessed. Your aura's blue, you know?"

Ginnie snapped the book shut. "What are you doing back here, Sunshine? I thought Uncle Ro told you to stay backstage."

"No, that never came up. I can't go in the light box, or below stage, or in any of the offices. He didn't say I can't come sit out here. How can you see what you're doing?"

"I can't." She stuffed the sketchbook and pencil back in the bag and started to get up.

"You want me to read your cards? I read tarot, you know?"

"No, thank you. I have to go now."

"I read them already, you know? I do that, read them first just to make sure there's nothing terrible coming up. If there is, I don't like to talk about it. Yours isn't so terrible. But you have black spots, you know?"

"I don't know what you're talking about. I have to go." She fled.

She found Gray in his office. He looked as tired as she felt. The manuscript was on his desk. Kirby had stripped the room of all but the basic furniture: the desk, two chairs, a filing cabinet. Gray had added nothing of his own. It looked barren and uninhabited.

"I have to talk to you," she said at the door, and waited for his nod. She entered, closed the door behind her, and crossed the room to stand before the desk.

"You've got to get that woman out of the theater. She has to go."

"Sunshine? What's she done now?"

"Never mind specifics. You know how it's been with her. She's . . . she has to be out before auditions start."

He stood up. "I wasn't aware that I was to take orders from you. Is this a new thing, or are you presuming a bit too much?"

"Damn it, Gray! You know how disruptive she is! She's driving people bananas! And for what? Why should anyone have to put up with her?"

He snatched up the play. "This is why. Listen." He read the first page, then the next. He was a very good reader, better than many actors she had heard reading. He slammed the manuscript down again and glared at her. "Say it! It's good and you know it!"

She nodded. "It's good. I'm surprised, but it's good. Your work or hers?"

"Hers! I have to force her to read each line, say each line and then tell me what she wants them to say, and then get that on paper, but it's hers. And it's damn good."

"I don't care! If she were writing a masterpiece, if she were writing *Faustus* I wouldn't care! It isn't worth it to the rest of us!"

"If you can't control your own temperament, maybe it's your problem, not hers!"

The door opened and William stuck his head in. "Private fight, or can anyone get in on it?" Directly behind him was Ro. He gave William a push and they both entered. The office was very crowded suddenly.

"Ah, you know, on this side of the building, the walls are pretty thin," William said apologetically.

"That woman's out there hanging on every word," Ro said in an icy tone.

"Well, let her hear!" Ginnie yelled. "Let everyone hear! What do you think it's going to be like around this place when she starts doing tarot readings for the cast? Can you imagine it? 'I see a catastrophe, a terrible accident. Avoid dark men.' Bullshit!"

She suddenly passed William and Ro and yanked the door open and screamed, "Get the fuck away from this door! Get out of here and let us have some privacy!"

48

"I wouldn't say anything like that," Sunshine said, smiling gently. "I told you I don't say when things look bad." She smiled at the men vaguely and turned, wandered slowly down the narrow hallway toward the costume room. Her shopping bag clinked and clanged as she moved.

"She minds you," William said doubtfully to Ro. "Order her not to read the cards."

"Then she'd turn up with chicken entrails or a crystal ball or something," Ginnie snapped. "You can't think of all the things you'd have to order her not to do. It's don't-put-beans-up-your-nose time with her."

"Simmer down, honey," Ro said then. "How long do you need with her?" he asked Gray.

"Another week at least. She's doing good work right now. It's just that she has to wander about and think from time to time. Maybe I can keep her confined to the office when she's here."

"Maybe you can make time move backward," Ginnie muttered.

"Maybe you've got some kind of personal problem you're taking out on her," he shot back at her.

"And after you're through writing her play for her, what then? You know damn well she's not going away until it's staged and she plays prima donna at opening night. If you order her to stay out of the theater, she'll hang out at the door smiling at everyone who comes in. My God, she's an albatross!" She pulled the door open. "I'm edgy, and bitchy, and tense, and mean as hell, buster, and it's not because I have a problem. It's because I have work to do and want to do it and this is how I get. I don't need you, or your discovery, to add to any of those things. I'm going home and I won't be back until she's gone. Call me when it's over." She slammed the door behind her.

Gray sank back into his chair and expelled a long breath.

Ro went to the door. His face was composed, his voice flat as he said, "This is your problem, Gray. Solve it before tonight." He left.

"We'd better have a little talk," William said. He pulled a chair around to face the desk and sat down. "There are a couple of things that I don't think you understand yet. One is that Ro won't put up with a lot of hassle where Ginnie's concerned. And less where the theater's concerned. That's just how it is with him. Now what are we going to do about Sunshine?"

Gray shrugged helplessly. "God, I don't know. Laura won't let me take her to the house. We can't work in that room she's renting. I tried and it's hopeless."

"There are several possibilities," William said slowly. "One's here, and that's out. Believe me, Gray, that's really out. Ro knows how Ginnie works. She prowls backstage, out in the auditorium, in the light box, out in the shop, and then she settles somewhere drawing like a maniac. And up again. She walks miles in this stage, and she lied when she said she gets mean. Usually she won't even see you or say a word to anyone. And we've all learned to leave her alone. She's too good to upset, you see, and Ro knows that. He won't let you, or Sunshine, or anyone else upset her. It's not even a choice between her and Sunshine. No choice to it. And I'm afraid that there wouldn't be a choice between you and her, either. Just how it is."

Gray nodded, knowing it also. That meant his house, he realized, and he knew Laura would have to accept it. She had no choice either.

William went on. "And when Ro said by tonight, that's what he meant. He'll want to know exactly how it's been settled, and he'll want to know by tonight. So, it's her room, or your house, or rent an office, or something." He stood up. "I'll talk to my wife about her. Maybe she can stay out at my house during the day until the show opens. Shannon's sick, she might even like having someone in to read the cards, make herb teas, just coddle her generally. I'll see about that."

Gray rose, too. He held out his hand and William shook it. "Thanks. I'll tell Ro I'm getting her out of here, at least until rehearsals."

When Gray told Laura, she stared at him, her eyes wide and frightened. "Don't you see what's happening?" she whispered. "We're acting out her play."

She remembered what he had said about entering another reality, living it, making others accept it. But not me, she wanted to cry out.

"I don't have a choice," Gray said tiredly. "It won't be for long, a week at the most."

Silently she went to the kitchen to start dinner. The next afternoon when Gray returned from the theater to work with Sunshine, he found her reading the cards for Laura.

"What are you doing here? I told you to come at two."

"I didn't want to make you wait for me, so I came early," Sunshine said, smiling her gentle, soft smile.

He looked at Laura. Very brightly she said, "Well, I'm off to the university. I'll work until five or a little after. See you later."

Too bright, too cheerful, he knew, and felt helpless to do anything about it.

It was cold outside, a week before Christmas, and Laura drove instead of walking as she usually did. That had been as silly as she had known it would be, she told herself. Sunshine was mildly crazy, not dangerous certainly, but not quite normal. Auras and tarot cards and prophetic dreams! Silly woman. Still, the words played around and around in her head like a tape loop.

"Danger in water. Money all around. Dreams and illusions, fantasies lead to danger in water, death in water."

EIGHT

"**Y**ou want to see it?" Ginnie asked Peter, indicating her large sketch pad.

He joined her in her workroom, stood by her desk.

"Okay. The stage is pretty bare for the whole thing. The desk is the symbol of Big Nurse's authority, right? When she's on stage, the light is cold blue, but subliminal, not blatant. There are three levels, one with her desk, one that the inmates use to approach her, the guards use, and so on. That's where they have the sessions. And the lowest level is where the patients talk to each other. When Mac is on stage the light is warm, yellows, reds, again subliminal. The fishing scene has a sky cyc and blue lights running along the floor. Bobby can do amazing things with those lights. The desk is the boat with the men hanging on to it, one or even two of them on top it, and the upper platform is gone. They've taken the authority to themselves. Then, for Mac's death, there's only one level. The desk is his bed where Chief kills him. Moonlight comes through the big

52

window here. That's where Chief bends the bars and walks away, into the moonlight."

She looked at him waiting for his response. His throat felt too tight to speak. Finally he said, "It's terrific, really powerful."

She sighed. She was tired, and by now the idea that had hit her with such force seemed self-indulgent, incomplete.

"I wish you could come with me. I really want to show you off to my folks."

"I know. I wish I could."

"Yeah. Well, remember you promised me New Year's Eve. And the whole week starting on the seventh."

"I didn't either," she said indignantly.

"I know, but you will. Wait and see. I'll be back on the thirtieth. Take care of yourself. Get some rest, okay?"

"I'll be at the airport. Be careful driving. There's new snow on the pass."

He nodded and kissed her and left. Before his car was out of her driveway, she was back at work, humming softly to herself the Moritat from *The Threepenny Opera*: "When the shark has had his dinner/ There is blood upon his fins./ But Macheath he has his gloves on:/ They say nothing of his sins. . . ."

Ginnie saw Laura and Gray at a party now and then over the holidays, but she did not go to many, and did not stay long when she did, and they did not mention Sunshine, or the rift she had caused briefly. Ginnie knew that Gray was as busy right now as she was; they were the two busiest people of the theater group at the moment. He had all the plays to update, alter, shorten or lengthen, whatever, and she had her preliminary drawings to get done by the first of the year. As soon as he handed copies over to Anna Kaminsky she would hurl herself into work, too, on the costumes, but for now Anna was free, as were most of the others.

Sunshine was going to William's house every day to keep Shannon company. She had decided that she could cure Shannon's defective heart with her herbs and a regimen of vitamins and fruit juices. Shannon, William reported, was thriving on the treatment.

Laura was terrified of Shannon. She had met her only once and made excuses to avoid seeing her again. The only way Shannon could get William's attention even momentarily, she believed, was through illness, and it was frightening to her that a woman would prefer that to being alone. When she mentioned her theory to Gray he looked at her as if she had committed a particularly nasty blasphemy.

For the most part she stayed home and stared at the small Christmas tree she had decorated, did a little work for her employer, who had gone to Indiana for the holidays, and waited for Gray to come home, or for Gray to finish what he was doing and talk to her, or for Gray to get ready to go out to dinner or to a movie with her. Waiting, waiting, she thought, that was her life here in ash land.

Gray had told her about the big fight with Ginnie and Ro over Sunshine, and she often found herself praying that Sunshine's play would be so bad, that she would make such a nuisance of herself, that Gray would get in such trouble over her that Ro would simply fire him and they could go back home and life would be as it had been.

The day after Christmas Ginnie told her uncle that she had given Peter the model for the production of *Major Barbara*.

"You gave it away?" He tried belatedly to keep the surprise and shock out of his voice.

"For Christmas. He really liked that one."

"Ginnie, those models, they aren't for things like that. They belong in the archives, in a collection."

She was sitting in the yellow chair, he was on the couch facing her. She had given him eggnog and cookies, her contribution to the holiday spirit. Slowly she said, "They're mine, Uncle Ro, not theater property. Like my sketches, my notes."

"No, you're wrong. They belong to the theater, not to you, or me, to the theater."

"It's not a body that can own anything. It's a building where we make things happen, but it's nothing in and of itself," she said emphatically.

He shook his head. "That's what it was when I first came to Ashland, a shell, abandoned, in disrepair, ready for the wreckers, but now . . . I hope you'll come to know it's more than that. It really is more than that, Ginnie, or it wouldn't matter about the models. I'd see it burned to the ground before I'd turn it over to a holding company, or a board of directors who saw it only as a way to make a good return on their investment."

"Well, the theater doesn't own me," she said firmly. "You know I've had offers to do sets for other theaters. I can work anywhere, send in my designs, models, finished drawings. I don't have to be there even. I don't have to be here, as far as that goes."

"But you do. I've seen those sets done by a designer in absentia. No heart, no soul. They could get them out of the book. Yours aren't like that."

"You're prejudiced," she said, and bit a cookie in half.

"I noticed that you didn't take any of those offers."

"I'm not ready. I still need to travel, see more and more theater all over the world, see what other people are doing, see how other people live. I didn't say I'd never take on outside work, just not now."

"And where are you planning to travel this year?"

"I've been thinking of South America. Peru maybe." She put the other half of the cookie down; it tasted stale and too dry.

Ro drank his eggnog and for a moment she thought the conversation had ended. Then he said, "Isn't that where Peter is going when he gets his Ph.D.?"

"He says digging in Peru is the greatest," she said with a grin.

He stood up and stretched and then, looking at her narrowly, asked, "Honey, do you love him?"

She hesitated. "I don't know. I'm trying to decide, I guess." She was trying to love him, she wanted to add, but she didn't know how; she was afraid of it.

"Well, I have to get along. You'll have the preliminaries done over the weekend? I'd like to see them before you show them to Gray, if you don't mind. I expect to have his promptbook for that damn play by this weekend. It'd better be decent."

55

"Are you holding him to showing you all of them?"

"You bet I am. I'm afraid my confidence in him was shaken over this mess with Sunshine. *Sunshine!* for God's sake! More like foul weather, if you ask me. You're looking tired. Pack it up and get some sleep, okay?"

She smiled at him and kissed his cheek. "Nag, nag."

"That's my job," he said and left.

Peter returned for New Year's Eve and they spent the evening at Bellair Inn, where they had dinner, then danced until two.

Peter was packing up his apartment; he already had taken a carload of things to southern California and had left his car there. "I have something to show you," he said mysteriously. "I can't wait. But I'm not willing to do it until you can appreciate it, not while your mind is completely on theater sets."

"Peter, be reasonable. I can't take off a whole week right now."

"You turn in the drawings for Gray to look at on Monday or Tuesday, right? That's what you told me. The following Monday there are auditions and you want to be back by then. But what do you have to do during that week? Even if you make changes, you can't start until after Gray's had a chance to look them over, and you know as well as I do that he's going to love them. You won't work on the models until after the cast is chosen and you've heard the readings. You said that."

"My God! Do you remember every word I've ever said?"

"Yes. I'm going to leave you strictly alone until Friday, when I'll arrive with dinner makings. And detailed plans for our week. Meanwhile, eat. Sleep. I love you."

She could do it, she knew. There was still a lot of work to finish, but by Friday afternoon she could be done. As for a whole week off right now, she was still certain she could not do that, but a few days surely. Four days, five? She went back to work.

There had been rain off and on for a week. Laura sat at the dinette table and talked to her mother, who reported three inches of snow on the ground. They had had a white Christmas, she said. Laura called Marianne next and heard about more snow and parties and how hard it was to get anyone to replace her. She gazed out the window at the dripping trees and found herself weeping. She could not explain it to Marianne; she simply hung up on her friend. She would say the connection was broken somewhere along the line. For a long time she wept. Everything she did was wrong, she kept thinking. She had complained about not having the car and he had put on his raincoat and walked to the theater; Ginnie had driven him home hours later. She complained about not going anywhere and he took her to one of their parties where she was miserable. And tonight, when she wanted him to go to a movie with her, and listen to jazz in a tavern with her, he had to go to a damn high-school play and check out the kids. When he asked her to go with him, she practically screamed no at him. No more plays, no more performances, no more theater, even if it was in a high-school auditorium and the kids were wonderful.

By the time Gray arrived with the car, she was carefully made up, no traces of tears remaining.

"I'll drop you off at the movie," he said. "I'll go on to the school thing and meet you at the bar at nine or nine-thirty. Would that satisfy you? We can stay as long as you want."

She shrugged. The movie house was only two blocks from the tavern and it was a reasonable concession, but she was in no mood even to pretend she was pleased with it. Neither spoke when they left the house.

Peter had brought steaks, salad greens, potatoes. "I knew you would skip food," he said reproachfully. "Look at you, five pounds lighter than last week."

She eyed the steaks hungrily and moved out of his way. It was not that she didn't get hungry when she was working hard, it was only that real meals were a nuisance and she ate whatever she could find that did not require cooking. Cereal, peanut butter, fruit.

"Anyway, I'm done," she said, seated at the table where he brought her guacamole and tortilla chips. Fattening foods, she thought, and ate gratefully.

57

"I knew you would be. There's a map on the table. I marked our trip for tomorrow. Want to take a look?"

It was a topographical map with a yellow highlighted line that weaved in and out of the hills to the northwest. "What's there?"

"You'll see when we get there. The woods are wet, remember to bring some extra socks."

"And snowshoes?"

"Nope. We won't be going up. In fact, it's lower than it is here. Eight hundred feet maybe. Now, no more questions."

They would take their first trip and return to her house, he told her over dinner, and on the next day, Sunday, on to the coast, to Whale's Head. There were cottages with fireplaces, overlooking the ocean, and a gourmet restaurant ten minutes from them. . . .

He took her hand. "Okay? I'm not asking for any commitment, not for more than the next week anyway. The rest can wait."

"It isn't fair to you," she said softly.

"It's much better to be me in love with you than to be anyone else on earth," he said. "That's as fair as I expect life to be." He squeezed her hand slightly. "Okay?"

She nodded. "I have to get the sketches to Uncle Ro in the morning, and tell him I'm going."

"Can't you do that tonight? I want us to start without anything hanging over us, just you and me—no work, no problems."

"You win. I'll write him a note and leave it with the drawings at the theater. That's where he'll go first thing in the morning anyway."

"Good. I'll come and we can pick up my gear and be all set to leave at the crack of dawn."

It was raining very hard when they left the house. Ginnie drove down Pioneer Street and turned into the alley by the side of the theater. The rain drummed on the car.

"I'll take the stuff inside," Peter said. "I have to get out at my apartment, anyway. No point in both of us getting soaked."

"You'll need a key, and there's Gray's raincoat on the backseat. He left it there a few days ago. You know where the office is?"

He nodded and dragged the raincoat over the seat, struggled to get it on and couldn't in the car. He draped it over his head and took the portfolio and key from her.

"Don't put it on his desk," she said. "Just leave it on the table. He's sure to see it first thing there."

"Right." He opened the door and dashed out into the driving rain. Ginnie watched him enter the theater through the stage door, then turned off the windshield wipers and headlights to wait for him. If this kept up into the morning, she thought, it would be one hell of a hike in the woods. Maybe he would call it off, do something more sensible, like curling up in her house before the fireplace and napping all day. She smiled slightly. Peter had had her out in all kinds of weather. He didn't seem to notice if it was raining or not. Like Christopher Robin, she thought, he didn't care what it did just as long as he could be out in it.

She was content, satiated with good food and good wine, warm, and sleepy. Not only did she not eat often or properly when she was working hard, she also did not sleep on schedule. She tried to remember the past ten days, when and how long she had slept at a time. It was a blur. Not enough, she decided, yawning.

She was not sure how long she had been waiting for Peter when she realized that it was taking him too long. If Spotty had cornered him, she thought, she would be out here waiting forever. She gave him another minute or two, then got out of the car and ran to the stage door. She expected it to be closed and locked, but Peter had not pulled it to, and she pushed it open and went inside. There was a dim light on in the backstage area. It cast a feeble glow down the hallway to Uncle Ro's office, where she could see a brighter light outlining the partly open door. She went down the hall to the office and pushed that door open.

"Peter?" she called, and then she saw him, and she screamed.

NINE

Gus Chisolm had been the chief of police for eleven years, and during that time there had been murder done, robberies, whatever mayhem people found to commit against other people and property. His first act when he arrived and saw a body was to call the sheriff's office. All murders were handled by that office. He was glad it was like that. Now he surveyed the office from the doorway glumly. Burglar caught in the act? More than likely. One of his men was at the door, another was checking the other entrances of the theater. A search would have to wait for more personnel. He went back to Spotty's room where Ginnie sat like a marble statue, with just about that much color in her face. She stared straight ahead, exactly as he had left her. She needed a doctor, he thought, and wished the officer he had sent out to find Ro Cavanaugh would hurry on with it before the sheriff's detective got there. He knew Steve Draker would want to question Ginnie right now, and to his eyes she was not fit to answer even one question.

On the table by her chair was the coffee that Spotty had poured for her, placed in her hands. Gus picked it up and said, "Ginnie, drink some of this. You'll have to answer a few questions."

Obediently she took the cup and sipped from it and returned it to the table.

Gus sighed and pulled a straight chair around to face her and sat in it. "Ginnie, didn't you see anyone at all? Someone come out the door and run, maybe?"

"No."

"Do you remember what happened?"

She nodded.

He wanted to shake her, to make her cry, faint, do something, to make her face stop looking as dead as Peter Ellis was. He patted her arm and stood up. Spotty was watching her with an expression of worry also. Gus motioned to him to step outside the small room.

"Do you know who her doctor is?"

"Jack Warnecke, more than likely. He's Ro's doctor, leastways."

"I think we shouldn't wait for Ro. You'd better go to a phone and call him. Tell him what she's like, what happened here. Tell him to bring something for her." So to hell with Draker, he thought. She needed something. He had known Ginnie first when she was a kid living with Ro, then since she had been back in town working in the theater. He never had seen her like this and he didn't like it. To hell with Draker.

Ro arrived before Draker. He came in with Walt Olien, who reported: "He was at Jake's Place with Jerry Alistair and a couple of other people. They drove over from the high school together."

Gus returned to Spotty's room where Ro was holding Ginnie, looking almost as pale as she was.

"My God, my God," he said over and over.

There were raindrops on Ro's shoulders and his shoes were wet, Gus saw. But anyone who entered the theater tonight would have wet feet. The alley was awash and a small lake was in front of the stage door. Ginnie was not responding in any way to Ro.

61

A deputy came to report that the theater was locked up tight, as was the shop out back. He had glanced in various rooms, but had not made a real search. Then Draker arrived with his crew and officially the case was out of Gus's hands.

Gus went with him to the office and waited while he looked over the scene. Peter Ellis was stretched out on the floor with the side of his head caved in from a heavy blow. There was an upset wooden chair that he must have hit on the way down; nothing else seemed out of order, except for a bronze statuette of a clown that was lying by the doorjamb. It was covered with blood on one end. Gus told Draker what he knew about it, damn little. Steve Draker was a thin man of forty with an intense stare that Gus hated. He always looked like he was trying to see clear through you, he thought, when they returned to Spotty's room. He watched Draker make himself comfortable in a straight chair within touching distance of Ginnie. Ro still held her against his chest.

"I have to ask her a few questions," Draker said. "Would you mind stepping over there."

Ro was on his knees in front of Ginnie's chair. He moved to the side and sat on the arm, and held her around the shoulders.

"You're Roman Cavanaugh?" Draker asked. Ro nodded. "The young lady looks perfectly calm to me. If you don't mind moving out of the way . . ."

"I do mind," Ro said. "Can't you see that she's in shock? Her doctor's on his way now. I don't want you to bother her until the doctor says she's all right."

"Miss Braden, do you feel able to answer questions?" Draker asked, turning his penetrating gaze on her. She nodded. "Good. What happened here tonight?"

"He's dead."

"Yes. We know that. Why did he come here?"

"To bring my sketches."

"Were you with him?"

"Yes."

"Who killed him, Miss Braden?"

62

"I don't know."

"But you said you were with him."

She looked straight ahead without responding.

Ro tightened his grip on her shoulder. His face was darkening with rage. "Damn you," he said. "This can wait for the doctor."

"Mr. Cavanaugh, I have a job to do. Don't interfere, or I'll have you escorted out to wait. Miss Braden, did you see who hit Mr. Ellis?"

"No."

"Where were you? Why didn't you see it happen?"

"I was in the car."

Draker leaned forward. "Just tell me what happened. I don't want to draw it out of you a word at a time."

"I came in and he was dead."

"Why did he come in? Why didn't you bring in the sketches?"

"It was raining. He wore Gray's raincoat. He was closest to the stage door."

"My God," Ro suddenly said in a horrified voice. "What if she had come in first? That could have been her!"

There was a silence in the room for a minute. Gus heard Jack Warnecke's voice raised in argument with one of the sheriff's men. He stepped out of the room and walked the length of the hallway, saw Jack near the door where the argument was going on.

"Gus, will you tell this man I'm Ginnie's doctor? I demand to see her."

"She's back this way," Gus said. He did not know the name of the deputy who was standing in the way. Coolly he added, "I'll take the responsibility. Get out of the way." The deputy hesitated for a moment, then moved, and Jack followed Gus.

"Miss Braden, why were you trying to close the office door when Spotty found you?" Draker asked, just as the two men entered. He scowled at Gus, his eyes very narrow and shadowed.

"I don't know," Ginnie said in the same dead voice.

Jack went to her and held her wrist, looked at her eyes, backed off a step, and said, "That's all. I'm giving her a sedative. Ro, is there someone who can stay with her tonight?"

"I'll call Brenda. After we're through here, I'll go up to her house, too."

"Good. I'll take her home now and wait for Brenda. Come along, Ginnie."

She stood up.

"Just hold on a minute," Draker said furiously. "I'm not through with her yet."

"Yes, you are," Jack said. "If you pursue questioning with her in this shape, I'll file a complaint, and if I have to I'll testify that nothing she says is reliable. She doesn't know what she's saying. Come on, Ginnie."

"For God's sake!" Ro said to Draker, who had moved to block the way. "You know where she lives, where she'll be."

Draker finally nodded. "I want to see her first thing in the morning. Alone."

"With an attorney," Ro snapped.

Jack led Ginnie out. She moved like an automaton.

Laura and Gray were in separate bedrooms. She stared at the ceiling dry-eyed and replayed again and again the furious scene that had led to her stamping out of the living room, to this room. It had been raining when she left the movie; that had started it, she thought now. A cold, miserable rain that had soaked her almost instantly. He had not been in the tavern when she got there. The jazz pianist had packed the place and she had not been able to get a table, or even a place at the bar. She had stood, cold, wet, more unhappy than she had been in years, in a mob of people she neither knew nor wanted to know. And finally he had come, almost as wet as she was. He had surveyed the crowded tavern bitterly.

"This is your idea of fun?"

"Let's go home. I'm freezing."

"And miss the music? And have you complain I won't go anywhere with you? No way. I want a drink. Besides, it's raining."

"I know it's raining, dammit! Look at me! I'm soaked! You had the car. You lost the umbrella. I didn't have a nice big black umbrella, or a poncho, or a raincoat. I want to go home. Give me the car keys. It's my car, remember?"

Silently he turned and stalked out; she followed. The rain was bitterly cold, relentless. Great puddles had formed in every dip. Her toes ached with cold and she was shivering too hard to drive. And she was crying. Only her tears felt warm on her cheeks, burned her eyes, the rest of her was freezing. Neither spoke when they reached the car in the parking lot and he opened her door, walked around to the driver's side, got in. He drove too fast for the terrible visibility. She hoped he would wreck the car, injure her, be sorry . . . Her tears came harder. The rain on the windshield was too much for the wipers to clear off, and between her own tears and the tears of the car she was blinded.

When they were in the living room, he handed her the keys. "You'll have to beg me to drive it in the future," he said in a voice as hard as ice.

"I won't beg you for anything! I supported you! I quit my job for you! I drove you halfway around the world! When have I ever begged for anything, or even asked for anything? You just take and take and take. You use people and never even notice what you're doing!"

"That's what you think? That I used you? All you've done since we came here is bitch. Is that why? Because you think I was using you?"

"Well, didn't you? Don't you? And now I'm not as useful to you as I was. I can have my own car back. You're finished with it. Now the boss's niece can play my part, drive you here and there. Are you just waiting for Peter to leave before you move in on her? Do you think I can't see?"

"I think that," he said flatly, "I'm going to bed."

"So am I. In the other bedroom."

"Good."

"Damn you to hell! Just damn you to hell!"

The next morning she left before Gray was out of the shower. At the university she learned that Peter had been killed; it was all anyone was talking about. She closed her eyes to hide the instant relief that swept her. The doom she had sensed in ash land was not her doom, thank God. Very quickly her relief vanished and she thought of the terrible things she had said to Gray, and she thought, now Ginnie is really free.

Brenda had talked Ro into going home at two in the morning. There was no place for him to sleep, she had pointed out. She was taking the couch in the living room. Reluctantly he left after looking in on Ginnie, who was in a deep drugged sleep. He was back by eight, half an hour before Draker arrived with one of his deputies.

"How is she?" Draker asked.

"I don't know, calm anyway, still shocked, of course. She's in the kitchen." Ro led him through the foyer, up the stairs to the kitchen where Ginnie was having coffee. Brenda had made breakfast for her, but it was untouched.

"Good morning, Miss Braden. I hope you're feeling better." She nodded.

"Good. Miss Gearhart, Mr. Cavanaugh, would you mind going into the living room." Brenda left. Ro hesitated. "If she wants an attorney present, that's her right," Draker said. "Do you, Miss Braden?"

"No."

"Ginnie, if you want me, just call. I'll hear you." Ro studied her face for an answer. She barely nodded, and he left the kitchen.

The deputy sat down at the table, out of Ginnie's range of sight, and opened a notebook.

"Miss Braden, I want to say first that I'm very sorry. I do sympathize. I found your note to your uncle saying you were going away with Mr. Ellis for a few days. Will you tell me about that?"

"I don't know where he wanted to go. To Whale's Head. I don't know where else."

"Just tell me about your evening with Mr. Ellis, exactly what you did, when you went to the theater."

She moistened her lips. She looked as if she had been sandbagged, he thought, still pale down to her lips, with the staring eyes that he had seen on others who hadn't yet quite faced what had happened. He waited patiently.

Haltingly she told him about dinner, about the sketches that she had to deliver, about Peter's talking her into taking them to the theater on their way to get his things at his apartment so they could get an early start today.

"So it was raining when you left the house here. Do you know what time it was?"

She shook her head.

In her toneless voice she described driving down Park to Pioneer, into the alley on the side of the theater. She stopped again.

"Did you see any lights on? Your uncle's office is on that side of the building. Were there lights?"

"I don't know. I didn't notice. The rain . . ."

"Okay. You drove to the stage door, then what?"

"Peter said he would have to get out at his place anyway, he might as well be the one to take the portfolio in. Gray's raincoat was in the back. He put it over his head, over the portfolio, and went in."

"How did he get in? Did he ring for Spotty?"

"He used my key."

"Okay. Go on."

"I turned off the wipers and headlights, and there was just the rain. After a while I went in and he was dead."

"Let's take it a little slower, Miss Braden. He had your key. The door locks automatically when it closes. How did you get in?"

"It wasn't closed tight. Sometimes it doesn't and you have to push it. It just opened."

After she cried, Draker thought, she'd be all right. She probably was still full of Jack Warnecke's dope, feeling nothing, her voice distant, her eyes not seeing much of anything. He got up and poured her cold coffee out, filled her cup again, and brought it back. "Take some of it," he said and waited until she swallowed a mouthful or two. "Now, you pushed the door opened. What did you see?"

"Nothing. Spotty was in his room. I went down the hall to Uncle Ro's office and he was there, dead."

"How do you know Spotty was in his room?"

"I don't know."

"Was your uncle's door open?"

"A little." She held up her hand to show about three inches. "Go on."

"I opened the door and went in and he was on the floor. He was dead. I don't know what I did then." She shook her head, as if trying to clear a memory, then sighed. "Then you came."

"Did you touch the doorstop?"

She shook her head.

"You must have stepped over it, or put it in the way yourself. Did you see it?"

"No."

"You know which doorstop I'm talking about, made out of bronze, about this high?" He indicated twelve inches or so.

"The clown," she said.

"Yes. It was in the doorway when I got there. Did you move it?"

"I didn't see it."

"After you saw Mr. Ellis, what did you do? Did you touch him to make sure that he was dead?"

"No. He was dead. I knew he was dead."

"What did you do?"

"I don't know," she said faintly. "I can't remember doing anything at all. I was in Spotty's room and Uncle Ro was there and you came."

"You screamed, Miss Braden. Spotty heard you. Where were you when you screamed?"

"I didn't know I screamed."

"And you had to leave the office again because Spotty found you in the hall. Do you remember leaving the office?"

She shook her head.

"Spotty said you were pulling on the doorknob, trying to close the door. The clown doorstop prevented you from closing it."

Her eyes remained blank, almost unfocused, and again she shook her head.

"Were the lights on?"

"I guess they were. I could see."

"Did you see which lights were on?"

"No."

"Did you have to enter the office to see Mr. Ellis?"

"I opened the door and walked in and saw him."

"Did you step over the doorstop?"

"I don't know."

He took her over it again and then came back to several points but got nothing more from her. Finally he motioned to his deputy, who had made notes, and he stood up. "Get some rest, Miss Braden. I may have to ask you some more questions later. We think he must have surprised a burglar. Miss Braden, do you think anyone could have mistaken him for Gray Wilmot?"

"No."

"He was wearing Wilmot's raincoat over his head, is that right?"

"Yes."

"That's a fairly distinctive raincoat. Not many men here wear them at all."

"It wasn't on his head. I saw his head. . . ." She looked at her hands in her lap.

"Yes. Well, it's a possibility, but we think he walked in on a burglary. I'll be going now. Thank you, Miss Braden."

TEN

"She should have gone down to the funeral," Ro said unhappily to Gray, over lunch five days after the murder. The murder was all they thought about, even if no one spoke openly about it. The detectives kept coming around, asking questions, getting in the way, accomplishing nothing except to keep everyone uptight; he knew they could not continue in that state indefinitely, not and put on plays at the same time.

"Maybe I should ask her to start work on the models now, not wait for the auditions."

Ro shrugged. "Maybe. Not her routine. Doubt that she'd do it."

"I'm tempted to complain about the sketches, pretend I don't like them, have her do some of them over. Might get a rise out of her, jar her out of this mood."

"I don't think we ought to play any games with her," Ro said heavily.

"Yeah, me too." Gray became silent.

After a long time during which they finished their food and had coffee served, Ro said, "I hear that you and Laura are separating. Sorry."

"Good Christ! Where'd you hear that?"

"I don't know. No secrets in this town, I'm afraid. Sunshine found out first, I bet."

"It's been coming for a long time," Gray said. "She doesn't like it here and hates the weather. She'll probably head back East eventually."

They both looked out the café windows at sleeting rain that was falling steadily. The weather forecast was for snow by the weekend.

"Well, some like it fine, others hate it. I asked you to come with me today so we can talk about Sunshine's play. I read it—God, I don't even know when. It's okay. Not great, not what I would have picked, but you did a good job with her on the rewrite."

Gray lifted his coffee cup to hide the small rush of triumph that he knew would show in his expression, but Ro was not looking at him. He was still gazing moodily out the windows, his thoughts on Ginnie.

"Ginnie's mother went crazy, too, when her husband was killed," Sunshine said to Laura. They were in Laura's kitchen drinking rose-hip tea. Laura hated it and wanted coffee, or even a stiff drink, but Sunshine had insisted on brewing her special tea because Laura had a cold and she could cure it, she had said with her gentle smile. "And Ginnie stopped talking for more than a year. So I guess she went crazy, too."

Laura looked at her in disbelief. "How do you know all that?"

"Shannon tells me. She likes to talk about how it used to be. Sick people are like that, you know? It seems the less future they have the more they live in the past."

"How did Ginnie's father die?"

"Their house burned down and he died in the fire. Ginnie nearly died, too. Ro saved her life. He's really crazy about her, you know? Maybe that's why. People like people they help more than others."

71

Laura sipped the foul tea. Poor Ginnie, she thought. No wonder she was so withdrawn, so . . . absent. Twice in one lifetime to have violence hit like that. No wonder. She glanced at her watch, then asked, "Sunshine, why did you call me? Is there something you want?"

Sunshine smiled. "You're nice to me, not like the others. They don't like me because I scare them too much, but you've been nice. I read your cards again last night. I wanted to tell you."

"They don't dislike you," Laura said without conviction. "They're all just very busy."

"They're scared because of what I might tell them. They're superstitious, all of them."

"Maybe they just don't believe in the cards, that sort of thing. A lot of people don't. I don't. Not really."

Sunshine's smile did not falter; her pale, vague eyes examined Laura, then flicked over the room. "You should go away," she said. "Back home. Real soon."

Laura felt frozen, immobilized. Finally she whispered, "What do you mean? Why?"

Sunshine stood up and started to gather the various garments she had taken off when she entered. A sweatshirt over the plaid shirt, a jacket over that, a poncho . . . "You know," she said with assurance. "The cards said you know, you're the woman of wisdom, and what you know is dangerous unless you go away. I'll leave the tea. Drink some of it every few hours, you know?"

"I don't know what that means," Laura said and heard a thrum of fear in her own voice.

Sunshine looked at her for a moment, then said softly, "You know. Go away, Laura, real soon, you know?" She picked up her shopping bag; it rattled and clanked.

After Sunshine left, Laura continued to sit at the table. Go away, she told herself. Go away now. Pack up your stuff and leave. It's your car and he won't touch it anyway. She got up and poured the tea down the sink and started a pot of coffee. All she could think of was going away, but not without him, not alone. There had to be a way to get him to leave with her, there had to be. She could burn down the theater, she thought, and she shivered, thinking about Ginnie's father dying in a fire. But it would take something that drastic, that final, she knew.

It snowed several inches on Saturday and on Sunday Laura wrecked the car. She was on her way to the drugstore to get something for her cold, which had worsened considerably. She sat helplessly clutching the wheel when the car went out of control on the icy hill and slid sideways into a tree. She was unhurt, but the car had to be towed to a garage and they said it would be a week before it was repaired. Go away, she thought almost desperately, and now she could not, not for a week. As long as it had been her choice to remain in ash land, she had felt somehow protected, somehow secure, but now with the choice removed, she knew herself to be vulnerable and her fear grew.

On Monday the temperature was sixty-five, the sun was brilliant, and crocuses were blooming as if by magic. Good sign, William told Eric, who nodded, and even smiled faintly. The weather always broke for auditions, Anna Kaminsky told Gray: a good sign for the coming season. A good sign, Ro told Gary Boynton, the shop foreman; an omen of better things to come. A great season was about to begin.

Ginnie wandered into the auditorium to watch the auditions that morning. She sat alone and watched without movement for several hours, then left quietly and went back home. She felt as if she could not get enough sleep anymore. She wanted little to eat, but she kept wanting to be in bed, to be asleep. Like a baby, she thought, and yielded to the urge to go back to bed even though the sun was shining and the air was warm.

She had sent Brenda home the day after, and that night she had sent Uncle Ro home when he said he wanted to sleep on her couch. She did not want anyone in her house, did not want people to bring her things to eat, to try to hold her hand, talk soothingly to her. She wanted them all to leave her alone, not say anything to her, not look at her. She pulled the covers up to her chin and fell instantly into that deep dreamless sleep that she craved.

For the first time since that night, she came awake again after a few hours. She was wide awake all at once, and her stomach ached with hunger. She got up and was surprised to find a big piece of ham in her refrigerator, and cheese, milk, fruit. Uncle Ro? Juanita? She could not remember who had shopped for her. After a few bites of a sandwich, she pushed it aside, but the milk was good, and the cookies she found on her counter. On the end of the table there was a stack of unopened mail, and there was the map that Peter had brought over that night. She drew it across the table and opened it, traced the highlighted trail with her finger. He had wanted to show her something.

She did not go back to sleep. She looked in her workroom at the drawings for the new sets and thought briefly about making the models, then closed the door and went to the living room, where she sat in the yellow chair in the dark and watched the lights of Ashland. There were always a few lights on, and the streetlights were on. Her mind was blank as she watched the pale dawn drown out the artificial lights. It was going to be another perfect day, she thought distantly.

At eight-thirty she stuck her head in Ro's office and asked for a cup of coffee. He bounded to his feet and ran across the room to clasp her against his chest.

"Ginnie! Oh, God, Ginnie girl! Come in, come in!"

She hesitated momentarily, not looking at the floor, unable to look at the floor, afraid to look. Ro had replaced the carpet; there was nothing to see, but she was afraid to look down.

Ro prattled about the auditions, about the new season, how good Gray's promptbooks were, and pretended not to notice her hesitation, her inability to look anywhere except straight ahead. He handed her the coffee and said, "What a mooch!" His voice was hoarse.

She found that she could walk into the office, could drink the coffee, but she had nothing to say, nothing at all. She felt as if she had been gone a long time to a very distant place and needed to become oriented once more. Her uncle did not press her; he talked. And in a few minutes she left him.

She watched the auditions all morning, but without interest, without noticing what they said, how they moved.

Ro asked her to join him and Gray for a sandwich during lunch break and she nodded and sat silently while they discussed the progress of the auditions, talked about one or another of the actors, the musical director.

"Ginnie, come out into the sun for a few minutes," Gray said when it was about time to start the afternoon auditions. "I want to tell you how much I like your drawings. And the sun is fantastic."

They walked out together, out through the parking lot on the side of the shop, onto the sidewalk and around the building, back to the stage door. Gray talked enthusiastically about her work; she listened. Again she could not find anything to say. Back inside, she searched for some response. "Thank you," she said in a low voice.

On the corner of Lithia Way and First Street Laura held on to a parking meter, stunned. She had seen them come out from the parking lot, circle the shop, and turn back in toward the theater. Gray had told her the auditions would go on all day, for most of the week probably. She knew this was just the lunch break. But watching them, she had realized what it was that she knew, and she felt weak suddenly. She was ill, feverish, drawn out by the sun in spite of her cold and chills and headache. And now she knew.

She released her grasp of the parking meter and began to walk again, trying to think, trying to decide what she should do. She walked a block, then turned onto Pioneer toward the theater. A lot of people were heading toward it, actors, Eric, William, the woman from the costume department. . . . As she drew closer to them, one or two spoke to her. Then she saw Ginnie walking toward her. She stopped.

75

"Ginnie, I wanted to come see you, but Gray said you didn't want company. I wanted to help, at least tell you how sorry I am."

Ginnie looked uncomfortable, at a loss. She began to walk a little faster. Laura turned and walked with her to the corner.

"If there's anything I can do," she said, "please let me." Without thinking she put her hand on Ginnie's arm, then drew it back hurriedly at the look of confused startlement on her face. "I know you've been hurt very much," she said impulsively. "I don't want to hurt you. I can help you."

"Thank you," Ginnie said finally in a stiff, formal tone. She could not soften it; she felt as if she had forgotten how to act with people, how to respond to them, talk to them.

Laura nodded and left her, and Ginnie continued her walk home. All at once it occurred to her that she had to go see what it was that Peter had wanted to show her. She had the map, everything she needed. She had her daypack ready. She walked faster.

Ginnie drove on a well-paved, well-marked road, then one that was potholed with crumbling shoulders, one that had been gravel-covered in some remote past, and finally on a logging road. They all hugged the valleys, wound around creeks, and gradually descended. She was relieved. Going upward would have taken her into a snow zone rather fast. In the valleys it was spring; the creeks were furious white-water torrents with runoff already cascading down the mountains, turning the water gray.

The road was little more than a track; she drove very slowly and began to worry about a spot where she could turn around. It was not a good road to back out on. Peter's map showed the road ending at a waterfall, she reminded herself. He had been here less than a month ago; he had found a place to stop, a place where he could turn his car. She drove on.

All at once she came to the waterfall and a rocky, flat area large enough for several cars. She turned the car to head back out, then switched off the engine. The voice of the waterfall sounded everywhere, echoing from the valley, from the trees, everything at once. It was not very loud, just everywhere, almost intelligible. She walked to the edge and looked down. It was only about eight feet of fall over the rocky outcropping, but the mountainside continued downward steeply here, making a chasm, and across it there was a wall of trees that seemed to rise straight up. She could make out the silver ribbon of another stream tumbling down. It was lost among the trees, then visible again lower, then vanished altogether. The tiny streams were carving away at the mountain, carrying the mountain to the sea grain by grain.

She continued to stand without motion for a long time before she went back to the car and got out the map. Turn left here and go on by foot along the crest of this ridge until it begins to climb, then turn left again, downward. Peter was good with maps, with trails that she could not even distinguish as trails; he had been here within the month, she thought again. The trail was here. She pulled out her daypack and put it on, locked her car, and started to look for the trail. A three-mile hike, he had said. That was nothing. He had had her out on ten-mile hikes, eight-mile hikes, all-day hikes. Three miles was nothing.

Miraculously, the trail was visible, even to her. Not a well-marked trail, not leveled and smoothed, but visible. She wanted nothing more than that. The sound of the waterfall faded so gradually that she did not know how long the woods had been silent when she became aware of the silence. It was a deep silence, as if it had been undisturbed for eons; all the echoes of all past noises here had had time to die. She walked carefully, reluctant to break that silence with rustlings, with snapping of twigs, or even the sound of her breathing. The woods were so thick that no undergrowth survived in the perpetual shadows, the needles so thick that their resiliency made walking almost effortless. The trail was not hard to follow, but she knew that was because she was still on the ridge; when she left it there would be no falling ground on both sides to keep her oriented. He had found the trail, she told herself; it was here. Then she saw where she should turn.

The trail had been level ever since she started on it; now one way

77

led upward, and to her left it went down. Although it started down gently, it soon became steep, and the trees changed. They had been the black firs that made for the darkest forests, with fir branches sweeping gracefully to the ground, and so close together that little light penetrated. Now the trees were the more open ponderosa pines with a scattering of madrones. The madrones were so smooth they looked as if someone had peeled them, sanded them down thoroughly, then polished them until they glowed red. The pine trunks were deeply incised, also reddish. The ambient light became warmer, tinged with pink.

The ground turned rockier; she could not move soundlessly, but it was all right because overhead the madrone leaves were whispering in the wind that was up there and not below. *Stranger in the forest. Who is she? What does she want?* Were they whispers of alarm? Or simply comments? The madrones were broad-leafed evergreens, the wisest trees in the world, Peter had told her. They could live without bark; they could take nitrogen from the air and put it in the soil where other trees could use it; they reclaimed land after fires ravaged it, or loggers. And they talked when there was no apparent wind; perhaps they made the wind, he had said.

There was no way to go except down, even though there was no sign of a trail now, then suddenly the way was level again, and the trees were spread apart as if by a gardener. She started to move forward, then remembered that she should mark her own trail or she would not know where to start up and out of this valley. Carry a good length of twine, Peter had told her when he instructed her about what to keep in her daypack. She got out the twine and cut off a length, tied it to a tree, then went into the parklike setting. And after fifty feet or so, she stopped and caught her breath.

She had been plunged into a valley of giants! The trees were like the sides of buildings, soaring upward to a canopy hundreds of feet over her head. These were ponderosa pines of legends, mammoth, too large to comprehend. Awed, she walked forward slowly, feeling as if she had come upon a holy place, a place where spirits lived. But the spirits were alien, indifferent to her. She touched one of the

78

giant trees; it was warm to her hand. She put her cheek against the trunk, touched it with both hands, and she whispered, "I'm sorry. I'm sorry." She didn't know what she said, or why, only that she had to tell those spirits something, that one thing, and that now it was all right to walk among them.

The trunks had diameters of at least twenty feet, thirty feet. She walked from one to another, touching them, feeling their aliveness, and then she came to a stop again. Rounding one of the giants had brought her out to face the biggest tree she had ever seen, so big it was overwhelming, almost frightening. This tree was twice as big as any of the others. It stood alone in a large circle it had cleared for itself; it glowed in the late afternoon light. She felt its power and found herself moving toward it without volition. When she reached it and put both arms out in an embrace, she looked straight upward and was overcome with vertigo. Slowly she sank to her knees and pressed her cheek against the trunk. She began to weep, silently at first, without any motion, then harder and harder, until she was racked by sobs and her grief shook her entire body.

When the outpouring of grief ended, she sat under the tree with her back against the trunk. Twilight came and soon the darkness deepened. She ate everything she found in her pack and put on her wool sweater, then a poncho and wool cap, mittens. Finally she wrapped herself in the space blanket and lay down on the thick bed of needles.

Sometime in the unrelieved black of night the towering trees she began to whisper. She talked to Peter, to the spirits of the giant trees, to the tree that had to be the god of trees, to the darkness itself. She talked of her childhood, of her mother, of things she had never mentioned to anyone, had not remembered in years. Eventually her voice trailed off and she slept.

In the morning she walked to the end of the small oval valley that had nurtured the giant trees for centuries. It was not more than two miles long, half a mile wide; all around it the mountain rose steeply, hiding this holy place. She returned to the god of the trees, and touched it reverently once more.

"I won't tell," she said softly.

When she found her twine marker, she untied it carefully, then moved away from that trail, not wanting to leave signs, not wanting to make the trail down here more conspicuous than it was now. She started the climb back up to the ridge. She was in no hurry, the going was steeper than she remembered; she rested and looked behind her, but the valley was invisible already, the secret well hidden.

It was after nine when she reached the waterfall once more. She dug in her pack and found matches, and on the rocky ledge she burned the map and dipped water from the creek to wash away the stain of carbon. Satisfied, she got in her car and started the drive back. She was very hungry. She would stop in the first restaurant and have a huge breakfast.

When she got out of her car in her own driveway, a sheriff's deputy appeared from her front stoop and walked toward her.

"Miss Braden, Lieutenant Draker wants a word with you down at the theater."

She stopped. "Why? Can I see him after I have a shower, change my clothes?"

"No, ma'am. He wants you now. I'll take you in."

"But . . ." The deputy touched her arm as if to grasp it, force her; she flinched away from him, turned, and headed toward the car parked on the street. She had not even noticed it when she drove up. Another deputy was inside behind the wheel. "Can you tell me what's happened?" she asked.

"The lieutenant will tell you." He opened the door, and after she got in, he got in beside her. She had her daypack on. When she started to take it off, he helped her, then held on to it.

At the theater the first thing she saw was that auditions were not going on. Eric and William were huddled with Brenda and Anna; Bobby and Amanda White were talking at the stairs to the dressing rooms. Other actors were in a clump before the wardrobe room. She felt a rising panic.

Some of them turned to look at her with open curiosity; William started to move toward her. The deputy waved him back.

"Where is Uncle Ro?" she demanded. "Tell me what happened, dammit!"

"This way, Miss Braden," the deputy said, taking her toward Spotty's room. "The lieutenant wants to talk to you in here."

The room was small, only ten by twelve, cluttered with Spotty's narrow bed, an overstuffed chair, a table with a white Formica top, two straight chairs that went with it. There was a hot plate on the table, dirty cups, a paper doughnut bag. There was a television on a second table and a stack of magazines, more magazines on the end of the bed. Spotty usually straightened up the room before going home; the mess in here now alarmed her even more. She stood in the middle of the room; the deputy stayed by the door.

After a few minutes Draker entered. He surveyed Ginnie with narrow eyes. "Where were you all night?" he asked abruptly.

"Tell me what happened! Is Uncle Ro all right? What's going on here?"

"Miss Braden, we are conducting a preliminary investigation in the death of Laura Steubins. It's my duty to tell you that anything you say may be used in evidence, and it's your right to have counsel present."

Weakly she sat down in one of the straight chairs.

ELEVEN

The trouble with owning a snowblower, Charlie Meiklejohn thought, wrestling the machine into the garage, was that you felt obligated to use the damn thing instead of being sensible and hiring someone with a tractor to come and dig you out. His face was hot and he was sweating, but his feet were frozen. And that, he thought, was the trouble with the human heating system. Not enough here, too much there. Brutus, the gray tiger-striped cat, stared at him malevolently through slitted yellow eyes. Now Charlie spoke out loud. "I didn't bring the snow. I didn't order it. I don't like it any more than you do, so fuck off."

Brutus flicked his tail and stalked in front of him toward the back porch and the cat door into the kitchen. Brutus hated snow even more than Charlie did. But Brutus hated rain, and fog, and mist, and open country, and company, and a long list of other ills to which he was subjected. What Brutus liked was life in New York City with his own fire escape and his own crowd of night prowlers.

Charlie looked more bearlike than ever, Constance thought when he came into the kitchen. He was dressed in a down parka that seemed to expand his figure outward alarmingly. He put his boots on newspapers to drip and began to peel off garments. His hair was damp, very curly, shiny black, with only an occasional gray hair in no particular pattern. It would go salt and pepper, she often thought, and then silver, and he would be quite distinguished-looking. She timed the process of making Irish coffee so that when he was finished unwrapping, she was ready to place the steaming mug in his hand.

"I'd take you over a whole flock of Saint Bernards any day," he said gratefully.

"I think it's a herd," she said. "Or maybe a school. Or a snarl?"

He grinned at her and sipped the scalding drink. Just right. No whipped cream to muck things up, enough Irish to taste, and coffee thick enough to stand up to the whiskey. Just right.

What she didn't say, he thought, even more gratefully, was that if he hadn't told the Bradens to come on today, he would not have had to clear the driveway; he could have spent the afternoon before the fire with the other two cats who hated snow as much as Brutus did and were smart enough to stay inside and wait it out.

The kitchen was warm and fragrant with the aroma of Swedish limpa bread that was in the stove now. The recipe had been Constance's grandmother's, brought from the old country in her satchel along with her special cookie irons for the fried cookies that Charlie loved and Constance would make only at Christmas because they were not all that good for him. He had to watch his weight. Since he had retired, his tendency was to put on a pound now and then and never take it off again. He envied Constance her long, smooth body that never seemed to change. It was as alluring to him now after twenty-five years of marriage as it had been the first day he met and lusted for her.

They went to the living room where he opened the fireplace screen and stood with his back to the fire for several minutes. Brutus followed them and went straight to Candy, the orange cat with butterscotch eyes. He sniffed her ear and she jumped up and ran; he took her place on the hearth. Charlie laughed softly.

Constance nodded. The conditioning was textbookish, she thought. At first, when Brutus wanted to torment Candy, or eat her share of the food, or simply raise some hell in general, he had bitten her ears with some ferocity. Candy was a born coward; she ran. Now Brutus simply sniffed her ear and she fled. Any day she expected to see the same outcome if Brutus merely turned his wicked yellow eyes in the direction of her ear.

"That damn cat's too smart for his own good," she said. She sat down in the wing chair; when Charlie sat down it was in his ancient Morris chair with the hand-carved lions on the arms. She sighed with contentment now that he was inside, no longer cursing the snow. She knew it was harder on Charlie living out in the country than he liked to admit. Ostensibly he was writing a handbook on arson and how to detect it, but for several weeks now the snow had marooned them, isolated them, and he had started to pace, absently at first, then with more energy. Like Brutus, she thought, and never said that.

Years ago they had made the down payment on this country house; they had spent summer vacations here, fixing it up, getting it ready. Was it like most dreams, she wondered, hollow when finally achieved? Instantly she denied the idea. It was just the snow and the middle-of-the-winter inactivity that were getting to Charlie. Since retirement, he had taken on investigative work now and then, but for the last few months there had been nothing that had interested him enough to stir out for. Meanwhile, her own book on the comparison of various psychological therapies that had sprung up in the past dozen years was advancing even faster than she had hoped for. Constance was a psychologist; when Charlie retired, she had quit her teaching job at Columbia, sighing a prayer of relief that they both had been able to get out of New York intact. Or almost intact. Charlie had scars that she knew no one else could see. She knew where they were, how painful they could become from time to time. Twenty-five years on the New York City police force left scars of one kind or another.

"The funny thing is," Charlie said suddenly with a touch of surprise, "is that after I'm done with the damn snow again, I feel pretty good."

"Another one?" She suspected the Irish coffee had contributed more than a little to his feeling of ease now.

"Later."

She took both cups to the kitchen and checked on the bread. It was ready to come out. For the next few minutes she was busy, then the doorbell sounded and she returned to the living room in time to see Charlie ushering Dr. Morley Braden and his wife Louise into the house.

Charlie introduced her and she helped Mrs. Braden off with her coat, mink. Dr. Braden's coat was vicuña. They were old, Constance thought with surprise, in their seventies at least. Mrs. Braden looked it even more than her husband. He was straight and vigorous with iron-gray hair and steady, clear blue eyes. Mrs. Braden's eyes were hidden behind thick glasses. Cataracts? Constance wondered, and realized that they could not have driven themselves up from New York City. It was a two-hour drive, and in this weather, with snow on the various roads throughout the Northeast, she doubted that they would have started out alone.

"Do you have a driver?" she asked as Charlie led them into the living room.

Dr. Braden studied her with interest. "Yes. I was going to ask if it would be possible for him to come inside and wait."

Charlie went out to bring him in and Constance offered coffee, tea. Courteously they refused. Dr. Braden settled his wife into a chair before he sat down. Charlie returned. The driver was in the kitchen having coffee, he said, and took his chair.

He looked from Dr. Braden to Mrs. Braden. "What can we do for you? I'm surprised you didn't ask me to come into the city for a talk."

"Phil Stern warned me that you probably would refuse," Dr. Braden said. "He also said you were the two people we should talk to. That meant we had to come to you." He took a breath, then said, "We want to hire you both to investigate two murders in Oregon. We are afraid our granddaughter is going to be charged with them."

Charlie glanced at Constance. She looked relaxed, mildly interested. He knew she was content to spend the rest of the winter snowed in, working on her book, planning the spring garden. He knew also how much she hated murder cases.

He said to Dr. Braden, "You'd better tell us what you can about it. If the police are looking into it, ready to bring charges, you may want a lawyer more than another investigator." He was thinking that probably this was not for them, not if it had gone this far. He could not decide if he was sorry or glad.

Phil Stern was a friend from college days, now an independent insurance broker. Charlie and Constance had done a few things for him before. And Phil was jealous as hell, Charlie thought also, because he was still working and Charlie was retired. Phil had called to talk about the Bradens he was sending their way. Dr. Braden, he had said, was not the richest man in the world, but he was not counting pennies either. He had pioneered in microsurgery and, although he no longer did surgery himself, he was still one of the experts in the field, in great demand as a speaker, a seminar guest, workshop leader, all that sort of thing. Phil handled his insurance, and when Dr. Braden had asked for advice about investigators, he had supplied Charlie's name.

Dr. Braden did not speak immediately. He gazed at the fire as he collected his thoughts. "I think I have to start with some past history," he said finally. "Louise and I had one child, Victor. He was intelligent, creative, happy, everything parents always hope for and seldom get in a child. We loved him very much." Mrs. Braden gazed toward the fire with her clouded eyes and nodded slowly. He went on. "He was a student at Stanford, pre-med, when he met a girl, Lucy Cavanaugh. She was pretty, gay, talented, I grant all that. He fell in love with her, and presumably she reciprocated. We tried to talk to him, postpone any decisions until he was finished with his education, but it was hopeless. They ran off together. He dropped out of school and they went to Europe for nearly a year. There were . . . We argued bitterly, I'm afraid, and he didn't write, or call. . . ."

Louise Braden's hands clutched each other. She looked down at her small, pretty shoes.

Dr. Braden's pause was longer this time. Finally he continued. "We didn't know when they returned to the States. They didn't get in touch. I had a detective locate them for me in Ashland, Oregon, and I went there in the summer that their child was three years old. She was a lovely child, very much like Victor as an infant, busy, precocious, charming. I'm afraid I bungled it. I threatened him and his wife when I should have accepted whatever he wanted. I tried to make him agree to give up that life, to return to school, become a doctor. It wasn't too late, I kept saying, and he looked at me as if I were a stranger. It was far too late. Then he said that he was leaving Ashland as soon as the second child was born, in six months. They were going to Paris, where he would study art and architecture, not medicine. A week later he died in a terrible fire. He was twenty-five years old."

His voice did not break; it simply stopped working. He looked at the fire. Charlie got up and added a log, poked at it and sent sparks up the chimney. Brutus protested in a deep voice and moved back a foot or two, then curled up again and tucked his nose under his tail.

"Lucy miscarried that night," Dr. Braden said at last. "Virginia— Ginnie, they called her—was hospitalized for observation. She was in the house. Roman Cavanaugh, Lucy's brother, saved her life. I saw him bring her out; his shirt was on fire, his hair smoldering . . . It was horrible. Horrible."

Now his voice broke. "God help me," he said, "I blamed her, Lucy. Her own suffering, the suffering of her child, my grandchild, Ro's burns, none of that mattered. I blamed her for ruining my boy's life, destroying him. I left Ashland, left them all, and when I came to my senses, months later, she was gone with Ginnie. Out of sight. Ro swore he didn't know where they were, and I guess he was telling the truth. He sent her money through a lawyer, and the lawyer would not reveal her whereabouts. I tried to find her, find our grandchild, and I failed."

His wife touched his arm. She said in a wavering voice, "I made him fire the detective. I was so certain that she had found another man, someone richer than Victor even, married, changed her name and Ginnie's name . . . We were so sure we understood her, it seemed the proper thing to do finally."

Charlie waited for a time, then asked, "Who was Lucy? Ro? Why were you so certain she was after his money?"

"Victor told us about her," Dr. Braden said heavily. "It was sordid. Her father was in radio, an announcer or something, gone most of the time, finally all the time. Her mother had a string of boyfriends. Lucy was twelve years younger than her brother, Ro. When she was about ten, he was gone, going to school and working. One of the boyfriends frightened her. I don't know if he molested her or not, but she ran away, went to her brother, and he kept her with him after that. He took her to the West Coast, cared for her, saw that she went to school, apparently did everything for her. They had no money, except for what he earned, but he was making a name for himself as an actor. Did some commercials, directed a little, things of that sort. The three of them, Victor, Lucy, and Roman Cavanaugh, went to Europe then to Ashland when Ro went there to buy the theater and rebuild it. When Victor's will was probated, there was only sixty thousand dollars in the bank, and the house that had burned to the ground. But when Victor was twenty-one, he had inherited a million dollars. It was all gone, spent, vanished. I know a million dollars isn't a vast fortune, but still, in five years . . . I blamed her, of course. But I don't know what happened to it. There were no papers, or if there had been, they were destroyed in the fire. Nothing in a safety-deposit box, nothing in a lawyer's office, nothing."

"Did the brother get the money?" Charlie asked bluntly.

Dr. Braden shrugged. "Who can say? He never admitted it if he did."

"Okay, so we have the background. What's happened recently?"

"Yes. Last year I was in San Francisco to give a speech at the AMA meeting there. The hotel had a stack of tourist-attraction pamphlets—wine tastings, shows, things of that sort. There was one about the Oregon Shakespearean Festival in Ashland. It's rather famous, you see. I glanced through it and found a second announcement concerning Ro's theater, Harley's. The announcement said that the sets were by Virginia Braden.

"After I was finished in San Francisco, I went up to Ashland," he said, his voice firm again, his eyes steady. "The sets were marvelous; she's very talented. But she was not in town. I talked to a lawyer there, hired him to inform me when she was home again, to find out everything he could about her past from the time her mother took her away until then. I could have asked anyone, I think now. It seems an open story up there. Her mother was killed in a car wreck when Ginnie was thirteen and Ro has taken care of her since then."

"To the rescue again," Charlie murmured.

Mrs. Braden suddenly said, "Lucy never remarried. She was never involved with another man. All those years we were so wrong about her. So wrong. And then I had to become ill, just when we could have met Ginnie, I had to become ill."

Dr. Braden patted her arm. "Ginnie was back and Louise had to have surgery. We decided to wait until spring and then take a trip to the West Coast, go to Ashland, spend a few weeks getting acquainted with our granddaughter. We planned to go at the end of February, be there for the openings of the new shows of the season." He took a long breath and let it out slowly. "The lawyer I hired called me yesterday. Early this month a man was killed in the theater. Ginnie was present. They were lovers. And Wednesday a woman was killed and Ginnie was gone all night and won't tell anyone where she was. It seems the man and woman had been seeing each other, having lunch, things like that. The circumstantial evidence, according to the lawyer, is damning enough, he thinks, to justify an arrest. But, of course, she didn't do it."

"How do you know that?" Constance asked softly. "You've met her, haven't you?"

Mrs. Braden looked at him sharply and slowly she nodded. "Last summer," she said. "You went back last summer, didn't you?"

"I had to see her," he said, looking at the fire. "I couldn't put us through all that again until I knew. What if she had turned out to be what we thought Lucy was? What if she was mean, hard, greedy, God knows what? I had to know before I told Louise anything about it. I went back. I didn't tell Ginnie who I was. I watched her, talked to her even. She was kind. You know how it is when you get to be our age? People don't want to be bothered if they don't know you. I can give a presentation, hold an audience of thousands, sign books, do all that, and have a waiter snub me because I'm old."

His voice was too matter-of-fact, Constance thought; he had learned to hide himself thoroughly. Had he appeared brutally cold to his son? Probably.

"Why didn't you tell me?" his wife asked, not looking at him. "After you met her, why didn't you tell me?"

"You were too ill at first," he said slowly. "Later . . . I don't know. I wanted you to meet her for yourself, not spoil that first meeting."

"You were still punishing me for making you stop the search," she murmured, examining her hands, rubbing one of the enlarged veins, then another.

"I've never held you responsible," he said gently.

"What if she actually did it?" Charlie asked coolly then.

"She didn't." He stretched his legs and shifted in his chair. "If they charge her, she'll need an attorney, naturally, but I don't want her to have to go through any of that. I want you to find out who did those murders and spare that girl any more grief. We owe her that much," he added in a lower voice. "God knows, we owe her that much."

"Dr. Braden," Constance asked then, "why did you come to us? What else is there?"

"You tell me something first," he said. "How did you know I'd met her?"

"Your expression when you talked about her. You were seeing her in your mind's eye."

"That's why I want you, too. Phil Stern called you a gifted psychologist; I think you've shown us that his opinion is justified. Ralph Wedekind, he's the lawyer in Ashland, he says they're saying Ginnie's crazy. She needs help, Miss Liedl, your help as well as your husband's."

"Have you been in touch with your granddaughter?" Charlie asked. "Does she know you're hiring us?"

"No."

Constance pursed her lips and Charlie went on. "Do you think that's wise, Dr. Braden? Suppose strangers came up to you and started asking questions about your personal life, your activities?"

For the first time he looked uncertain, grieved. "I'm afraid she might refuse our help," he said faintly. "Please, don't tell her unless it's necessary."

Charlie glanced at Constance and nodded.

Dr. Braden had brought the correspondence from the lawyer, his report on Ginnie and her uncle. Wedekind would arrange accommodations, he said. He was waiting for a call, anytime. He would meet them at the airport in Medford, drive them to Ashland, brief them, do whatever he could to assist them.

The Bradens prepared to leave shortly after that. As Charlie got their coats, Constance asked, "Why are you doing this, Dr. Braden? Hasn't her uncle always taken care of her? Don't you think he'll take care of her now?"

He helped his wife out of her chair and held her arm carefully until she was steady. "He might," he said, "but I want it to be us this time. For once I want us, the two of us, to take care of our own."

"You understand that, don't you?" his wife asked. "After all these years . . . she's all we have now."

"Of course I understand," Constance said, but even as she was saying the words, she wondered if they understood fully, if they were fooling themselves. How hard would they work to eradicate all traces of the trail of guilt they had brought with them from the past?

"Now," Charlie said after they were gone.

"Now what?"

"Now I'll have another Irish coffee. I'll make them."

"If I have a drink now, we won't have dinner until ten. And if you have a drink, I have to. I refuse to let you start being a solitary drinker at this stage in your life."

"What stage is that?"

He started for the kitchen and she followed. "Middle-aged, unemployed, drifting, restless, so bored you're willing to take a very messy case just because it will get you out of the house."

"Hm." He measured coffee beans into the grinder, ran water into the kettle, and placed it on the stove. He then rummaged in the cabinet for the Irish whiskey.

"It's on the counter," she said.

"So you think it's messy," he commented, taking the bottle to the table.

"Murder's messy by definition. And this one's messier than most because there are too many nasty echoes from the past."

"He was an arrogant son of a bitch, I bet, ordering his son into medical school, trying to keep him out of that girl's bed, trying to run his life in every way, I bet."

"He's still an arrogant son of a bitch," Constance said. "Not telling his wife that he met Ginnie. And coming here with a check already made out. He's just learned to hide it better." She watched Charlie pour steaming water over the ground coffee in the filter. "Why did you say yes? You hate this kind of thing as much as I do. What if she really did it? He won't thank us, that's for sure."

Charlie stirred the water and grounds. He thought that made it drip through faster. "You know how long our driveway is?"

She blinked. "Couple of hundred feet. Why?"

"Nope. It's three and a half hours of blowing snow and digging snow. Believe me, I know. I figure a little time in Oregon, which I hear is very nice, then on down to San Francisco, which I know damn well is nice, and from there it's five hours to Hawaii. I want to see a volcano in action. Rivers of fire. Hot sunshine. No snow."

"Have you also thought of who we can get to come out here this time of year?"

"Sure. Cousin Maud and that dumb ox of a husband of hers. So they'll clean out the freezer and drink everything in the house. Let them. We'll be on a blistering beach sipping mai tais. Ah, it's ready." He finished making the Irish coffee. They ended up eating cheese and bread in front of the fire, sipping their drinks. Outside, it had started to snow again.

TWELVE

Ralph Wedekind was a powerful-looking man in his middle years. His face was tanned, weathered; many lines converged at the corners of his eyes. He met Charlie and Constance at the Medford airport and drove them to Ashland. His speech was deliberate, without any affectation or accent that Constance could discern.

"What I'd like to do, if it's okay with you folks, is take you to the inn and let you get registered and settled and then come back in an hour and take you to dinner and talk. Would that suit you?"

"Sounds good," Charlie said. He wished it had not suddenly turned dark. Coming in to land, he had seen snow on all the mountains and had felt doomed, trapped wherever he went by winter. The road was clear, but he knew that could be misleading. Snow could be lurking in every shadow, in banks along the secondary roads.

The inn turned out to be a private mansion that had been

converted to a bed-and-breakfast hotel. It was spacious and very beautiful, Victorian, impeccably maintained. A broad curving staircase led to their two rooms on the second floor. When Constance looked at Ralph in surprise, he shrugged.

"Dr. Braden said two rooms in the nicest place we have to offer. This is it. Oh, here are car keys. I had a rental car delivered. It's in the driveway. A Buick."

Then he told them he would be back in an hour and left. Mrs. Shiveley, one of the owners, led them upstairs.

"Please, don't bother with the bags," she said pleasantly. "We'll have them brought up in a few minutes." She was plump with greenish eyes and auburn hair in a single braid halfway down her back. She, too, looked as if she spent a lot of time outdoors.

"When you wake up, ring for coffee," she said. "We'll bring it right away, and breakfast about half an hour afterward, unless you prefer to set a time. We'll serve breakfast in the sitting room. Lunch and dinner are available, but we have to know ahead of time, an hour at least. All right?"

"Fine," Constance said, feeling almost dazed by the treatment Dr. Braden was providing.

Mrs. Shiveley opened the door to their sitting room and ushered them inside. The room was spacious, with wide windows on two sides. The furniture was antique, the rug a Kerman. The bedroom was equally large and well furnished. In the sitting room a bar had been arranged with a bottle of bourbon, an ice bucket, and several glasses. Mrs. Shiveley opened a door on a chest to show them various mixers and several bottles of wine. "If there's anything at all we can do to make your stay more comfortable," she said, "please let us know. Coffee is available from six-thirty in the morning until midnight from the kitchen. If you would like it, we can bring a coffee maker and coffee things up for you to use. And there usually are snacks in the kitchen. Sometimes, if we know our guests will be here in the afternoon, we serve tea, but not unless we know ahead of time." She cast an experienced glance over the room, smiled at them, and left.

"Well," Charlie said, pleased, and headed for the bottle on the table. Constance went back to the bedroom and saw that while they had been in the other room someone had brought up their bags. She was as delighted with the house as Charlie.

"Like it?" Ralph asked when he picked them up later. He was grinning.

"Are you kidding? I may never leave," Charlie said.

"When I told Dr. Braden how much it cost, he didn't even hesitate. He wants you to be comfortable."

The drive to the restaurant was short, mostly uphill. Their table was at a window overlooking the town. It was like a postcard vista.

Ralph called their waiter by his first name, and was called by his. "He's my leader on the rescue team," he said after they had ordered. "Ski rescue," he added. "Do you ski?"

"Some," Constance said. "But probably not on this trip."

"Definitely not on this trip," Charlie said.

Drinks were served and then Ralph said, "Dr. Braden called me last night about the problem of keeping him and his wife out of this. We decided to let me be the one to hire you. You can refer any questions back to me and I'll stonewall as long as I can. If Draker makes noise, I may have to tell. He's the detective on the case out of the sheriff's office."

"Do you know Virginia Braden?" Constance asked. "If she asks you who's paying the bill, then what?"

"Everyone knows everyone in a town like this," Ralph said, glancing around the restaurant. He had nodded to several people as they entered. "I've known Ginnie these last five years, and I knew who she was before she went away to school. I know her uncle much better, of course. We're in several of the same organizations, end up at the same civic-affairs meetings, the same parties. It's a very small town." He had touched his martini to his lips briefly, put it down again, and now moved the glass back and forth an inch or so, obviously not interested in the contents.

"I talked to Ginnie today," he said. "I asked her if she would back me up if I just said I was having someone look into this mess on her behalf. She wanted to know who was paying the bill, naturally, but she accepted that I was not free to tell her. She's not stupid, by the way. She knows she's in trouble."

"How much trouble?" Charlie asked.

"It's bad. You want it now, not after dinner?" Constance and Charlie both nodded. Ralph sipped his martini as sparingly as before. "Okay. The first one, Peter Ellis. He and Ginnie were friends, casual lovers, I think. They were planning to go away for a few days, but she had to deliver sketches at the theater first. They went that night. She waited in the car while he took them inside. He used her key to get in. She watched him unlock the door, then turned off the headlights and didn't see anything else. When she got tired of waiting, she went in and found his body. His head had been smashed with a bronze doorstop. No prints on it. Just smudges. That's her story.

"There's a watchman, Spotty. He got there around eight, as he usually does. He's not due until ten, but he spends his nights there and likes to watch television in the evening. He looked around when he arrived, checked the doors in the shop out back, then in the theater. Everything was locked up. He went to his room and made coffee, turned on the television. He heard Ginnie scream at nine-eighteen. He looked at his clock when he heard her. He found her in the hallway outside the office where the body was. She was trying to pull the door closed and the doorstop was in the way. She was in severe shock. She has no memory of leaving the office, of seeing the doorstop, or trying to close the door."

Their waiter brought salads and bread and they were all silent until he left again.

"The theory was that a burglar got in somehow and Ellis surprised him. It was as plausible as anything, I guess. More plausible than believing Ginnie did it. There was another possibility, though. Ellis was wearing the raincoat of the new director that night. It was raining pretty hard and he slipped it over his head, covered the portfolio. Ginnie had given the director a ride a day or two before and he left his coat in her car. Ro raised the possibility that the killer thought it was Gray Wilmot. The coat is black, the only one just like it I've seen around here."

Charlie cut the bread and they all began to eat their salad. In a few minutes Ralph went on.

"Ginnie was in a really bad state for the next week or longer. Not talking, not eating much, I don't know. Not there, is how someone put it. You know what I mean?"

"Sounds like severe depression," Constance said. "Not emotional depression, clinical."

He nodded. "I guess. Anyway, she was just beginning to show signs of life again when Laura Steubins was killed. And this one is harder because Ginnie won't cooperate and tell us where she was that night. She says only that she spent the night in the woods."

Charlie looked at him in disbelief. He smiled faintly. "I know it sounds crazy, but it isn't. Not really. People do that around here, even in the winter. I believe that's what Ginnie did, but she has to say where, lead others to the place to see that someone actually did spend a night there, prove it before the next hard rain washes away every trace. She says she doesn't know where the spot is and no one believes that. I don't believe it."

"What happened to Laura Steubins?" Constance asked.

"No one knows much. People saw her meet Ginnie outside the theater shortly after noon that day. They walked away together. Ginnie says they parted at the corner; she went on home and put her stuff in her car and took off for the woods. Laura wasn't seen that afternoon. At five she called Gray Wilmot, the director—they were living together, at least in the same house—and told him she wouldn't be home for dinner. He was eating with one of the theater people anyway. She was seen in the restaurant where Ro Cavanaugh was having dinner with a couple of other people. She spoke to Ro and left and no one saw her again. She was found in the river the next morning, her head smashed in. The autopsy put her death at about nine the night before. Ginnie returned to her house at about one in the afternoon, and that's where it is now."

"Motive?" Charlie asked.

Ralph shrugged. "There isn't any. They're saying Ginnie was upset because Ellis was seeing Laura. He got her a job at the university and had lunch with her a couple of times. But he and Ginnie were going out of town together for a few days. Doesn't sound like much of a motive to me. He was in town to clean up some business and spend a few days with Ginnie, then he was going down to California to finish his Ph.D. work. He was crazy about Ginnie."

"You knew him, too?" Constance asked.

"I met him a few times. And I saw them together a couple of times. He was serious. I don't think she was."

"Why are they saying Ginnie is crazy?"

"When Ellis got killed she went into the shock I told you about, wouldn't talk, all that. When they told her Laura Steubins was dead, she went silent again, but this time not from shock. She just won't say where she was and Draker is acting as if he thinks she was pretending before, pretending shock. He's convinced she really is crazy. He thinks her silence proves it."

They ate silently for several minutes.

"That was Wednesday night?" Charlie asked. When Ralph nodded, he continued, "Why the rush? Your Lieutenant Draker seems in an awful rush to settle on any one person this fast."

"Everyone else connected with this mess had an alibi one night or the other, or both. Ginnie was available both times. Draker's been around for seven or eight years. He did a big investigation the year he came, made a tremendous drug bust after a lot of good work, and made a name for himself. He wants to keep up his reputation maybe."

"If he's really settled on Ginnie, that means his investigation will be skewed," Constance commented.

Ralph nodded soberly. "That's how I read it."

Constance was frowning slightly. "That argument seems pretty circular, doesn't it? He's satisfied that she did it; her silence proves both her guilt and that she is crazy. Most people start from the other side: She's crazy, therefore she's the killer." Charlie looked mystified, and she continued, "Well, Ginnie must be passing for sane, as sane as most people, anyway, or he wouldn't have to reach quite so hard to label her crazy. Why does he want the label for her?"

Ralph sighed. "You'll hear this from someone or other, it might as well be me. They say that when her father died she became autistic for over a year. It was only after her mother took her all the way out of here that she began to recover. And they say that she started the fire that killed him, playing with matches. That seems to be enough for Draker. He equates autism with insanity, and as far as he's concerned she was never cured, only in remission until someone crossed her."

Charlie whistled softly. "How old was she?"

"Three." He glanced at his watch. "Well, you've had a long day, and so have I. I have a packet of stuff for you in the car. A map of the town showing where the theater is, where my office is, things like that. My office will be available for you if you want it for anything."

"Just a couple of things," Charlie said. The waiter cleared the table, poured more coffee without being asked. Good waiter. "First," Charlie said when they were alone again, "you said Ginnie has agreed to the investigation, strangers asking questions, all the rest of it. What about the others? Her uncle, for instance?"

Ralph sighed. "I talked to Ro this afternoon. He thinks I'm running scared over nothing. He's clinging to the burglar theory, and he thinks Laura was out with someone who got nasty when she wouldn't play. She wasn't raped or anything."

"Just killed," Constance murmured.

"Yes. Anyway, Ro will cooperate just as long as he isn't too inconvenienced, just as long as his people aren't too distracted from the business. He warned me that they are going into rehearsals in just one more week and there simply won't be time for anything else then." He looked troubled. "I'm afraid Ro isn't going to see anything he doesn't want to see. Having Ginnie accused of murder is one of those things he doesn't want to see."

"And the others?"

"They'll do what Ro tells them to do. And, of course, they're all really fond of Ginnie. Most everyone is. Ro said you can go in and out of the theater when you want to, but you can't interrupt any of the readings or the rehearsals or anything else. Catch people in the halls, I guess." He shrugged helplessly. "They're show people, not quite like anyone else. If Ro ever realizes that Ginnie is in real danger, it'll be a different story, but it might take a baseball bat to drive that into his head."

"Okay. We'll work around that. The other thing: You've said everyone knows everyone here, no secrets. Do you know that they're homing in on Ginnie, or is that a guess? And if you know, how? Do you have sources that are reliable?"

He looked distinctly uncomfortable now. "I know," he said after a pause. "I don't know this detective all that well, but Gus Chisolm, who is our chief of police, is also a good friend of mine. They aren't letting him in on everything, but he hears things. He's reliable."

"Good. And finally, is there a schedule somewhere of when they'll all be in the theater, when we can meet them?"

"I added a schedule to the things in the packet for you. I think there's a nine-o'clock call for readings. What that means I can't tell you," he added dryly.

"So we get to learn how they put on a play," Charlie said easily. He looked at Constance; she shook her head slightly and they were ready to leave the restaurant.

In their sitting room later, Charlie and Constance went through the packet of articles, reports, maps that Ralph had provided. It was very thorough. Ginnie was in good hands, Charlie decided. Dr. Braden had picked a good attorney. They read the many profiles of the theater people with interest and studied their photographs. Ro had been written about most, as was to be expected, since he practically had willed Harley's Theater into existence and prosperity.

Constance left to take a bath, yawning widely; she had little faith in newspaper feature articles, having seen her own words distorted too many times in the past. Charlie continued to read.

She returned in her gown and robe, frowning. She was pink from the hot bath; clinging to her forehead were tendrils of hair so pale that they were invisible until they flashed in the light. "If she's guilty," she said, "I think Dr. Braden sees my role here as providing a case for mental illness. I don't like being used like that."

"Hey, hold on a second. That's a great big leap. You left me too far behind."

"He must have heard the rumor that she started the fire that killed his son. He was on the scene, remember? Now there's a killing spree going on and she might be implicated. She must be crazy. I testify eventually that she's incompetent, was incompetent at the time of the murders; she goes somewhere for a cure. Period. Used."

Charlie grinned at her indignation. "So let's hang the rap on someone else."

"You bet your sweet fanny," she said. "Let's go to bed."

His grin turned into a soft chuckle and he started to flick off lights.

THIRTEEN

"Ladies and gentlemen," Gray said, "I want to outline the procedure for the coming week. Each morning at nine I'll read a play, in the order of openings. Starting tomorrow the cast will read in the afternoon. We'll begin with *The Climber* today, and tomorrow at one that cast will gather in this room and read. I don't want you to try to memorize your lines yet. This afternoon, tonight, simply read through the play a few times, think about your character a lot. We may be doing some improvisations, so be prepared."

He looked at the people around the table, then picked up the play. Constance and Charlie had met him and most of the others in Ro's office that morning. Gray was pale and drawn, with dark hollows under his eyes. As haggard as he appeared, however, he looked robust and in perfect health compared to Ginnie. She was ghostly in her pallor and almost gaunt. Everyone was tense except Sunshine. Her eyes were glowing with excitement; it was her play they were going to read, she had whispered to Constance. At the table in rehearsal room A was the cast for the first play of the season. Gray was at the head of the table; at the other end was Eric Hendrickson, the stage manager. In a second tier of chairs were the costumer, the technician, the sound and lights people, others Constance and Charlie had not met. Ro stood by the door, then seated himself next to Ginnie, out of Gray's line of sight. Ginnie sketched as Gray read, paying little or no attention to her hands, turning pages silently, sketching very fast.

"She can draw in the dark," Sunshine had whispered to Constance, who believed it.

Gray read very well. Quite often he stopped reading and talked about the actions, or the dialogue, the characters. His analysis was impressive. Constance watched the expressions on the faces of his attentive audience and knew that his was a godlike position.

When he finished there was applause; he looked surprised. Constance turned to Sunshine and said, "Congratulations. That's very good. You must feel proud."

Sunshine nodded, her smile happy and wide. "I wanted to rewrite it again and he"—she nodded toward Ro—"said he'd wring my neck if I touched it again."

"Are you going to be around all week?" Constance asked. "Perhaps we can talk to you."

"Oh, I'll be here. They said I can watch everything to do with my play. I'm not usually allowed in the theater, you know? They said I was disruptive because Ginnie got mad at me for talking to her, you know?"

"When was that?"

"Oh, a long time ago. She kept moving around out front in the dark and I couldn't believe she was drawing in the dark, you know? I think she was in a trance and if I'd known that I wouldn't have spoken to her. You shouldn't when people are in a trance, you know?"

"You're probably right," Constance said carefully. "When did they let you back in?"

"For auditions, but then he"—she looked toward Ro—"thought I made Ginnie leave that day and threw me out again. He"—this time her gaze stopped on Gray—"said I could come in for the readings and the rehearsals, but I'm not supposed to talk to any of them, you know? Do you want me to read your cards?"

"I'd like that," Constance said. "I'll let you know when I have time, when it's convenient for you. See you later, Sunshine."

Charlie was at the door motioning to her. "There's a meeting in Ro's office," he said when she joined him. "The people with keys who were around when Peter Ellis was killed. Ro says his office is the logical place, probably the only place where no one can overhear."

Ginnie and Gray were already out of the rehearsal room; the actors were gone. A clump of people remained at the table talking. She followed Charlie and the other men to Ro's office.

Charlie took control as soon as everyone was in the office. He would have made a good director, Constance thought with satisfaction. He had Ginnie and Gray on the couch, Ro in one of the easy chairs, Juanita in another one. Eric and William were in straight chairs, as was Constance. Charlie stood before the semicircle they made.

"I know you've all been through hell already," he said matter-of-factly. "I'm afraid I'm going to have to put you through it again. I don't have access to the police records, unfortunately. Now, does anyone else have a key to this building?"

"Spotty," Ro said. "That's all. Kirby Schultz had one but he gave it back to me before he took off."

"Good. Now, let's go through this logically. Someone could have been inside the building earlier and simply stayed after everyone else left." William was shaking his head. "Mr. Tessler?"

"Duane Higgins was overseeing the workmen in the auditorium," he said deliberately. "He checked them out. I did the same backstage."

"I see. But in theory someone else could have slipped in during the day, hung around all evening. We can't prove a negative, you see. It could have happened. It's the sort of straw that defense attorneys cling to. That's one possibility." He turned to Ginnie. "Did anyone know that you and Mr. Ellis were coming here that night?"

"No. We decided at dinner. I didn't even know it until then."

Charlie nodded. "You see how that goes. If our anonymous stranger did hang around, what for? Not to waylay Mr. Ellis, since he couldn't have known he would show up. Not to steal something, surely, or he would have done it and gone by then. We can't prove that no one was here all that time, but neither do we have to act as if we believe in it. That means that someone with a key entered the theater that night, and if you're certain that only you few people have keys, that means it was one of you. Or the watchman. Did Spotty have a grudge against Mr. Ellis?"

Ginnie shook her head. "He had met him once or twice at the most."

"If Mr. Ellis walked in on Spotty in the office, so what? Is there a safe in the office, Mr. Cavanaugh?"

"No. There's nothing of real value here. During the season there's money in a safe out in the auditorium office, but not off season."

"So again, what if Mr. Ellis had come across Spotty in here? He worked here, belonged here."

"That applies to all of us," Ro said impatiently. "It wouldn't have been a surprise to find any one of us in here."

"That's the point I was coming to," Charlie said softly. "That's exactly my point. Now, what the police have against Miss Braden, Ginnie, is purely circumstantial evidence, or so I've been told. If we can place any other person in this office, that evidence will also be circumstantial unless we can also come up with a motive for murder. I know you've all told the police where you were that night, maybe many times. Will you go through it again, please? Mr. Cavanaugh, will you start?"

"This won't get you anywhere," Ro said sharply. "If they'd been able to put anyone else in here, they would have."

"Did they question you as a group?" Charlie's voice was bland. "Sometimes that shakes a memory; hearing someone else say something reminds you of something you hadn't thought of before."

"They questioned us separately," Ro said with great weariness. "I had dinner alone in a restaurant and at eight went to the high school to see a production. I always see their productions. At nine-fifteen or so I went to Jake's Place, a bar, with several other people, and I was there when the police came looking for me."

"Did you see people at the high school who know you? Did you leave and return?"

Ro glanced at Eric, then Gray. "They were both there. Maybe a dozen other people that I talked to at one time or another that night. I started to leave when Gray did, but it was raining too hard and I didn't have a car or an umbrella or even a raincoat. He was out before I could catch him for a ride. I hung out there until the play ended and got a ride with Jerry Alistair."

"Thank you," Charlie said, and turned to Eric. "Mr. Hendrickson?"

"I stayed at the high school until the play was over and then went straight home. I got there about nine-thirty. My wife was up. We watched television the rest of the evening."

"Now see," Charlie said, beaming at them. "Here's someone who could have been at the theater at the right time."

Angrily Eric said, "I took a friend home that night. He's my next-door neighbor, a teacher at the school in the drama department."

Charlie sighed and looked at Juanita.

"I was in Medford all evening. Dinner with friends, then a movie. I got home at one in the morning."

William had been home with his wife and Sunshine, he said, when it was his turn. At eight-thirty Sunshine helped Shannon get ready for bed, then he drove Sunshine home. It was raining but he didn't know what time it was when he dropped her off. He stopped in a convenience store and bought a candy bar, then went home.

"You got out in the rain to buy a candy bar?"

"Yes. Sunshine made dinner that night and it was some god-awful mess with rice and parsley and peanuts. I was hungry."

"And you knew the person who waited on you, I suppose?" Charlie's voice was gloomy now.

"Stu Lavelle. He works here as a stagehand during the season."

Charlie sighed again. "Mr. Wilmot?"

"I was at the high school until a few minutes before the play ended. I didn't want to get mixed up with the other cars all trying to leave the lot at the same time. I knew Laura would be waiting for me at the bar. She was there when I arrived. We went home."

"Time?" Charlie asked without much hope.

"I picked her up a little after nine. I don't know exactly what time it was."

Charlie looked at Ro and said softly, "You see how it is, Mr. Cavanaugh? On the basis of circumstantial evidence, they have enough to arrest your niece today."

Ro was pale now. His voice was ragged when he spoke. "You did that to demonstrate something, didn't you? You win, Mr. Meiklejohn. What do you want?"

"Full cooperation from you and all your people here. I'll want to ask a lot of questions and it's going to take time. I don't want you to interfere when I use that time."

Ro nodded. "Whatever it takes." He looked at Ginnie. "It's going to be all right, honey. We're all going to help."

"Aren't you going to ask me?" Ginnie demanded of Charlie.

"We'd like to talk to you at your house," Charlie said. "After lunch, this afternoon."

"That was a gamble," Constance said in the car when they left the theater. "You were lucky."

"I wanted to test the reliability of Ralph's contact, the chief of police. He said they all had alibis for one or both nights, and so far, he's right."

"Not Gray," she commented. "Unless someone else in the bar can confirm his time. And William's alibi isn't all that hot, either. Not unless he drew attention to the time in the store."

"It seemed a good idea to let them all believe we swallowed it whole," Charlie said cheerfully. He was driving along the river that ran through town. On the other side of the street was Lithia Park. The street they were on was lined with parking places, all empty. "This must be about it," he said, and pulled into one of the parking places. "About a mile in. Let's walk a bit."

It was a cool, overcast day with no wind. The river was raging grayish-white and nearly to the top of the banks, only about fifteen feet across, but loud. On a path across it several runners appeared, trotted easily into view and out of sight again without glancing at them. Charlie walked closer to the river and looked at the banks.

The earth was dark and soft-looking, laced with many rocks. Large rocks jutted out of the water, made ripples in it. Charlie found a small stick and tossed it into the water; it was swirled around and carried away quickly.

"The bank was a mess, according to the report," he said. "About a mile from the entrance. Let's see if we can find the spot." They walked slowly and stopped when they came to a roped-off area where the bank was eroded, badly scuffed. Silently they studied it.

The whole area had been trampled a lot, but the place on the bank was only about two and a half feet wide where the earth was gouged out, scraped-looking.

They were twenty feet from the nearest parking spot, a hundred feet from the nearest streetlight. It would be very dark here at night, Constance thought. She looked upriver at a bridge, downriver at another one farther away. Who would have seen anything here, heard anything? And it was only a mile from downtown.

"Someone must have had some pretty muddy shoes," Charlie said absently. His own shoes were already muddy. He backed away from the bank. "Let's walk a minute." There was a footpath between the parking area and the river; in some places trees or bushes hid it from the street. The bridge turned out to be for traffic. All the others they had seen had been foot bridges. They walked to the middle of the bridge and looked back at the roped-off area. Their car was not visible from here; none of the parking spots were. The river was very swift and shiny.

Constance was studying the spot they had just left, frowning slightly. Finally she said, "It just doesn't make any sense, does it? Laura came out here with someone, parked. They got out and walked to the bank. Why? You couldn't see anything at night. They fought and she ended up in the river. But why get out of the car at all? And if she was trying to get away from anyone, she would have gone the other way, not toward the river. And it couldn't have been much of a fight, the messed-up spot is too small. People who are fighting move around a little more than that, don't they?"

"Maybe she didn't go in at that spot at all."

Constance looked at him and waited.

"Suppose you want it to look as if you fought on the riverbank. You'd know you had to make a bit of a mess, but remember it was dark and that spot is a good distance from a light. No one would turn on car lights in order to see. He did the best he could in the dark, I'd say."

"But why mess it up at all? What for?"

"To hide the fact that there's no blood, maybe?"

"You think she was killed somewhere else and brought here? Killed in a car? Not with that head wound. A heavy object just behind the right ear. Not easy to do in a car."

"I know. The report suggests that the killer picked up a rock and used that, then tossed it in the river. They didn't find it, obviously, and even if they found a thousand rocks, they'd be pretty well scoured. Try to find a particular one among them. Let's see where this road goes."

They continued across the bridge into the park itself. The road dead-ended at a small maintenance building. There was a turn-around gravel drive. No one was in sight. The trees in the park were magnificent, huge, beautifully shaped madrones, firs, spruces. An almost vertical cliff that paralleled the river was the park boundary. It was covered with trees and bushes; a path or two seemed to go straight up it.

"You could hide an elephant brigade in here," Charlie commented.

He began to poke around in bushes that grew lush on the riverbank. He leaned over and came upright again with a three-foot-long, partly decayed branch in his hand. With a guilty look he went to the bank and started to gouge at the soft, muddy earth. It crumbled at a touch. He nodded and tossed the branch into the water and backed away, then looked at his feet. "I could have done it with hardly a drop of mud getting on me." he said.

They started to walk back to the rented Buick. "Charlie, I really hate this. Why would anyone put the body of a woman in the river? It's . . . it's too crazy. People know that autopsies determine the time of death and cause. No one these days would expect to fool experts into thinking she drowned or anything."

"I don't know why," he said, agreeing with her. Television had educated most people about such things. He looked at his watch. "I have to have something to eat before we tackle Ginnie. How about you?"

FOURTEEN

Ginnie led Constance and Charlie into her living room. Almost before they were seated, she demanded, "Tell me who hired you. I have a right to know."

"Ralph Wedekind," Charlie said. "I thought you did know. He said you did."

"Who hired him? Was it Peter's family? His parents?"

Constance said, "Does it matter so very much? You could ask Ralph for a lawyer-client contract, you know, to be sure he's working in your interests."

Ginnie looked taken aback and abruptly sat down on the yellow chair. Constance and Charlie were on the couch.

"Do they do that?" Ginnie asked. "Write out contracts of that sort?"

"Of course, if you want one. I would, in your position. Why not give him a call and tell him you want it."

"Excuse me," Ginnie muttered and left them. A moment later

they could hear her voice from the kitchen; it was too low to understand the words. She came back. "He said he'd have it in the mail today. Thanks. I didn't think of that."

"I understand your concern," Constance said. "For all you know, someone might be trying to close the trap even more."

"At the theater, what you said about one of us . . . Do you believe that?"

"If the key's the deciding factor, it has to be one of the people who have the keys," Charlie said. "May we call you Ginnie? And please call us Charlie and Constance, or else you run into the Mr. Meiklejohn and Ms. Liedl problem. It confuses a hell of a lot of people. They probably all think we're living in sin."

Her smile was not very pronounced, but it was there flashingly. "Okay."

"I know you've told everything a million times," Charlie said. "But not to us. Would you mind going through it all once more?"

She started to speak in a toneless voice and he held up his hand. "You've memorized all that from too much repetition. Let's do it a different way. We'll ask questions, jump about a bit, maybe, and you just say what comes to mind. One word or a paragraph, whatever."

She was gripping her hands together so hard the knuckles were white. Constance signaled Charlie and said, "Ginnie, it relaxes you if you draw while you talk, doesn't it? Why don't you do that?"

Ginnie looked at her hands and sighed. She got up and crossed the room to the paisley bag she always carried and rummaged in it. Suddenly she dumped everything out on the floor and scattered the items—two sketchbooks, half a dozen or more pencils, a penlight, pens, a paperback book . . . "It's gone."

"What's missing?" Charlie asked lazily.

"My other sketchbook, the one I've been using." She picked up one of the two on the floor and returned to her chair. "I must have left it in Uncle Ro's office, or the rehearsal room."

Later, Ginnie could not remember which one of them asked which questions, or even what questions they asked specifically, but

113

she had found herself talking about her life with her mother, about going to college, doing graduate work, moving to Ashland.

"After Mother died, Uncle Ro overreacted. I think he was afraid I'd go into a worse depression than I already was in," she said that afternoon. "He took me to England and France and Italy. He always took me to see big things—cathedrals, Stonehenge, castles, that sort of thing. At first I didn't want to go. I didn't even know him, but he was wise. I know that now. The things he made me look at were all so much bigger than anyone's personal grief. He was wise."

"And your mother hadn't told you about him?"

"No. She never talked about anything in the past. Even when we moved from one city to another, she never talked about the last city. I didn't realize how strange that was until years later. It was what I was used to and I accepted it." A puzzled look crossed her face, left it again. "One time," she said then, "she said something about the theater here, about Uncle Ro. I had forgotten it until this minute. I had a part in a play at school, a Shakespeare play, and she said she had always wanted to play Shakespeare, and he, her brother, hadn't let her. She said she ended up playing Cressida to his Pandarus anyway." She shook her head. "I don't know what she meant and she wouldn't say anything else about it."

"Why wouldn't he let her do Shakespeare, I wonder," Charlie mused.

"Now I understand that part. He'll never do any Shakespeare because of the Oregon Shakespearean Festival. That's their territory and he wouldn't encroach on it for anything."

"And that's the only time she mentioned him, or Ashland, any of this past?"

"I can't remember anything else."

"You and Peter were actually planning on two trips, weren't you? One all-day trip, then back here, and then on to the coast for a few days?"

"Yes."

114

"Why weren't you planning to camp out overnight and then go on to the coast?"

"It was rainy."

"But you camped out other times in the rain."

She ducked her head and mumbled, "I don't know. He didn't want to this time."

"Did they impound your car when you got home after being in the woods?"

"Impound? You mean take it away?"

Charlie nodded.

"No, but they had a bunch of men in the garage examining it all afternoon. I think they took mud samples. I know they were all through my daypack."

"And they didn't find a map. And that made them believe you knew where you had been well enough that you didn't need a map. Is that right?"

"Yes."

Charlie felt Constance signal and looked at her, waiting for her to pick it up. One time their daughter, Jessica, had demanded to know how he knew when Constance was signaling; she couldn't see anything, she had said indignantly. Charlie had answered, "She tickles me under the left shoulder blade with invisible fingers." Jessica had flounced out with a disdainful glance. But it was as true as anything else he could have said about it, he thought, watching his wife.

"What would happen," Constance asked gently, "if you led them to this secret place? How would they desecrate it?"

The lead broke on Ginnie's pencil. "I don't know what you mean."

"Not mountains, or canyons; there are too many of both, and even if you found steep mountains or deep canyons, they would be very like all the rest, wouldn't they? Something big. Trees. Giant trees? Was that it? Was that what Peter discovered and wanted to share with you, but not camp out among them, not disturb them with fire and tents?"

115

"How do you know?" Ginnie whispered in fear.

"Well, as I said, not mountains or valleys or canyons. Not an archeological site, because that would have to be disturbed in order to investigate it. And he didn't want to camp out there, just go and look and leave it alone again. That's what you did, isn't it?"

"I slept under the tree." Her voice was so low it was almost inaudible; her gaze was riveted on Constance as if she could not look away.

"Did you need a map to find the place?"

"I burned it the next morning when I came out again."

"What would they do to the trees?"

Ginnie finally looked away. "They'd go in with augers and drills and take core samples. Photographers would go in, make a better trail. Maybe they'd make a state park or something, or loggers would take the trees down. People would carve their initials in them, build fires everywhere. . . ."

"We won't tell, but one day you might have to. You understand that? Could you return there if it becomes necessary?"

"I'm not sure. I think so, but I can't be sure. How did you guess?"

"You were healed there, weren't you? Not completely, perhaps, but the process began there and is continuing, the way the cathedrals and Stonehenge started the process when your mother died. Something bigger than anyone's personal grief, bigger than life, awesome. Something holy. Here it would be a tree, or trees."

Constance glanced at Charlie; his turn again. She leaned back in her chair.

"Ginnie, exactly what did Laura say to you that day outside the theater?"

"I told you. She was sorry, she wanted to help. . . ."

Charlie was shaking his head. "Her words. Close your eyes and think of her words. Get the scene back first."

Obediently she closed her eyes and the minutes dragged before she opened them again. She picked up another pencil and began drawing, evidently paying little or no attention to her hand. It looked eerie to see the pencil moving without supervision. "She said, 'I don't want to hurt you. I can help you.' and 'I know you've been hurt very much.' Something else . . . 'If there's anything I can do, please let me.'" She became silent, her brow wrinkled in thought, and finally she said, "I can't think of anything else."

"Did you see Sunshine that day?"

"No."

"Why did you leave at that time?"

She shrugged. "I ate lunch with Uncle Ro and Gray and we walked outside for a minute. Everyone kept talking about how wonderful the weather was, sunny and warm, and I couldn't think of anything to say back to them. I felt as if I had forgotten words, simple everyday words that people use."

"Where did you walk?"

"Just out back, around the shop, and back in through the stage door. It was just a minute or two."

"Could Laura have seen you?"

She looked blank, then shrugged again. "I don't know. If she had been anywhere back there, or even on the corner, I guess so."

"You see the problem, don't you? If she had been going to the theater, why didn't she keep going? Why did she turn around and walk away with you? And where was she all afternoon?"

She looked miserable. She understood what Draker had meant by his questions, implying that she and Laura had spent the rest of the day together, that she had driven Laura to the park and hit her in the head there, pushed her into the river, and then had driven around most of the night terrified.

"Ginnie," Constance asked then, "what did your mother and Ro argue about? Why wouldn't she talk about him?"

"I don't know."

"We have to be going now," Constance said easily. "What you just said reminds me of when I was studying under this bear of a psychology teacher. He hated for the students not to remember word for word every lecture he gave. One day he roared at us: 'You will remember, do you hear me? You will remember, if not in words, then in sounds. If not in sounds, then in pictures. Your hands will remember even if your head doesn't.'" She smiled. "Why don't you keep that sketchbook here? Just so you won't misplace it at the theater. When can we see you tomorrow?"

"I'll be free after Gray's reading," she said in a low voice. "Right after lunch?"

"Fine. We'll see you at the reading, too. Get a good sleep, Ginnie."

In the car Charlie leaned over and kissed Constance. "You're a witch," he murmured. "And I like it."

"Is she really in danger?"

"I wish I thought she isn't. She put that sketchbook in her bag, you know. I saw her do it."

"Me too. I was watching her. It's as close to automatic writing—drawing—as you can get."

Charlie drove cautiously down the steep hill onto the main street. "We're due at Ro's apartment at six-thirty," he said. "And it is now five-ten. What I say is let's have a drink."

"Good thinking. Look, there's Sunshine. Can you endure her for an hour?"

"Might be a good time. Let's nab her and pump her full of liquor and get the lowdown on everyone all at once." He parked the car and they got out and caught up with Sunshine.

"Hi," Charlie said. "We're on our way to have a nice quiet drink. Join us?"

"I don't drink anything with alcohol," she said, smiling. "Or caffeine, you know? You know what alcohol does? It kills liver cells, like radiation."

"You can have orange juice while we poison our livers," Charlie said.

"They smoke in bars, don't they? I don't go where people smoke, you know? Smoke is worse than alcohol, you know?"

"There's an ice-cream parlor down the block," Constance said and smiled sweetly at Charlie.

"I am not interested in ice cream," he said emphatically.

118

Constance took his arm and steered him about. "I wonder how long it's been since I've had a strawberry soda. You know ice cream is full of cholesterol, don't you?" she asked Sunshine.

"They pretend dairy products are bad for you, but they aren't. Not if you exercise. I drink juices and raw milk at home, and herb teas. I can't get raw milk in restaurants. They pretend it's dangerous. Chocolate is bad, but strawberry's all right."

"I'll have a double chocolate milkshake," Charlie said grumpily.

Constance squeezed his arm. Actually he had a root beer. If he pretended hard enough, he thought, he might even convince himself it was real beer. He failed to pretend hard enough.

"I really like your play," Constance said after sipping her soda. It was as good as she remembered, she thought with surprise. So few things were.

"It's a good play," Sunshine said with her gentle smile in place. "I wanted to write about evil, how it kills everyone it touches, and I had to personify evil in a woman because women are mysterious, you know? Men can be really bad but they aren't mysterious. You always know why they're bad, what they want, but you don't know that about some evil women. You're the High Priestess, you know? And he's the Emperor. I'll read your cards tonight."

"I'm afraid we won't have time tonight," Constance said.

"That's all right. I always read them first and if there's anything bad I find it and don't talk about it, you know? I sort of talk around it."

"Have you read for the theater group?"

"Laura. The others are too superstitious. They're afraid I'll read for the actors and actresses and spook them. When the sun came out last week, they were all smiling and saying it was a good sign and then they say they aren't superstitious." She laughed softly.

"What did you read in the cards for Laura?"

She scooped ice cream from the bottom of her glass and looked at it. "I can't tell you. I never tell anyone what someone else's cards say, you know? It would make people nervous."

"I know," Constance said, sighing. "Do you use the Waite pack?

I used to read but I had to stop. People acted as if the cards told what would happen, not just say what might happen if they didn't do something. They simply didn't understand that they could change things by taking charge of their own lives."

Sunshine was nodding. "I use that pack, too. That's what I always tell people. I don't believe in determinism, you know? It isn't like you don't have control over your own life. Laura said wrecking her car was a sign that fate was determined to keep her here. She thought the cards agreed with that. But she could have got on a bus. I came here on a bus. She could have walked. Ro walks everywhere practically. She could have ridden a bicycle like Ginnie. But she thought it was fate." Sunshine leaned closer to Constance and said in a near whisper, "She was trying to make up her mind about something and wanted me to read for her. But I didn't have my cards. Ro looked in my bag and saw them one day and threw me out and said if I ever brought them back, he'd burn them. He would do that, you know? He thinks the actors and actresses are little children and he has to take care of them and the cards might upset them. So I didn't have them."

"What day was that?" Constance asked. "Do you want more ice cream?"

She wanted more. They waited until she had a dish of lime sherbet—better for you than real ice cream, she told them. Constance repeated her question.

"The day Ro thought I spooked Ginnie again and threw me out. He's always throwing me out."

"You mean the day Laura was killed?"

"She wasn't killed that day," Sunshine said gently. "She was killed that night, you know?"

"So you met Laura somewhere after you left the theater. Where?"

"William said I could shop for some things that Shannon wanted and take them out to her and be back at the theater by six with his car. William's nice to me. Shannon is, too. I was going to the store and saw Laura and gave her a ride and she said she wanted me to read, that she had a question she needed answered, and I told

120

her I didn't have the cards, but I'd go get them after I took the stuff out to Shannon. She got in the car and went with me. She waited in the car at the store and at Shannon's house. Then we went back to her house and I made her some more rose-hip tea because she had such a bad cold. She didn't like it, you know? Some people don't understand that sometimes the taste isn't the important thing. It would have helped her cold."

Constance nodded thoughtfully, then said, "You haven't told any of this to the police, have you?"

"I don't talk to police. They didn't ask me. You know the criminal mind and the police mind are exactly the same? It's circumstances that turns one into a cop and the other into a crook, you know?"

"I've heard that before," Constance said. She stifled a grunt when Charlie kicked her under the table. He looked sleepy-eyed, as if he might be dozing off and on. "How did Laura's question come out? I've never had any luck answering direct questions about what people should do."

"I told her it doesn't work that way. She finally asked what would be the outcome if she did A. And then what the outcome would be if she did B. Both were very bad."

"Did she seem to make a decision?"

Sunshine shook her head. "She kept going back and forth. Then she thought Gray was coming home and she didn't want to see him until she had more time to think. I told her if William was going to be busy until six, Gray would be, too, but she called him anyway and said she wasn't going to be home and he said he was eating with Eric and didn't care. And she said, 'I'll make you care, goddamn it,' but she already had hung up and he didn't hear her. That's when she decided, you know?"

"It sounds as if you may be right," Constance agreed. "Did she stay there when you left?"

"Oh yes. She was looking for something to drink, something alcoholic, you know? I don't hang around with people who are poisoning themselves, so I left."

121

"Sunshine, did she tell you anything to indicate what A and B were? It's very important."

Sunshine shook her head. "Just A and then B. I told her it works better if I don't know. That way I can't read anything into the cards, have any real influence, you know?"

She talked on until Charlie and Constance had to leave for their appointment with Ro. As they put on their coats, Charlie said in his soft and easy voice, his working voice, Constance called it, "Sunshine, thank you for talking to us."

"To her," Sunshine said, nodding at Constance.

"Right. To her. What you've told Constance is vital evidence, Sunshine. You must realize that. I know you're a good woman, a gentle woman with a lot of compassion for other people, a lot of understanding. I wouldn't like to see someone like you hurt because you withheld evidence, but you could find yourself in trouble over it. You have to go to the police, tell them what you've told us—Constance."

She shook her head, smiling gently. "I don't talk to police. I'll read your cards tonight. Good night."

"Well," Constance said after they were alone again. "Are you going to tell?"

"Eventually," he said. "Eventually."

FIFTEEN

Ro Cavanaugh's apartment had enough art to qualify as a museum, Charlie thought when he and Constance were admitted. There was a spacious foyer with a carved Chinese cabinet that held ivory and jade carvings. Above that hung a Chinese silk embroidery of a dragon in a garden. Before they could examine the objects in the foyer, Ro was ushering them into the living room, and it, too, was filled with carvings, paintings, statuettes, plates. . . . A flawless glass-topped coffee table with beveled edges had a pedestal made from a bronze dolphin with a patina that suggested centuries in the sea. A hanging lamp was made of twisted translucent porcelain in pastel colors. There were floor-to-ceiling windows on both end walls that reached up two stories. A balcony on the second floor overlooked the living room; on the wall up there were oversize paintings—Miró, Kandinsky, some Charlie did not recognize. He took a deep breath. He was afraid to touch anything.

123

"This is very lovely," Constance said, gazing from one object, one painting to another. The couch was covered with ivory velvet; the chairs with red-and-ivory-striped silk. At the far end of the room were a mammoth television receiver and a ten-foot-long cabinet with film cassettes. Around the corner from it was another, equally long cabinet with a stereo, records, and rows of music tapes.

"I pick up things when I travel," Ro said. "These are from Spain." He went to a chest and lifted a carved bull, done in dense black wood. There were other pieces—a matador, a picador. . . . Above them were the two symbols of the theater—the laughing face and the crying face, done in gold, or at least gold-plated. "Those are from England," he said, noticing where Constance was looking. "Irish gold. Now what can I give you to drink?"

"Anything except root beer," Charlie said.

"Martini?"

"That would be very nice," Charlie said.

As Ro started to cross the living room toward the kitchen, Constance asked, "Would you mind if I go up on the balcony and look at the paintings?"

He looked pleased. "Delighted. I'll do the mixing."

She went up the broad stairs from the living room, pausing now and then for another look around; the perspective changed everything again and again. On the balcony she went from one painting to another. Ro and Charlie were out of sight in the kitchen. She opened one of the doors and glanced around the room—his bedroom apparently, as neat and decorated as the downstairs. She did not enter. At the other end of the balcony was the second door. When she reached it, she looked inside that room also. Smaller than the other one, a spare bedroom. The bed was piled high with boxes and books. She was almost relieved that the entire house was not as neat as a showplace. When Charlie and Ro returned to the living room she was standing before the Kandinsky, a dizzying mélange of lines and colors.

"You like that one?" Ro asked from the living room. She nodded and started back down the stairs. "I do, too. The windows are east and west exposures; it changes from morning to night with the different quality of light." He handed Constance a glass when she joined them. "You might as well see the rest of my place."

He took them back through the foyer into a hall that led to his study. On the interior wall there were shelves and a collection of clowns. "This is what Draker wanted to see," Ro said, surveying them with a glum expression. They were molded, cast, carved from all kinds of materials—wood, bronze, silver, glass, china. Some were gaily painted, others not. All were beautiful. He pointed to one of the bronze ones. "That's a mate to the one at the theater, the one the murderer used."

Charlie picked it up. It was very heavy, bronze, fifteen inches tall, a thin, lugubrious clown. A hell of a weapon, he thought, but said nothing.

The desk here had the same cluttered messy look as the one at the theater, with papers in precarious stacks, magazines, some of them open, books with slips of paper sticking out, a road atlas. . . .

Ro led them through the kitchen to complete the tour. He dismissed it with a wave. "Hardly ever use it, except to mix drinks, or breakfast now and then. When Ginnie lived here, I had a housekeeper who cooked and I hated it. She liked things to be on time." He smiled grimly. "I fired her the day Ginnie left for college."

"It must have been hard, having a child on your hands suddenly. I'd be afraid to bring a child in here," Constance said.

"Well, she wasn't a little child," Ro reminded her. "She was thirteen. She was . . . disturbed. We went on a six-month trip and she seemed to mature a lot during that time. I understand that's common, a spurt in maturity about then. Anyway, she was a good kid. I increased my insurance coverage, just in case, but it wasn't necessary. She was a good kid always. And, of course, she was busy with high school and she took dancing lessons and voice, acting. For a time I thought she would become an actress, like her mother, but she decided backstage was more exciting finally. She's a gifted artist, could have gone into fine art, made it as a painter."

125

He was keeping an eye on the time, Constance realized. Now he said, "I made a reservation for seven-thirty. It's about a five-minute walk, maybe ten at the most. I'd offer to drive you, but I seem to have a dead battery. Damn cars are nothing but trouble, I just leave it in the carport most of the time."

"Well, we can drive, or we can walk. If it isn't raining," Charlie said. "You always walk, even if it's raining?"

"Sure. Why not? Only exercise I get, and Ashland's only so big, you know. You can get anywhere in town in ten minutes. If it's raining, I carry an umbrella. Leave them all over town, of course, but umbrellas are cheaper than car repairs and gas."

"Just wondering how you know you have a dead battery if you never use your car," Charlie said easily.

Ro gave him a shrewd look. "They came looking the day they found Laura. Wanted me to back it out of the carport so they could look it over. They gave up on it right off. Dust all over the windshield and a dead battery. I could have let it roll out of the carport, but then I'd have had to push it back in and I said they needed a warrant or something before I'd do that. They never came back with anything official."

He drained his glass and put it down. "You want another one? If we're late at the restaurant it won't matter. They'll hold my table all night if they have to. I'm one of their best customers."

"I need something to eat fairly soon," Constance said.

Ro started for the closet for coats and said abruptly, "That's why I didn't take it seriously, that Ginnie was in trouble with that pissant detective. They've been all over the place asking questions, going away again. Eric, William, Juanita, Gray, it's been the same with all of us. I assumed it was like that with Ginnie."

Over dinner Ro talked about starting the theater thirty years ago. "I knew the minute I saw it that it was perfect," he said. "Angus Bowmer had already started up the Oregon Shakespearean Festival again. It stopped during the war and then came back stronger than ever. I knew he was right, that you can make a small town into a great theater town, bring in people from all over the world. It's

126

happened here. Over four million people have come to Ashland to see excellent theater. I decided not to touch Shakespeare, that's Bowmer's field, and that just left me everyone else. I wanted a repertory group from the start. I used to say it was all for Lucy, Ginnie's mother, but I was kidding about that. I wanted to run a good theater from the time I first saw a live production. A bunch of amateurs doing *The Cherry Orchard*. They were terrible, the production was lousy, the sets old bed sheets and boards on orange crates, and it was the most exciting thing I had ever seen in my life. I was ten." He laughed at the memory. "Lucy wasn't even born yet and I already knew where I wanted to go, what I wanted to do."

"There must be a theater gene in your family," Constance said. "You, your sister, now Ginnie."

"And my father," he added. "He was in radio. He got me my first acting job on a radio station, back in the days of radio drama. A damn shame that died out. It was a hell of a lot better than anything on television. The sound effects, all those voices. You can make people believe anything with the right sound effects. A hell of a lot better. I made our mother see to it that Lucy got dancing lessons, voice, everything she needed to get a start. Our mother didn't like acting, theater, any of it. She was jealous, I guess, because that was all the rest of us cared about."

He seemed to be looking into the past, a distant expression on his face, dreamy almost. "Lucy was the star in my first production," he said. "She was four and a half. She cried because she was so scared of the audience at first, and then we couldn't drag her behind the curtain later. She wanted to keep bowing. She had learned how to blow kisses with both hands. The audience loved it."

"How old were you?" Constance asked.

Again he smiled. "Sixteen. I wanted to take the show on the road. Mother wouldn't let me. All I asked for was five dollars. I was sure we'd make enough to keep it running forever."

He needed little prompting to continue the story. He had gone to New York University and lived at home until his father left and the boyfriends started. By then he had had many jobs acting on radio and he thought his chances in Hollywood were too good to stay East; he had already made the move out of his mother's apartment and out of her life. He had thought then, and still thought, he admitted, that she had driven their father away.

"Then you and Lucy were reunited," Constance said when he paused. "Was that on the West Coast?"

His face became guarded. "She came out here," he said. "She didn't like living with our mother either by then."

"How old was she?"

"Twelve. Just a kid. Like Ginnie was when she came to live with me."

"Strange that Lucy didn't go to your father."

He shook his head. "She had no reason to trust him. He'd run out on us as far as she was concerned. Besides, I'd given her money and told her that was what it was for. If she ever decided to leave, to take a train and come to me."

Their waiter cleared the table, brought coffee. Charlie added sugar to his, and as he stirred it he said, "She owed you a lot. You provided for her, wanted to make her a star. Yet she moved away, took Ginnie away with her, and never even told Ginnie about you. Why was that, Mr. Cavanaugh?"

"None of that has anything to do with what's happening here now."

"Probably not, but if they try to prove that Ginnie's been disturbed in the past, they won't have to look much beyond the time she came to live with you. No secrets in a town this size, I understand. And that will send them into the more distant past. It'll all come out, whatever it all is. That's the trouble with murder, Mr. Cavanaugh. Nothing that was believed decently buried stays buried. It all gets dragged out and examined again."

Ro drank coffee, his eyes narrowed; he signaled to the waiter. "Just bring the pot, will you, Bill?" He waited, then poured for himself. Finally he said, "I'll tell you about it, Mr. Meiklejohn, but if you bring it up when you don't have to, if you exploit it in any way, I'll come after you. And I'll get you."

128

Charlie added more sugar to his coffee. "You seem to forget that I'm here to help her."

"I haven't forgotten," Ro said quietly. "I just want to make sure you don't forget that, either. This is ancient history, let's keep it like that. Lucy met Ginnie's father when she was in school. She was nineteen, he was twenty. Kids, both of them. Vic was crazy in love with her. She was a beautiful girl, talented, wonderful in every way. I didn't blame Vic for falling the way he did. I blamed him for insisting on marriage right off the bat. They were too young. His parents were well off, bound to raise a stink over it. I was on my way to Europe that spring. I'd already found Harley's Theater and knew it was going to be mine, but I had to see other theaters before I made a bid on it. Anyway, they decided to go, too, and the three of us were abroad for almost a year. By then Vic was twenty-one, no longer under his parents' control. They came to Ashland with me. Lucy was excited about the theater, as much as I was. Ginnie was born and then the fire between Vic and Lucy began to dim a little. He began to drink too much. I saw the same pattern there had been with my parents, one of them involved with theater, the other feeling neglected, left out." He sighed. "I blame myself. We were too busy for me to see what I should have seen. I was older than they were, I should have done something about them. We were all too busy. Hanging scenery, painting, taking multiple parts, learning lines, doing everything. All of us."

Constance wanted more coffee, but she was afraid that any motion might interrupt his flow. She waited. Charlie was unmoving; he looked sleepy.

"That day, the day Vic died," Ro went on, "I saw Lucy in town. She had said something about going to the doctor and I knew Ginnie had been sick with a cold. I assumed she had taken Ginnie for that. She passed me in her car and I followed her out to their house, to see how Ginnie was. It wasn't far, ten minutes out of town. The roads were unpaved then. Lucy was driving so slowly that I caught up with her and was right behind her when we turned the last curve and saw the fire. The house was blazing. Lucy jumped out of her car and started to run toward the house. I caught her and threw her to the ground. She was screaming that Ginnie was in there, Vic was in there. I can't remember much of the next few minutes. I was inside, found Ginnie, still in her room, terrified. I wrapped a blanket around her and ran out with her. The blanket was on fire, my hair. Ginnie was screaming hysterically, saying over and over, "I'm sorry. I'm sorry."

His face looked twenty years older than it had minutes before. Constance now poured the coffee for them all. He lifted his cup and drank without bringing his gaze back from that distant place. "Someone slapped out the fire in my hair. Someone tried to put Ginnie in Lucy's arms and she refused to take her. She was fighting to get free, to run into the house. She was screaming at me, "Why did you bring her out and not Vic? Let me go get him out."

Suddenly he shook himself. "Ginnie wouldn't say anything at all for the next year. Nothing. Lucy miscarried that night. She was delirious when they put her in the ambulance. She said it was Ginnie's fault, that she had been playing with matches. She had been spanked for playing with matches a week or so before that. Lucy blamed me for luring her to Ashland, for starting Harley's Theater, for everything. She blamed me for not saving Vic. She hung on for almost a year and then left. She said I'd never hear from her again and I didn't. I owed her and Vic money, a hundred thousand dollars. I didn't have that much cash, but I told her I'd send her money every month until it was paid, as long as she needed help, as long as Ginnie needed things. I gave her the name of a lawyer we had used in San Francisco and told her we could go through his office for the payments. She went to a different lawyer and I paid her through him until she was killed in an automobile wreck. Every month I begged the lawyer to ask her if Ginnie was all right, if she had recovered. It was three years before she responded and told him to tell me that Ginnie was well. Other than that I never did hear from her again."

Charlie let out a long breath and looked about for the waiter. He came almost instantly. "Three double cognacs," Charlie said. "Pronto."

No one spoke until they had the drinks. "Ginnie doesn't remember any of that," Constance said then.

"And I don't want her to," Ro said quickly. "You see why I want the past to stay back there where it belongs?" He drank most of his brandy in a large gulp. "When she came to me I thought I was being given another chance, a chance to do things right, not botch it again. She was too quiet, had nothing to say to me. We were strangers. I knew I had to do something, make memories for us to share. That's why I took her on a long trip, so we would have shared memories, something to talk about. Over the years she's become vivacious, happy, and busy. And now this. She's right back where she was then."

"If only she hadn't left town that night," Charlie murmured. "To bring our information up to date, will you tell us about that day and night?"

Ro shrugged. "When I heard that Ginnie had left, and I saw Sunshine, I thought it was her fault again. She bugs Ginnie, bugs everyone. I yelled at her to get the hell out—"

Charlie held up his hand and said apologetically, "Let's do it slower, if you don't mind. When did you last see Ginnie that day?"

"At lunch. She ate with Gray and me in my office. Then Gray talked her into a little walk around the building, to get some sun. It was a glorious day, everyone was up about the weather. Anyway, she went out with him."

Charlie nodded. "And when did you realize she was gone?"

Ro shook his head. "I don't know. An hour later, maybe more. You know what it's like now, people everywhere. I was here and there and quite suddenly realized that she had left again. She had been doing that. Coming in, staying an hour or so, then leaving. I thought that day that maybe she had come out of her withdrawal phase, and it upset me to have her gone again. I looked around for her then, and saw Sunshine in the costume room. She had orders to keep the hell out, but there she was trying on hats. I exploded at her.

I was sure she had said something to Ginnie. It was pretty public and ugly, my yelling at Sunshine."

"You didn't try to call Ginnie?"

He shook his head. "I'm afraid I had been hovering too much, getting on her nerves. She asked me and some of the others to please just leave her alone, and I knew she meant it. I didn't call."

"Okay. Did Sunshine leave?"

"Sure. She grabbed that bag of hers and ran, smiling all the time. That woman is a curse." He stopped, then continued in a quieter voice. "I worked until six or so, washed up, met friends here for dinner.

"And that's when you saw Laura? Before or after you had dinner?"

"When I entered the restaurant, she was over there in the lounge. I saw her when I came in at seven-thirty. I said hello to my friends at the table, then went over to speak to her."

"Why?" Charlie asked.

For the first time Ro looked unsure and uncomfortable. He made a slight shrugging motion, then said, "Nosy, maybe. She and Gray were having trouble. She was the outsider, and nothing seemed to make her feel welcome. I don't know why. I didn't stop to ask myself why. I just went over and said hello, asked about her cold. She looked terrible."

"Mr. Cavanaugh," Charlie said slowly, and very directly, "as far as the record goes, you're the last person who spoke with her that night, with the exception of her killer maybe. Let's do this word for word, if you can. You say she looked terrible, but how? Unkempt? Bloodshot eyes? Terrible how?"

For a moment Ro seemed ready to protest, then he sagged back against his chair and drew a deep breath. "It's just that we keep going over the same ground, over and over. She looked ill, feverish even. And she was staring at her glass as if at a crystal ball. When I spoke, she started and nearly knocked her glass over. Nervous, distraught even. That kind of terrible." He was watching Charlie closely; at his nod of encouragement, he went on. "I said I hoped

132

she was feeling better, and she said this medicine was helping. She meant the booze, held up the glass when she said it. And she said she had rose-hip tea. A and B, she called them." He closed his eyes a minute in thought, then went on. "I think that's when she said the rose-hip tea was one of Sunshine's many cures. And then she said did I know Sunshine was rewriting the play yet again." He rubbed his eyes now and shrugged. "I'm afraid I lost the rest of whatever conversation we had at that point. I was seeing red."

Charlie sighed. "I suppose you've tried to recall what else was said."

"I have. It couldn't have been much. All I could think of was that damn woman and her damn play and the trouble she was causing all of us. I cut my dinner short and left the restaurant early, I was so furious. At eight-thirty," he added with a grim laugh. "Trevor, the bartender, noticed the time. He said Laura left at ten after eight."

"So you were home again what, five, ten minutes later?"

Ro shrugged. "I just know I called Gray at a quarter to nine. I asked him if it was true. I didn't tell him where I heard it. I knew he hated for Laura to be chummy with that woman. He said he had threatened mayhem if she even hinted that she wanted to rewrite again. I didn't believe he could handle her. No one had been able to keep her out of our hair yet. Still haven't. She turns up everywhere, always underfoot. Anyway, I called William and Eric and asked them to come over. I wanted contingency plans if we had to yank the play at the last minute, and I was ready to do just that if that woman was driving Ginnie away. William and Eric came and we talked for a couple of hours. I wasn't paying much attention to the time. Eric said he left at eleven-thirty and that's probably about right. I had a nightcap and went to bed."

"And she was killed at about nine," Charlie said. "Do you know for sure what time you were making those phone calls? What time you called Gray?"

"A quarter to nine. I realized when I was dialing that he might not be home yet. He and Eric had dinner together to discuss the auditions. When I got him I knew I'd be able to reach Eric."

Charlie sipped his cognac, his expression unhappy.

"Look," Ro said. "She was in a bar, drinking alone. She was good-looking, lonesome. So someone picked her up and later on they fought. I just don't see the mystery about it."

"And Peter Ellis?"

"He walked in on a burglar, obviously. No one on earth had a reason to kill him."

"You may be right," Charlie said, even unhappier. "But if you are, Ginnie's in for a hell of a time. Unless those two unrelated murderers come forward and confess."

He glanced at Constance, who had been silent and watchful throughout the questioning. She was regarding Ro thoughtfully. "When you were talking to Laura," she said then, "what was her attitude? Was she still staring, looking at you, what? You said she was startled at first. More than you might have expected?"

He nodded. "I hadn't really thought about it, but yes. It was as if she had been so deep in her own thoughts that my voice was a wrench to her. Yes. And then she looked at me almost as if she was studying me, you know the kind of intent look people can assume. That didn't last long. She began to play with her glass, moved it back and forth, back and forth, and didn't look at me again. She might have glanced up when I left. Probably did, but no more than that."

"Moved her glass how?" Constance asked.

Ro glanced at Charlie, who looked as at sea as he felt. Constance watched as he picked up his brandy glass and put it down softly, picked it up and returned it to its original position, then repeated the action several more times. She smiled her thanks and looked at her watch.

"What was that for?" Charlie asked as they drove back to the inn a few minutes later.

"She hadn't made up her mind yet about A and B," Constance said. "It was evident in her earlier remarks about the drink and rose-hip tea, referring to them as A and B. And the glass, back and forth,

134

not making idle circles or just for something to do. Still going from A to B, back to A. What do you think?"

"I think it's funny that Ro keeps threatening to toss Sunshine out on her ear and Sunshine keeps hanging in there. Smiling."

SIXTEEN

"Charlie, come look," Constance called. She was in their sitting room before one of the wide windows. The clouds of the day before had left; today the sun was brilliant, and on the hills across the valley the clouds had deposited a dusting of snow. On the higher mountains the snow was dazzling in the oblique rays of the morning sunlight. She turned to look at the mountain behind the inn; there the snow was whiter, deeper-looking, and closer. The evergreen trees were startlingly green; the grassy meadow that was the backyard was summer-green.

Charlie joined her and put his arm around her shoulders. He made a grunting sound of approval at the view.

"Oh," she said softly, and pointed. At the edge of the meadow a deer was grazing.

Charlie squeezed her shoulder and went to the table for coffee. It had been delivered a few minutes earlier and in another few minutes breakfast would follow. They could sit and watch the deer

136

while they ate their own food—rainbow trout, croissants, poached eggs, melon. . . . Too much, Constance thought with contentment. The phone rang.

Charlie answered it. He said uh-huh several times, then, "Have you called Ralph? He'll want to go with you. . . . I'm sure, Ginnie. Don't go alone. Okay? Give us a call later. We'll check in often and call back if we miss it. And, Ginnie, take it easy. We'll see you at the end of the reading." He listened and nodded. "Don't let them scare you, that's the main thing right now."

There was a soft tap on their door and they went into the bedroom while their breakfast was being laid out.

"The detective from the sheriff's office is taking her for a ride right after the reading," Charlie said. "He says maybe retracing her path will make her remember where she went. And just incidentally let him try to find anyone he can who can put her in any definite location at any definite time."

"Poor Ginnie. What will she do?"

He shrugged. "Probably say maybe this way, maybe that way. She'll have to tell eventually. Not that it will make much difference. Out in the wilderness, no witnesses, no alibi. They'll be able to say she saw those trees last month, last summer, sometime."

They returned to the other room and started breakfast. Neither spoke for several minutes until Constance said, "I think we're having some of the best food I've had in years. And the prettiest scenery." The deer had been joined by two does. It was like a picture from a romantic illustration.

"It's okay," Charlie said. "But that damn snow is too close."

She laughed and pushed her plate back a bit.

"You going to finish that fish?"

"Can't."

He slid it off her plate onto his. "I think I'll skip the reading this morning. I want to catch Spotty, and have a chat with the police chief. Want to tag along?"

She shook her head. She knew it would go better without her. Spotty had been a police officer years ago, Gus Chisolm was still a

137

policeman. They would establish credentials, exchange stories a few minutes, test for mutual acquaintances, and then Charlie would ask his questions, and more than likely get full answers. The phone rang again and this time it was Sunshine calling Constance.

"She's read your cards," Charlie said with a grin, his hand over the mouthpiece. He gave the phone to Constance.

"Hi, Sunshine." She listened for a long time, then said, "This morning? I can give you a lift back into town afterward. Okay?"

Charlie had cleaned both plates and now emptied the coffeepot, dividing the coffee equally between the two cups. Yesterday morning they had eaten everything, and this time there had been quite a bit more. Tomorrow would it all be increased again, and then again? He hoped so.

"Well," Constance said thoughtfully after hanging up. "It seems that Shannon Tessler would like to talk to me, alone."

He laughed. "Thank you, Sunshine."

"So, you want to drop me and then pick me up again? Or have me drop you off?"

"I'd better walk," he said with a sigh. "Maybe even run."

Shannon Tessler was in her early sixties, twenty-five pounds overweight, and very pale with black hair that waved softly about her ears in an old-fashioned style that became her. Her eyes were bright blue and lively. Only her unhealthy pallor betrayed her illness. She must have been stunning as a young woman, Constance thought; even now she was quite attractive. There was a dimple high on her cheek.

"I made some blackberry-mint tea," Sunshine said softly. "It's a good spring tonic, you know? Do you want some?"

"No, thanks. I'm just up from the breakfast table. This is a lovely house, Mrs. Tessler."

It was turn-of-the-century clapboard, with high ceilings, lovely mellowed paneling and floors, and crisp white curtains. And not a single reminder of theater to be seen.

"It's too big for us now," Shannon said, "but we're used to it and

138

don't want to move. We just closed doors to rooms that we don't need anymore. Please, sit down. I'd like some of your tea, Sunshine, and then maybe you would leave us alone for a few minutes?"

Constance sat in a high-backed damask-covered chair, Shannon in a straight chair; she sat almost rigidly upright. She did not speak for several moments.

"Sunshine has been a blessing," she said finally. "I really think there may be something to all those herb teas that she serves. And, of course, she's company." She sighed deeply. "We're six miles from town here, but sometimes it feels like the end of the earth."

Sunshine brought a single cup and put it on a table at Shannon's elbow.

"Thank you."

"I'll go upstairs and work on my new play now." She turned to Constance. "My first one's so good I'm going to do a lot of them. I have a lot to write about, you know?"

"I'm sure you do," Constance said.

She left without a sound. Shannon picked up the tea and tasted it, nodded, and sipped. "It's very good. Are you sure?"

Constance smiled and shook her head. "What did you want to see me about, Mrs. Tessler?"

"Please, call me Shannon. Everyone does, always did. When I was a girl they called me Irish and I had to fight a dozen fights to make them stop. Aren't children foolish, fighting over things like that?"

Constance said nothing, waited.

Shannon put down the cup and folded her hands in her lap. "Forgive me," she said. "It's Ginnie. I wanted to tell someone about Ginnie and the fire. I know what the gossip is and it's all a lie, you see. But I didn't know who to tell, or what I should say. It's so difficult to refute gossip, so difficult. And I doubt that anyone would bring it up in any official way, but it influences the way people think about other people."

"Are you talking about the fire that killed Ginnie's father?"

She looked surprised. "Yes, of course. They're saying Ginnie started it and she didn't. The fire started in the kitchen, where Vic died, and she was in bed, nowhere near that end of the house. She was still in bed when Ro ran in and carried her out. They say that she had been playing with matches before and was spanked once, so she must have done it again. But that's wrong."

"How do you know?"

Shannon sighed even deeper. "A week or two before Vic was killed in the fire, the children were out back, here in our yard, and my son Jackie started a fire that almost got out of control in the woods. Everyone around here is terrified of wildfires, naturally. There have been some very dangerous ones from time to time. Lucy was here with Ginnie—they just lived a mile up the road—and together we got the fire put out. We were both very frightened. Four children, Lucy pregnant . . . It was a bad experience. But Jackie was responsible, not Ginnie. He was six."

"How did such a rumor start? Didn't you tell William?"

"No." Her voice was faint. "We were having a bad year, one of several bad years. . . . I hardly ever saw him, and when I did . . . we had little to say to each other."

Constance frowned. "Ginnie's mother must have told her husband, and Ro."

"I know she told Vic. They were both so frightened that they searched the house and threw out every match they found. They didn't smoke and there wasn't any reason to keep matches, so they got rid of them. I don't know if she ever told Ro. They'd had a fight over something and she swore she'd never speak to him again. Vic wasn't talking to him, either." She shook her head. "Those were very bad years in so many ways. That damn theater nearly killed all of us in those years. Every cent, every minute, every thought was for the theater, nothing else."

"What happened to Ginnie afterward? We've heard that she stopped talking."

"Yes. Ro moved her and Lucy into town, rented a house for them, and he brought in one specialist after another for Ginnie.

140

Nothing helped. He was nearly demented himself. Lucy blamed him for everything, everything. She turned on him in a way I wouldn't have thought possible. They had been so close before. At first I thought it was just what he deserved finally, but then even I had to feel sorry for him, the way she turned."

"Why do you say even you? Did you blame him for your problems with William?"

Shannon nodded and let her gaze slide past Constance, out the window. "We all loved him, you see," she said in a low voice. "Every woman he met must have loved him, and he just thought of the theater, Lucy, and Ginnie, in that order. It was all he cared about. He made me feel . . . I thought at first that he cared about me, but I was wrong. I was so wrong. So wrong. I was glad he finally was getting some of it back, some of the hurt, the pain, the loneliness. I was glad at first, but then I had to feel sorry for him, and even sorrier for him when Lucy went away and he really lost them both. But he's so lucky, isn't he? Now he has Ginnie back." She looked at Constance again. Tears were making her eyes glisten. "I was so sorry that Lucy didn't keep in touch. We had become friends, our children were playmates. I thought she would let me hear from her, but she never did. I was with her the night she miscarried, the night of the day Vic died. She was hysterical, out of her mind. She seemed to think that Ginnie had died in the fire, too. She kept saying he's gone and I lost his child and there's nothing left. I was afraid she would try to kill herself that night."

"Was Ginnie actually burned?"

"No. She was treated for smoke inhalation and shock. I saw her, poor little thing, drawn up like a baby, sleeping. I had baby-sat her so many times, she was almost like one of my own children, and she looked as if she had never seen me before, wouldn't say a word. She didn't cry either. I always thought that strange, that she didn't cry."

"I never worked with children," Constance said, "but I've read that shock and grief affect them like that sometimes. Does she know that they say she started the fire?"

"I'm sure not. Not unless it's come up now, since those terrible murders. All that was twenty-six years ago, and until now no one would have thought to bring it up, I'm sure. Hardly anyone around here was even here then."

"I don't want to tire you," Constance said, "but could you tell me how it was when Ginnie came back? Did you see her then?"

She nodded. "I saw her but she didn't know me. She had forgotten everything about Ashland, Ro, all of us. She was silent again. Not completely like before, but almost. She would say yes and no and things like that, but nothing else. No real talk, if you understand what I mean. It was heartbreaking to see her like that again."

"And Ro took her on a long trip," Constance said. "How was she when they got back?"

Shannon smiled. "Almost like a normal girl, not quite, not that fast, but almost like any thirteen-year-old, fourteen by then, I guess. Ro did a good thing. I've always wondered if he would have done that if the season hadn't already begun, if things hadn't been well started. We'll never know. She comes to visit pretty often, makes me think of Lucy when she was young. Our children are all grown, moved away to big cities. Not a one of them is interested in theater," she added, almost proudly.

"Look, Charlie," Gus Chisolm was saying, "I know Draker's an asshole, but he's a good detective. He doesn't like loose ends and he works to tie off each string thoroughly."

They were in his office; his feet were on his desk, his chair tilted back. Charlie had turned a straight chair around, was astraddle it, resting his chin on the back.

"Suppose you knew for a fact that Ginnie didn't do either one," he said. "Where'd you look then?"

"That's the problem," Gus said. "There isn't anyone else, I'm telling you. The only one of them who could have done it, besides Ginnie, is Gray Wilmot. He left the high school a few minutes after nine and no one knows when he picked up Laura in the bar. Why?

There's no reason that anyone's come up with. Because Laura and Ellis were having lunch now and then? It's a laugh. They were splitting. She was getting ready to go back East. What difference would it have made if she'd been having late-night dinners, all-night dates with Ellis? Wilmot didn't seem to give a damn one way or the other. But even if that could work as a motive, there's no way he could have killed Laura in that park. He was on the phone with Ro Cavanaugh just before nine. Now, unless you want two killers instead of one, that lets him out."

"Maybe she wasn't killed in the park," Charlie said.

"Yeah, I thought of that. But that's even worse. How'd he get her body to the river? Their car, or her car, was in the garage being repaired. The only way from their place to the river is through town. I don't think he hauled a body through town that night or any other night."

"And the other alibis check out," Charlie muttered, scowling at the floor.

"They sure do. William was seen dropping off Sunshine, and he was in that store all right. The kid who works there had his girlfriend in visiting, they both back him up. The store closes at nine, he was the last customer, chatted a few minutes. Eric was by his neighbor all night, gave him a ride home. Ro was in the high-school auditorium until he got a ride to Jake's Place."

"Was he with people all night there?"

"No. We have confirmation that he was there during the intermission at eight-thirty; he tried to get a ride with Gray Wilmot a little after nine, and did get a ride with Jerry Alistair at nine twenty-five. As for the night Laura was killed, he was either on the phone or with other people until eleven-thirty. Besides, his car hadn't been out of the carport since before Christmas. Hell, it wouldn't even start."

"And the rain started at ten to nine," Charlie muttered. "Doesn't it rain a lot here? Why were so many people surprised by it? No umbrellas, no boots."

Gus smiled genially. "We don't pay a lot of attention until it's actually coming down. The forecast that night was for clearing. It was a surprise that time. Ro's feet were soaked; Ginnie was soaked, Ellis was. Wilmot and Laura were both soaked. Way it goes. There was a real lake outside the stage door that night. My feet were soaked."

"Okay. Okay. So that leaves Spotty. Why not him?"

"No motive. But let's say he's a nut and doesn't need a motive. We have the same problem with Laura. He doesn't even own a car. And why go to the park with her anyway? Privacy? Hell, they could have danced the jig all night in the theater without anyone knowing."

Charlie glared at the floor. Spotty was incapable of it, he had decided earlier after talking with the watchman for half an hour. Not incapable of murder, but of leaving his job for the time it would have taken to get to the river and back. It kept coming home to those with keys, he brooded. The stage door had been replaced sixteen months ago, the locks changed, and only six keys provided, numbered, registered. Of course, copies could have been made in any big city. No copies had been made in Ashland; Draker had checked. But why? As far as he could tell, people wandered in and out all day long. Who would want to enter at night? And why? And if someone had entered and Ellis surprised him, why murder? Ellis seemed the most unlikely victim he could imagine. No enemies in Ashland, none at the university.

"Was Ellis going in or coming out of the office when he got it?" he asked after a time.

"Looked to me like he was done and coming out again. I've got some pictures from one of my officers in here somewhere." He hunted through a desk drawer and brought out a folder, shoved it across the desk.

The top picture was of Peter Ellis sprawled on the floor of the office. His feet were toward the desk, his head close to the round table. The black raincoat was partially wrapped around his body, clearly wet. There was another picture of his head in a close-up; Charlie did not linger over it. "Where does that door go?" he asked, showing Gus a picture of Ro's desk and a door that was open a crack.

"Little closet and through there to a john."

The hall door opened inward to the office, revealing first the easy

144

chairs and couch. Anyone had to enter entirely to see the desk area. Charlie peered closely at the pictures of the furniture: no coat, no book, nothing to indicate that anyone had entered, had been busy doing anything. The round table was bare; the desk the same kind of mess he had noticed the day before; nothing else seemed disturbed in the slightest.

"And all the lights were on?"

"Every one. Switch by the door turns on the lamps at the ends of the couch, but the desk lamp has to be turned on over there. Ceiling light's got a switch on the wall by the closet."

"How about lights in the closet and bathroom?"

"Closet light was on."

Charlie closed the folder. "So maybe it was a burglar. Why else turn on every damn light?"

"Crazy burglar to do a thing like that. Spotty made checks off and on all night, and Ginnie was sure the office door was open a little. It was dim in the hall and she could see the light from the office as soon as she went in the stage door. Some crazy burglar."

"Yeah. Well, I'm due to meet my wife in a few minutes. Thanks, Gus. Can't say any of this has been really helpful, though. Owe you a beer or something."

"No, you don't, Charlie. If there's any way to get Ginnie off the hook, I'm all for it. I'm just hoping you can find that way. I hate to admit it, but I'm stymied. There just isn't anyone else with enough opportunity both times. Give me a call if you want anything else. And I'd appreciate it if you didn't let on to Draker that I showed you the pictures, stuff like that."

On the sidewalk outside the office, Charlie gazed at the rolling hills across the valley, but it was a long time before he saw that the snow had vanished. The air was brisk, like spring in upper New York, he thought then, and suddenly he wished he and Constance were home with their cats and their fireplace and Irish coffees in front of a sparking fire. Constance had said in the beginning that this was going to be messy, and he was very much afraid that, as usual, she was right.

145

SEVENTEEN

Constance watched Sunshine vanish backstage, merging with the actors and various assistants and workers without effort. She wasn't supposed to be there yet, Sunshine had said, not until one, but as long as Ro didn't see her it would be all right. You know? Constance heard that soft voice in her head and turned away with a twinge of irritation. Sunshine could be trying, she decided. On their way back to town all she had talked about was what she had read in the cards for Constance and Charlie. All accurate enough without being very specific until she had said, "You're the High Priestess because you can see into people and because you're not afraid. Why aren't you afraid, Constance? Most people are, you know?"

"Oh, I'm as afraid as most people, I'm sure," Constance had replied lightly and Sunshine had shaken her head, still smiling.

But she wasn't afraid in the usual way, Constance had realized. She had taken years of training in aikido and that helped, of course.

She really was not physically afraid of anyone, and yet she had lived in terror for a long time in New York, especially the last ten years that Charlie had been on the police force. The odds got worse and worse, she had thought then, still thought. Every year he escaped life-threatening injuries made the next year that much more dangerous. Charlie had laughed at her, but had not been able to dissuade her.

The little side trip of thoughts had lasted only a moment, hardly interrupting the conversation. "You're not afraid, either," Constance had said. "It was very brave of you to leave everything and come down here among strangers. Especially a group like this one, so close to each other."

"People don't scare me," Sunshine admitted. "If you watch them, and read their cards and look for signs, for auras, things like that, they aren't so scary. You have to understand the relationships, you know? That's what was wrong with Laura, she didn't understand relationships, didn't even look for them. She just saw herself this way and that way. Like looking at the surface of a pond and not through the water to the bottom. If you can do that, you don't have to be afraid. They're all obsessive, you know? That's why Laura was unhappy. She was obsessive about Gray, and they're all obsessive about the theater."

"Aren't you obsessive about anything? Most people are. Weren't you obsessive about rewriting your play so many times?"

"Up to a point, but that's different. You want things right, you know? As soon as the promptbook was done, I was done. There will be things that come up in rehearsals, maybe, and I'll make little changes, but I'm doing a new play now."

"And you're not afraid of Ro?"

"Not really. As long as I leave Ginnie alone, he won't bother me. That's his obsession, you know? Ginnie is."

"I thought the theater was."

"That too. But mostly it's Ginnie. He thinks I bug her. He's afraid I'll read her cards and scare her."

"I never could read my own cards," Constance said, making a last

147

turn before reaching the theater. She wished the trip could have taken just a bit longer. "Can you read for yourself?"

"Oh yes. It's hard, though. You're so biased, you know? I'm the child of inspiration on my way to becoming Empress. You know how to read that?"

"I'm not sure," Constance said. "How did you?"

Sunshine laughed gently. "You know how. Thank you for the ride, Constance. See you later."

They had drawn up to the parking lot. Sunshine opened her door and left before Constance drove into the lot to park. Constance watched her for a moment, the awkward-looking bag clanking and jingling as the woman moved swiftly to the rear of the quonset hut. Well, she thought, the truth was that she did not know how to read that. She didn't know enough about the relationships yet.

She parked, entered the theater, and started for rehearsal room A, where Gray Wilmot was reading. She had just turned the corner of the hall leading to the rehearsal rooms when Ro emerged from one of them.

"Constance, I'm glad you're here. They're almost done, no point in going in there. Come with me, will you? I want you to meet Ginnie's doctor, my doctor. Did you hear that Draker's taking Ginnie for a ride, trying to make her remember where she was last week? Idiot! How can anyone tell one piece of these woods from another?"

Constance went with him to his office. Although he was talking about Draker and Ginnie, she noticed that he was quite aware of everyone they passed, everything going on. For a moment he stiffened, his stride broke, then he continued. Sunshine had slipped into Juanita's office.

"Jack, glad you could come," Ro said brusquely, entering his office.

Dr. Jack Warnecke was in his middle years, tanned, athletic. When Ro made the introduction, his handshake was almost too firm. Constance felt as if her state of health had undergone a complete scrutiny in that instant.

148

"Constance Leidl. Leidl. Of course, the psychologist! I've read your books. It's a pleasure, Miss Leidl. Or is it Ms.?"

"Or possibly Doctor," she said.

He looked taken aback for a moment, then laughed. "Sorry. Please, call me Jack. Do you like birds? Perhaps you could drop in for a drink, see my birds."

"For God's sake, Jack," Ro cut in. "Not now. Look, you've got to get Draker off Ginnie's back. He wants to drag her off on a wild-goose chase and I won't have it!"

Jack Warnecke raised an eyebrow. "How do you propose I do that, Ro?"

"You took her away from him once. Do it again. She has no business out being interrogated in a car with that man. He's trying to frame her. God knows what she might say while they're driving around."

Jack took a step toward the door. "Ro, that's impossible, and you should know it. She was in shock that other night, but she's fit now. I saw her just a couple of days ago and she's fine."

"She's not fine, goddamn it! She's as disturbed as she was when you said I should take her on that trip! Was she fine then?"

"Ro, you can't direct the world. The police are going to investigate and you can't make them stop. I can't. Sure, she's disturbed; so are you; so is Gray. It would be inhuman if all of you weren't. But she's well enough to be questioned. Tell her to give me a call if she wants to see me." He turned to Constance. "I'm in the apartment next to his. Please do come by. My wife and I would like to show you the birds. Cockatiels, a mackaw, budgies . . . Ro can tell you they're worth seeing. He feeds them when I'm gone. Take it easy, Ro. Just relax, will you? Ginnie's okay. See you later."

"Goddamn fool!" Ro stormed when Jack was gone. "He doesn't understand that she's in danger. You said you're a doctor?"

"Sorry. Ph.D.—psychologist, not a medical doctor. He's right. You can't direct the investigation." She smiled. "I said that just to bring him down a peg. Medical doctors seem incapable of calling anyone else doctor. He's no exception. Does he really have a lot of birds?"

"One whole room's been turned into an aviary. Our leases specify no pets, and spell out cats, dogs, hamsters, but no mention is made of birds, alligators, or rabbits. He decided to make an issue of it and started with birds and got hooked on them. I feed the damn things, all right. Stupid parrot nearly took a finger off once."

Jack had left the door open; now the noise level from backstage increased perceptibly. The reading was over. Ro sat down heavily at the round table and drummed his fingers on it. He looked as if he hadn't slept much the night before. If he had been unaware of Ginnie's danger before, he was making up for his ignorance now, Constance thought.

"I told Charlie to meet me here," she said. "Do you mind if I wait for him?"

"No. No. Make yourselves at home as much as you can, please. Ah, here they are." He stood up as a group entered the office. Ginnie and Gray were in front, then William and Eric, Bobby, the lighting director, others whom Constance had met, some she had not.

"It was a stupendous reading, Gray, really magnificent," one of the women was saying as they entered. "Inspiring, truly inspiring."

Eric was not frowning with his usual intensity and William seemed in deep thought. He nodded as if confirming something in his mind and looked surprised when everyone stopped moving and he was forced to stop also.

Ginnie was too pale, down to her lips. She was clutching her paisley bag in a hard grasp.

"Hi, Ginnie," Constance said. "Did you sleep at all?"

"Oh, hi. I didn't see you. Yes, as a matter of fact, I did sleep. I was a little surprised, but I did. Now I'm off. I'm supposed to be in Ralph's office in a couple of minutes."

"Wait a minute, honey," Ro said. "I'm leaving for lunch, walk down with you." He went to the closet near his desk and brought out a topcoat and put it on.

"Want me to hold on to your bag for you?" Constance asked.

"That's okay," Ginnie said. "I can just leave it here and get it later. You don't have to bother with it."

"No bother," Constance said and took it from her hand. "Remember, give us a call as soon as you're able."

Ginnie nodded and left with Ro. As they were going out, Charlie entered. Constance watched how he searched the room for her, how his expression changed subtly when he spotted her. She always felt as if they had exchanged long messages with that one swift locking of gazes. *Hello. How are you? I'm fine. It's okay. I love you.* And more.

Eric, Gray, and the woman who had been talking when they came in were in a huddle. Now Eric stepped back, nodding. An actress, Constance remembered. She was playing Big Nurse. She was shiny-eyed, gazing at Gray with open invitation in her eyes. He was oblivious of it.

The office was emptying, the backstage noise fading. Charlie waited until Gray was finished with Eric and the actress, then said, "I wonder if we could have a word with you, Mr. Wilmot? In here, maybe?"

Gray looked exhausted and wan. Silently he nodded and the last of the group left, murmuring. Charlie closed the door.

"I understand Ro often orders lunch in here," he said. "Maybe we could do that."

"Not for me," Gray said tiredly and sat at the table.

"Especially for you," Constance said. "Who does he usually call?"

Gray supplied the name of the restaurant and Constance placed the order while Charlie prowled the office. He looked at the bookshelves that lined one wall—all plays: comedies, tragedies, American plays, English, one-act plays. . . . He surveyed the desk but touched nothing on it. He understood the filing system Ro used; it was much like his own. You fish around and bring out what you were after, but if anyone moves anything, all was lost. He nodded at it and opened the door to the closet, peered inside. A

151

couple of jackets, a mackintosh, a pottery umbrella holder with two black umbrellas with crook handles. A smaller door opened to a tiny lavatory. Of course, Ro was always making coffee, he needed a water supply, his own john. A toothbrush, shaving gear, a large bottle of aspirin were in the medicine cabinet. There were fluffy towels on the rack, more folded on a shelf. The soap looked like butterscotch candy. He thought fleetingly of their cats back home. When he rejoined Constance and Gray, she was speaking.

"Why don't you see a doctor? A mild sleeping pill for a few days wouldn't dull you too much for work."

He shook his head. "Drugs and theater, they seem to go together, don't they? Except I can't do drugs of any kind. Wrong reactions to them."

"Mr. Wilmot, would you mind helping me with something?" Charlie asked then.

Gray looked at him expectantly, nodding.

Charlie picked a book from the shelf and handed it to Gray. He opened the door to the hall and looked out. "What I want you to do is come in, walk to the desk and put the book down and go back out. That's all. When I say 'Start.'"

Gray looked from him to Constance and shrugged. He went to the door and out to the hall, pulled the door closed. Charlie went to the closet and entered it.

"Start," he yelled.

Gray came back into the office with the book in his outstretched hand. It was only a few steps to the desk. He put the book down and turned and was to the door again before Charlie got out of the closet and caught up with him.

"Thanks," Charlie said, and retrieved the book, replaced it on the shelf.

"What was that for?" Gray asked.

"One more little scenario first," Charlie said. "Do you mind?"

"Of course I mind, but let's have it. What this time?"

"I want you to lie down. About here, I think. Your head about here." This time Gray was even more reluctant; he started to shake

152

his head, but Charlie was not looking at him, was studying the floor instead. Gray took a deep breath and got down on the floor. Charlie watched him stretch out rigidly, then said, "Let me fix your arms and legs. . . . That looks about right. Now the chair . . ." Carefully he turned a chair over on its side, then stepped back to survey the scene. Gray's feet were two steps from the desk, one leg partly drawn up under him, one hand outstretched almost to the chair. Charlie opened the door all the way; it cleared Gray by less than an inch. "Okay," he said then. "That's all."

Gray was ashen when he got up and brushed himself. "That's how Peter Ellis was found?"

"Yes. As a director, how would you stage the action that would lead to that final scene?"

Gray looked at the closet, then at the floor where he had lain. A frown creased his forehead as he studied the room considering it. Finally he said, "Not the way I thought it was before. I thought someone was in the closet and got him on the way out. That's what Spotty seems to think. But he would have been farther down the room, nearly out the door, wouldn't he?"

Charlie nodded.

"And why hit him at all in that case?" Gray demanded. "If someone was in the closet, he was out of sight. Why dash out and kill someone?"

Again Charlie nodded. There was a tap on the door then and Constance admitted the waiter with a tray. He looked at them curiously as he arranged the lunch things. "Ro ain't here?" he finally asked.

"Nope. How much do we owe you?" Charlie replied.

"It goes on the tab," the waiter said and slowly backed out, examining the room as he did so.

"Probably never saw a room where murder has been done," Charlie commented. "Let's eat."

Gray's color was better. Having a problem to solve seemed to improve his circulation, Constance noticed. He ate little, however.

Suddenly he put down his sandwich and said, "Ginnie couldn't have done it, could she? She would have had to come in first, go to the desk and get the statuette and wait for him to turn around and move away one step. What for? Where was he hit?"

Charlie touched his head just behind and slightly above the right ear. Gray said more positively, "She couldn't have done it. He was my height and she's what? Five-six, -seven?"

"It's the kind of thing experts get rich arguing in court," Charlie said. "A bullet track is easier, but even that isn't foolproof. But you were going to tell me how you would stage it."

Gray regarded him steadily for a moment, then turned his gaze to the desk. "The clown was usually on the end of the desk. I never saw it used as a doorstop, anyway." He paused, thinking. "Ellis came in and walked to the desk and put the portfolio down. Since no one could have come leaping out of the closet, picked up the clown, and caught him that fast, he must have seen whoever it was. Maybe even talked to him a minute, while the killer picked up the clown and came around the desk. As soon as Ellis had turned his back, taken a step or two, the killer hit him, sent him sprawling forward. Would he have fallen like that?"

"Probably. Might have clipped the table on his way down, and for certain hit the chair, knocked it over. But go on. Then what?"

Gray swallowed a bite of sandwich and drank coffee, still thoughtful, before he answered. "He must have run, and at the door realized he was carrying the clown and dropped it. Out through the double doors to the shop, I'd say, or Ginnie would have seen light around the stage door when it opened. The doors open from the inside unless they're padlocked, and Spotty doesn't put on the padlocks until after his ten-o'clock check. Once outside, he was home free."

Charlie righted the chair he had turned over and sat in it. "That's how the police will reconstruct it, I'm afraid."

"What's wrong with that reconstruction?"

"Well, it rules out mistaken identity, for one thing. The killer had time to get a good look at him and knew it was Ellis, not you, in that raincoat. And for another, if the killer had been a burglar, would Ellis have turned his back on him?"

Gray finished his sandwich and drained his cup. Constance refilled it for him and he nodded thanks. "Is that what you wanted to see me about? That little demonstration?"

"Actually no. You have to get to the cast reading at one, don't you? That leaves almost an hour. Would you mind filling in a few details for us? We're still trying to get the complete picture for both nights."

"Sure," Gray said with a touch of weariness. "Where do you want me to start?"

"I have a question," Constance said then. "I've been wondering why you didn't go back East for the funeral."

Gray looked startled. "Her family didn't like me. I would have been in the way. I wasn't welcome in their house when Laura was alive. I sure as hell would not have been welcome when she was dead."

"Was she leaving you, going back East?" Constance asked.

"Yeah. Everything blew up when we got here. She didn't like the small town atmosphere, and she couldn't get a job that she felt was right for her."

"Ellis got her the job, is that right? Were the four of you friends?"

"Not really. I met him a couple of times only. He got us our house, too, but because of Ginnie, not us. He would have done anything for her."

Constance glanced at Charlie and leaned back in her chair.

"Why don't you just fill in the details of both those evenings for us," Charlie said easily.

Gray took more coffee and looked at it. "We'd been having a lot of arguments, one after another. That night it was the same thing. Laura got mad when I said I had to go to the high-school play. She wanted me to go to the movie with her, but I seldom go to movies, and I thought it might be important to see the quality of the kids' performance. We get some of our actors from the high school, of course. Anyway, that's what we agreed, that I'd drop her at the movie and see the production, and then meet her in the bar. We had planned to spend an hour or more there listening to jazz, but we were both soaked and she was furious, and we came home."

"Whoa," Charlie said with a grin. "Too fast. Why did you take the car? It was hers, wasn't it?"

"It was hers. I had to drop off the promptbook for Sunshine's play here, and the high school is on the other side of town. It just seemed simpler that way. It's only two and a half blocks from the movie to the bar. In fact, it was her idea that we do it that way, less trouble for both of us. And I'd join her faster that way," he added bitterly.

"So you saw Eric and Ro. When?"

"I got there a few minutes before eight and they were already there. We spoke but didn't have time to talk. I saw Ro again at the intermission at eight-thirty or so. He introduced me to a couple of people. Jerry Alistair, for one. It was hot in the auditorium, people were milling about, going outdoors for cigarettes, things like that. I told him I'd left the promptbook for him. Then we separated and I didn't see him again that night."

Charlie looked at him thoughtfully. "When did you leave?"

"A little after nine. I didn't notice exactly. It was raining and I realized that Laura would be getting wet. The movie got out at nine-ten. I drove right to it, but it was already emptied, and I went on to the bar. I had to park a block away, and by then I was pretty soaked too."

"Where did you sit in the high school?"

Gray looked exasperated. "In the last row, aisle seat, nearest the parking-lot exit. I knew I wanted to get out before it ended."

"When you and Laura met at the bar, what did she say?"

Now Gray's expression was murderous. He stood up and looked at his watch. It was twelve-thirty; he could not plead that he had to get to the cast reading yet. He started to pace. He had good recall and he was a good mimic. He repeated what Laura had said, then added, "I told you we'd been having trouble. We were both bitchy. When we got home it turned into a real fight and she ended up in

156

the second bedroom of the house. She stayed in there from then on."

Charlie stood up and stretched and now Constance also left the table and leaned against the desk watching Gray. He was looking over the shelves of books of plays.

"Gray," Charlie said softly, "was Laura interested in money? Would she have tried to blackmail anyone?"

Gray's reaction was swift. He turned from the shelves and leaped toward Charlie. Constance, almost in slow motion, caught his wrist and he found himself sitting down hard on the floor with a grunt.

Slowly he pulled himself up and sat in one of the chairs at the table. He rubbed his wrist, watching Constance warily.

"Do you know that she wouldn't have tried to blackmail anyone? Really know it?" Charlie asked in the same low, pleasant voice, as if he had not noticed the incident.

Gray shook his head violently. "She wouldn't have done that!" He started to talk about Laura and their relationship, about Laura and Ashland, Laura and Sunshine, Laura and the night they had had dinner at Ginnie's house. He talked rapidly, his voice harsh, his face strained. Suddenly he jumped up and went to the door. "I'm responsible. I know that. She was right about that. It's all my fault. She called me the climber. Maybe I was, maybe I still am. Maybe I saw myself in that damn play. Her father called me, they all know I'm responsible for everything that happened here. I can't deny it. I'm not even trying! I've got to get out of here for a few minutes. Christ, it's almost one!" He left so fast he was almost running.

EIGHTEEN

"Let's get the hell out of here before Ro comes back from lunch," Charlie said. "I've about had it for one day."

"Amen." Constance drew on her coat, collected her purse and Ginnie's paisley bag, and they left the office in time to see Sunshine enter through the stage door. The cast members for her play were already gathering backstage. Charlie steered Constance past them all, out through the double doors that opened onto an alley. Directly across the alley was the shop with open doors. To the right was the parking lot.

"I parked over there," Constance said.

Charlie nodded and kept walking through the lot onto the sidewalk, where he stopped and looked up the street in the direction of Lithia Way.

"Laura was on that corner at exactly the right time to see someone leave," he said. "The question is, who?"

They retraced their steps to the other alley that led to Pioneer

Street, and again he stopped. "This is where Ginnie parked and waited for Ellis. No way could she have seen anyone go out that back door from here. All right, let's beat it."

"You don't think all those alibis will hold up?" Constance asked as they reached the Buick. Charlie opened the door on the passenger side for her and went around to get in before he answered.

"Ro was right about this town," he said as he started to drive. "You can walk from end to end in ten minutes, and you can drive in just a couple of minutes. I've been all over it today. I know. Anyone could have left the high school, driven over here for something, and met Ellis. Two minutes to get here, a minute to bash in his head, two minutes to get back. Who'd miss him? Same with William. Drop off Sunshine, a minute to the theater, get Ellis, and be in the store less than two minutes later. Even Sunshine could have hightailed it over after William left her."

"That makes it completely unpremeditated," Constance said slowly. "Not even time for an argument to develop."

He nodded. "That's the hitch. Look, there's Ro's car." He had driven on the street behind the apartment complex. The carports were like stair steps, each one a foot or two higher than the last. The car parked there was a two-seater Fiat. It looked like an antique. Constance told him about Jack Warnecke, Ro's next-door neighbor with the birds. His carport was empty. Charlie drove on and made a left turn at Main Street.

"There's the moviehouse. One block to Lithia Way, another block to Pioneer, half a block to the bar where they met. Three minutes, at the most. Say she took a minute or two to get her coat on and actually leave, that puts her on the corner at about fifteen after nine."

"If she saw Gray . . ." Constance said thoughtfully, "as mad as she was about getting wet, that might have been the last straw. She was jealous of the theater, of course, and everyone connected with it."

"The only one she couldn't have seen was Ginnie."

"Or Juanita. Does her alibi hold up?"

"Definitely. Half a dozen people will swear she was in Medford."
He turned again and this time went down Water Street. He nodded
toward a restored Victorian house. "That's the boardinghouse where
William dropped off Sunshine. Three blocks from the theater." He
drove on past a Greek restaurant, past a wooden bridge. The river
was no less swift here in the middle of town than up in the park; the
banks were steep and rocky. He turned away from it onto a different
street. "Let's go home and put our feet up and brood. Okay?"

"Sure. What were you looking for?"

"Some other place where Laura's body could have been put in
the river. Not easy. Too many cars, streetlights, no approach to the
river by car. No one can tell how far she was carried by the river
before she was caught up in the boulders."

As he drove back to the inn she told him about her visit with
Shannon. His only question when she finished, as he parked the car
at the inn, was "And what did Sunshine say your cards foretell?"

She laughed softly. "Poor Sunshine. No one wants her to read for
them except Shannon."

His gaze was on the hills across the valley. "You know what I like?
Snow that goes away by itself." The hills were brilliantly green
without a trace of snow. He turned to grin at her. She was frowning
absently. "What is it?"

"Oh, the town, how accessible everything is to everything, five
minutes from here to there, no matter where either point is. People
made so much of alibis, remember? What good are any of them in a
town that size? Who would miss anyone for five minutes? Even
Sunshine. She said she worked on a new play the night Laura was
killed, but who's to say if she did or didn't? I bet in a house like that
boardinghouse of hers, no one pays any attention to the goings-on
of the residents."

"You're right. I asked."

"About Sunshine? I was just making a point. Why would she do
it? She didn't even know Peter Ellis, and Laura was about the only
person around here to give her the time of day."

"Why would anyone else do it? I'm afraid that Draker's hunt for circumstantial evidence may be the only way to go about all this, and let motive take care of itself. On that basis, of course, the strongest case can be made against Ginnie. Let's go in."

Constance was reading a copy of *Troilus and Cressida*, Charlie gazing out the window. They had been quiet for almost an hour. Suddenly Charlie stood up and said, "I can make a case for just about all of them. Too messy. I don't like it."

Constance put her book down and waited. When he seemed absorbed in the scenery again, she cleared her throat. "Eric?"

"He's easy. He wanted the job that Gray landed. He was next in line, as far as he was concerned, and Ro brings in this young man with practically no experience. He knows that Gray left the prompt-book for Sunshine's play at the theater; he overheard Gray tell Ro. He gets bored with the high-school kids and goes to the theater to read the promptbook, maybe with the idea that if it's as bad as they all seemed to think it was, that would be his chance. Ellis comes in with Gray's coat over his head and when he turns to leave, Eric swings, just as Ellis let the coat fall around his shoulders. Too late. He's dead and Eric knows he needs an alibi and hightails it back to the school."

"But everyone agrees that no one would mistake Ellis for Gray," Constance reminded him. "He would have seen his face."

"Maybe not. Everyone's assuming the lights were on when Ellis entered the office, but maybe they weren't. Eric could have turned them on just to make everyone jump to that conclusion."

She considered it, then said, "And Laura? How could he have managed that? He was at Ro's apartment until eleven-thirty, and on the phone to Ro at nine-ten."

"Remember that nine-o'clock time of death is approximate, could be off half an hour, or even more, either way. He leaves for Ro's house and meets Laura and she tells him she saw him the other night and he slugs her. He puts her body in his car and covers her with a rug, a blanket, something, and goes on to Ro's. When he leaves, he drives up the park road, gets rid of her body, and then goes home."

Shuddering, she said, "And Gray? You can see a way he could have done it?"

Charlie picked up the map Ralph Wedekind had provided them. "Look, here's his house, up a pretty steep hill. Everyone says he would have had to go down the hill, through town, up the park road, but that's not quite so. See, he could have stayed on the hill. They could have taken a walk together, talking, ended up on the ridge overlooking the park, here. That park's really in a canyon, with Park Drive winding around the crest over it for several miles. They get to the edge of the cliff and their argument gets worse and he hits her, kills her instantly. She topples over the cliff and goes rolling down the slope. It has dozens of paths up and down it; we saw them, remember? Steep as hell, but obviously used. He goes sliding down after her. She wouldn't have bruised since she was already dead, but she would have been covered with mud, her clothes torn, scratched up, probably. And that's why he puts her in the river and messes up the opposite bank, to make it appear that she went in there. He figures the swift water will tumble her about, account for the shape she's in. Then back up the cliff, the same streets home, and cleanup time."

"Oh, Charlie," she sighed. "We're going to have to talk to that detective, aren't we?" He nodded. "And Ro? Do you see how he might have killed Ellis? He's about the only one who wasn't caught out in the rain that night."

"I'm working on it," he said, and the telephone rang.

It was Ginnie, back from her ride with Draker and Ralph Wedekind. She sounded miserable, Constance reported, as she and Charlie got their coats on again to go to her house.

"Oh, I want to glance through her sketchbook first," Constance said. She started to flip pages, then stopped and examined a page, then another. "Do you remember the scene in *One Flew Over the Cuckoo's Nest* where the Indian kills Mac? Doesn't he smother him with a pillow?"

"In the book he does. Why?"

He looked at the sketch. It was the setting for the play, with the nurse's desk looming large in the background, file cabinets on one side, and in the foreground the figure of a man on the floor, one arm stretched over his head, his legs drawn up. His arm concealed his face.

"She's good," he murmured, and looked at the previous pages. Different views of the same setting, some with figures, some without. There was a sketch of the desk being used as a bed, a man lying on it, someone standing over him holding a pillow. "Here's that scene," he said. He turned more pages—the window with Chief walking away, the boat scene . . . None of the sketches was complete; the details were not the same from one to another, as if she had been trying out this, then that, just to see how well they fitted.

"That isn't the position Peter Ellis was in, was it?" Constance asked, again studying the sketch that was out of place in that play.

"Nope. Not a thing like it. I wonder what's in the missing sketchbook."

"Maybe nothing much. I just told her to remember yesterday. That's why I wanted to snatch this before someone else had a chance to."

Charlie looked at her suspiciously. "When did you tell her to remember?"

"When I told that silly story about a professor yelling at his students. I gave her hands permission to remember even if her head doesn't, and I think it took. Let's go see her."

Charlie thought of the look of wariness that Gray had assumed after Constance put him on the floor, and he sympathized. Gray didn't know the half of it.

He had insisted years ago that she take self-defense classes, and as soon as their daughter was old enough, that she take them also. When Constance protested one day that they were being taught how to kill people, he had said grimly, "If anyone ever touches you or Jessica and you don't take care of him yourself, I'll kill the son of a bitch and that will be murder one, premeditated, cold-blooded murder. If you do it, it's self-defense." He had meant exactly what he said and they both knew it. She had become very good indeed. In the beginning of her lessons she had demonstrated some of her new skills on him, but one day when he invited her to show him what they were practicing, she had said quite kindly that she had better not.

Ginnie admitted them and led the way to the kitchen. "I just put on coffee," she said. "Do you want some?"

"That would be nice," Constance said. "Was it awful?"

"He's such an asshole!" Ginnie muttered. "He really believes I killed Peter and Laura! He believes it!"

She poured coffee and started to arrange a tray. "Let's just have it here at the table," Constance said and sat down. Charlie sat opposite her, leaving space for Ginnie at the end between them. She brought the coffee things to the table and sat also. She was still too pale, but there were spots of color on her cheeks and a glint in her eyes that had not been there before. He had made her angry, Constance thought: a good sign.

"I brought your bag and stuff," she said. "Did the other sketchbook turn up?"

A puzzled look crossed Ginnie's face. "It was on the table in the rehearsal room when I got there. I must have dropped it yesterday. I guess Mrs. Jensen found it when she cleaned this morning."

"That's good. It would have been a shame to lose all that work."

"Oh, it wouldn't have been lost, not really. Sometimes I don't even look in them again. I have the preliminary sets drawn up, and at the readings I might get an idea or two, a nuance I missed, something of that sort. Once I draw it, it seems to stick in my head. For instance, today I realized that I hadn't made the hospital look institutionalized enough, and I added more file cabinets, rows and rows of files. They'll be way in the back and an orderly will go to them now and then as background. People won't consciously notice them, but they'll add to the feeling of bureaucracy an institution

164

has." She opened the paisley bag and pulled out all the sketchbooks; there were four of them.

Constance had looked inside only the one. She wished now that she had examined all of them. "What did you think of yesterday about Sunshine's play? I saw you drawing like mad all through the reading."

"Nothing much." She began to flip through the sketchbook as she spoke. "It's pretty low-budget, not a lot we can do with the sets. Sunshine had action going on in every room of the house and I got that down to the living room only."

Suddenly Charlie felt the invisible fingers on his back and he leaned forward very slightly to look at the page Ginnie had stopped at. The same figure was there in the same position. Ginnie hardly even glanced at it, but turned another page.

"Here it is. I decided to cut away about half of the flats for the living room so that the audience can see through it to the mountains in the background."

She had not seen it, Charlie realized. She had been blind to that intrusive figure. There were sketches of a woman on the couch obviously dying or dead, but that one figure had not been the same. If he had not already seen it in her other book, would he have paid any attention? He could not answer his own question. Constance was idly turning pages in the sketchbook they had looked at earlier. She glanced at the page Ginnie was showing her and nodded.

"That should be very effective. Is that what they call a practical rock?"

"Yes. It's to be about eight feet high, high enough so the actor can actually be seen climbing it. . . ." She talked on, apparently blind to the fact that Constance had placed one of her pencils near her hand.

"Well, these are all so good. You're very talented. I suppose that detective went on about the fact that you're an artist, with fully developed visual memory. It's tempting to think that visual artists must be able to remember everything they've ever seen and reproduce it on demand. I imagine he's still bothered that you didn't see that doorstop in your uncle's office. He might even think you're lying, or something."

"He wanted to know if I studied acting in school," Ginnie said in a low voice. "All drama majors have to."

"I bet he did. I can just imagine him ordering you to remember. 'Of course you can remember!' Just like my professor ordering our hands to remember."

Ginnie was staring at Constance now, nodding.

"Start at the beginning of that trip with him and pick up the pencil and tell us about it," Constance said in her pleasant low voice. Ginnie picked up the pencil without looking at it. Constance slid the sketchbook under her hand, opened to the page with the man's body on the floor. Ginnie apparently did not notice, but as she began to describe her interrogation in detail, her hand began to draw. Charlie exhaled very softly and watched the hand in fascination.

Neither of them interrupted Ginnie as long as her hand kept drawing. When it stopped, Constance laughed and said, "That's enough of that. What a terrible trip that must have been for you." She reached out and took the sketchbook and casually slipped it into her purse. "Charlie, didn't you say you wanted to ask Ginnie something?"

"As a matter of fact," he started, searching for something, anything, to ask, "I wondered if Ro objected to your traveling so much?"

"Not really. You can't do theater work in a vacuum. You have to get out and see other theaters, how other people are doing sets, costumes, all that. He travels a lot himself, that's how he knew about Gray. He saw a production of his last year."

Constance stood up. "Thanks, Ginnie. I know you still have your models to make and we shouldn't keep you any longer. It must be difficult to keep on working right now."

"Thank God I have work to do," Ginnie said fervently. "As long as I'm working I don't think, not really think. It's like coming out of

166

a daydream when I realize it's midnight and I've been working for four or five hours."

"Or a trance?" Constance said. "I've heard artists describe it like that. An altered state of consciousness that is like a trance more than anything else."

"That's right," Ginnie said a little self-consciously. "That's how I'd talk about it with another artist, but not usually with outsiders. They think you're crazy if you talk like that."

Not until they were in the car heading down the hill did Constance ask, "Charlie, did you get a look at the drawing?"

"I sure did," he said grimly.

Ginnie had finished the sketch. The man was stretched out on the floor, an overturned bottle near his hand, a chair upset at his side. There was a kitchen table with a plate that held cheese, a loaf of bread with a knife stuck in it, a very short candle burning on a second plate. A door was open a few inches behind the figure on the floor. A kitchen sink with a pot or pan in it, an open window behind it, part of a refrigerator . . . A typical kitchen, except that there was a body on the floor.

NINETEEN

There were two messages waiting for them when they got back to the inn. The first was from Lieutenant Draker. Charlie returned his call while Constance hung up their coats and put away papers they had left on the table in the sitting room.

"He's coming over in five minutes," Charlie said. "I don't think he's happy. You want to call Dr. Warnecke?" His was the second call.

She nodded and took his place at the telephone. Jack Warnecke answered at the first ring. "Constance," he said, and she grinned, "could you and your husband join us this afternoon for cocktails? Sandy, my wife, is so eager to meet you both."

She accepted his invitation and called him Jack and was smiling broadly when she hung up. At Charlie's raised eyebrow she shrugged and said, "It's called one-upmanship, played among doctors and other professionals all the time. We're due at his place at five."

"That blows tea again," he said regretfully. "Maybe Mrs. Shiveley could send up coffee now. I used to hate it when people drank beer or booze in front of me when I was on duty and had to say no and be polite and just watch."

"Poor baby," she murmured and called Mrs. Shiveley for coffee.

"You don't understand," he said indignantly. "Suppose it's ninety-five outside, you're covered with sweat right down to your BVDs and this slob in shorts and a tank top is having a frosty glass of beer."

"So you arrested him and tossed him in the slammer," she said, laughing.

"Damn right. Every time."

The coffee and Lieutenant Draker arrived practically together. Mrs. Shiveley was arranging the cups on their table when Draker knocked on the door. Mrs. Shiveley was angry that he had come upstairs alone, unannounced.

"What do you mean coming in here without permission? This is not a public house, young man. Get out this instant." She turned to Constance and Charlie. "I'm very sorry. I'll call my husband and the police instantly."

"I am the police," Draker said icily.

"Where is your identification?"

He showed her his ID and looked past her to Charlie. "Tell her it's all right. Let's not have a stupid scene."

"Are you Lieutenant Draker? We're expecting the sheriff's detective, Mrs. Shiveley. Thanks for your concern. You are Draker, I take it?"

"I'm Draker." His face was flushed a dull red, his eyes nearly closed.

Wired too tight, Charlie thought, and smiled genially at him. "Come on in. We ordered coffee for you. Thanks again, Mrs. Shiveley."

Her gaze that swept the detective was cold and unapproving. Wordlessly she nodded and left, closed the door softly behind her.

"This isn't your average Howard Johnson motel," Charlie said comfortably. "She takes good care of her guests. Sit down, won't you. I'm Charlie Meiklejohn, and this is my wife, Constance Leidl. What can we do for you, Lieutenant?"

Before he could respond, Constance asked brightly, "Cream? Sugar? Look, Charlie, she brought some pastries. They're fresh out of the oven!"

"What a wonder she is!" Charlie said with enthusiasm and popped one of the tiny savories into his mouth. "Mmm."

"She's spoiling us so much, we may never leave," Constance said to the detective, who was still standing in the center of the room. "Please, sit down. Let's all sit here at the table and try the pastries."

What the hell had happened? Draker wondered furiously. Charlie Meiklejohn was sitting down, poking at the plate of biscuits; she was pouring coffee as if they were having a party. Angrily he yanked a third chair back and sat in it and knew instantly it was a mistake. If he looked at Constance, he couldn't see Charlie without turning his head. They both gazed at him with good-natured innocence.

"I don't know what you think you're doing here," he said finally, choosing Charlie as his target. "You're not licensed to practice in Oregon. I checked." He turned to include Constance in time to see a smile on her face.

"Sorry," she said. "You just reminded me of a friend of ours. He won't go to a doctor, he says, until they stop practicing and know what they're doing."

"Try one of these," Charlie said, pushing the plate toward him. "You know, I think they all have different fillings. That woman is a marvel."

Draker ignored the plate and said to Constance, "Let me tell you something about Jackson County. It's a conservative county, one. You might not get that impression if you just hang around Ashland here, because it's a university town, and the theater people are from outside for the most part. But when it comes time to impanel a jury, it's county residents who are sitting in the box, and they don't trust fancy New York psychologists and fancy New York detectives, and

170

hey sure don't believe in pleas of incompetency. And number two," e said in a hard voice, "we don't have unsolved crimes hanging ver us, and our cases don't drag on for years."

Now he lifted his coffee cup and drank. They both continued to atch him with interest. He looked from one to the other and added eliberately, "And they tend not to trust the word of women who are leeping with men they haven't got around to marrying yet."

Constance nodded. "Should that be number one, Lieutenant? Vould they convict her on that alone?"

"You'll claim that she was crazy, not responsible, and I say that he's putting on an act. They'll decide which of us to believe."

"I can put William Tessler in the theater long enough for him to ave done it, and Eric Hendrickson, and Gray Wilmot," Charlie aid lazily. "And probably Roman Cavanaugh."

"You can try," Draker said. "But it won't wash with any of them. Io motive. And I don't buy coincidence working twice, not with llis and then with Laura Steubins."

"You're absolutely right," Charlie said. "I don't either. What rime lab do you use?"

"Oregon State. Why?"

"Just wondering. Isn't that Ernie Stedman's show?"

"Now you tell me you used to work with Stedman. Right?"

"Oh, no," Charlie said very gently. "I taught him. Honey, when id I do that series of workshops in San Francisco? Seven years ago? ight? It was the same year you gave the keynote address to the iternational psychologists' meeting in Copenhagen." He looked at)raker and added, "We went by way of Tokyo. I did a couple of orkshops there."

He was being laughed at, Draker realized with cold rage. This astard was patronizing him, laughing at him. Abruptly he stood p, almost upsetting his chair. He caught it before it fell and he felt ie way he had as a boy in his aunt's house. Aunt Corinne had lways made him feel as if his hands were grimy, his hair ncombed, his knees dirty. She never said anything, but it was in er look of patient resignation, as if she were simply biding her

171

time until he grew up, and meanwhile she could bear his presence only by detaching herself from him at a great distance. He could not remember a visit to her house in which he did not spill something, or drop something, break something, stumble, or in some way make a fool of himself. She had never laughed openly, or even smiled, as her two daughters had done again and again, but her eyes had a way of brightening that he had come to dread. He looked at Constance and saw the same kind of bright interest.

"Lieutenant," she said directly, "Ginnie didn't do either of those murders."

"That's what you're paid to say," he snapped, and started for the door. He looked at Charlie. "You just leave my business to me."

Charlie grinned at him. "You never did actually say what you wanted to see us about, did you?"

Draker felt his stomach muscles tighten in a way that meant heartburn later. "What I came to tell you," he said harshly, "is that when I call for a grand jury hearing, you're going to be subpoenaed and you have no privileges here. None. You'll either testify and repeat what she's told you, or I'll get you for perjury and or contempt of court." He yanked the door open and slammed it behind him.

Charlie was regarding the plate of savory pastries and now he nodded. "I bet she keeps them made up in the freezer ready to heat in a microwave on demand. How else could she do them?"

"Oh, Charlie."

Although the Warnecke apartment had started out identical to Ro's, it was like entering another country—a tropical rain forest, perhaps. Ten-foot-tall orange trees and an avocado tree nearly that tall pressed greenery against the floor-to-ceiling windows. Hanging pots with vines dangled from stainless-steel rods suspended from a bar across the end of the living room. A four-foot-long aquarium had been turned into a cactus garden, with brilliant fluorescent lights creating the glare of a desert. Two of the cacti were in bloom with flamboyant red flowers.

172

Sandra Warnecke was in her middle years and comfortable with herself. She was strongly built without being too heavy, and she had a directness that was engaging.

"I've never met private detectives before," she said, surveying them both frankly. "And I must say you two don't look the part. Martinis, wine, a straight slug of something? What can I get you?"

"Martini," Charlie said; Constance nodded.

"But first the birds," Jack Warnecke said. "Come on, come on. Sandy can do the mixing. They're upstairs, except for Pretty Boy, and he's hiding in the orange tree, sizing you up."

The birds were free in the room that in Ro's apartment was a second bedroom. Here, part of the balcony and the room had been done over with plants—in buckets, tubs, redwood planters, on glass shelves at the three windows. A macaw screeched at them; two cockatiels twisted their heads eyeing them; a flock of budgies darted from one tree to another in a spray of blues and greens, chattering as they flew and even more when they landed. A bright yellow finch edged along a branch closer and closer and finally flitted to Jack's shoulder and pecked at the seam of his jacket.

"Dinwiddie," he said, and stroked the bird gently with his forefinger."

"Are they all named?" Constance asked.

"Sure. That's Wallace, and Stan and Ollie over there, and the budgies are Grumpy and Sneezy and so on. I have to confess I can't always tell them apart. Except for Pretty Boy, and he stays in the living room with us. He's the only talker among them, but he tells us everything that's going on."

Half of the balcony had been enclosed with screening; on it there were perches, a swing, feeding dishes, and water. When they started to leave the room, the budgies followed and crowded close together on perches and the swing, chattering.

"They want a treat for good behavior," Jack said, grinning. He pulled a small bag from his pocket and emptied it into a feeding dish. Sunflower seeds, raisins, crushed corn. The budgies swarmed to it and began to eat, scolding each other, elbowing each other out of the way, keeping up a constant barrage of chatter. On the other side of the screen another budgie landed on a perch and said very clearly, "Pretty boy, pretty boy. Hello, Jack."

"I thought that would bring him out of hiding," Jack said. He opened the door to the cage, letting Pretty Boy in, and left the noisy budgies to their treat. Pretty Boy flew to Jack and landed on his shoulder. It stayed there when they went downstairs again.

"They're wonderful," Constance said to Sandy, back in the living room.

"They're all his," she said, looking at Jack with affection. "We had to have an understanding about them the first week. I said I wouldn't feed a damn bunch of birds, clean up after them, or do anything except look at them. He didn't think I meant it, and for a day no one fed them. He gave in. I just look at them."

"Do they have to be fed every day?" Charlie asked. "We can leave food for our cats for several days. They complain, but that's life."

"Twice a day," Jack said. "Water's even more crucial. They have to have fresh water at all times. That's why I made a deal with Ro. He looks after them when we're gone, and I look after him. Fair trade. I asked him to drop in, by the way."

"We spend Christmas in Honolulu," Sandy said. "Our daughter lives there. Ro takes us to the airport, complaining bitterly about the rain, of course, and almost as soon as we arrive his postcards start to arrive, too. He mails them before we even leave town, from the airport! Things like, Pretty Boy had babies, or Wallace bit the cleaning woman, or something. He's not fond of the birds, he says, but he buys them grapes and pumpkin seeds. He left a tape for Pretty Boy once and taught him four-letter words. We never know when they'll come popping out."

"He says if we ever get another mynah bird he'll teach it Hamlet's soliloquy. We had one that died a few years ago. Now that's a real talking bird!"

Pretty Boy landed on the coffee table and Sandy said, "Scat."

174

Pretty Boy said, "Damn, damn, damn," and flew off, back to the orange tree.

"Before Ro gets here," Charlie said, "I'd like to ask you something, Jack. If you don't want to answer, that's fine. You know why we're here, of course, what our reasons are." Jack nodded. "About Ginnie. When she came back here after her mother died, how disturbed was she?"

Jack glanced at Sandy. She nodded slightly, stood up, and took Charlie's glass to refill. "I'm not a psychiatrist," Jack said slowly, "but 'disturbed' isn't the word I'd use. She was depressed. Maybe severely depressed. She was going through her own puberty crisis, and that made it worse, losing her mother so suddenly. They never had lived in one place more than a year or two, I understand, and she had few real friends, and until she came here and met Ro, she had no other family that she was aware of."

"Did you advise him to take her on a trip?"

"I don't know. His idea, mine. It seemed a good idea. She was a skinny kid with great saucer eyes and nothing to say to anyone. She hung out at the theater a lot, not saying a word, just there. Something had to be done."

"Did you advise counseling, psychiatric help of any kind?"

"No. We talked about it a couple of times, but I felt that she would come around. My God, it was a shock. Anyone would have reacted."

"Thanks," Charlie said, accepting a glass from Sandy. "Just one more thing. How sick is Shannon Tessler? Is she too ill for me to ask her a question or two?"

Constance felt a jolt of surprise and saw the same surprise on the faces of both Jack and Sandy.

Jack lifted his martini and sipped it, thinking. This time he did not consult with his wife. Looking at the olive in his glass, fishing for it with a pick, he said, almost carelessly, "You can ask her anything you want. She's about as ill as I am."

The doorbell rang and he looked relieved. "That's probably Ro. Excuse me." He went to open the door.

Ro looked worn and tired. He was dressed in a blue suede jacket, navy slacks, the best-dressed man in town, but for once his appearance was not dapper and advertisement-perfect. There was a slump to his shoulders now, and his walk was without its usual bounce.

Jack looked at him critically when Sandy handed him a martini. "You sleeping, Ro?"

Ro greeted Charlie and Constance, thanked Sandy, and sat down before he replied. "Hell no. And you wouldn't either if Ginnie was yours. I'm worried about her, Jack. Really worried."

"Well, you're not helping her any by staying awake all night. I'll give you something. I've got some samples upstairs." He left.

Ro looked at Charlie. "Do you think they'll let her go away for a while?"

"I don't know. I doubt it."

"She needs to get away, get some rest. They haven't ordered her not to take a trip."

Jack returned with a small bottle. He handed it to Ro, who slipped it into his pocket without looking at it. "Take a couple of them half an hour before bed."

"Thanks. I'll do that. Right now there's just so damned much to do. . . ."

"If I were you," Charlie said to Ro, "I'd talk it over with Ralph Wedekind before I advised Ginnie about a trip. It could be damaging."

Ro sighed. "You have a daughter, is that right?" Constance nodded. "You know how it is then. When they're small you want to arrange the world for them, and you can almost do it, make things come out all right most of the time. When they're small it's not so hard, is it?"

"It's always tempting to think that when they're grown up you won't have to worry about them anymore," Constance said. "The worries are just different ones."

Pretty Boy flew to Ro's chair and perched, saying, "Hot shit, hot shit." Sandy shooed him away and he left, saying, "Damn, damn, damn."

176

"And that's your fault," Sandy said with resignation.

Ro grinned. "If he could project just a little bit more, I'd make him a star."

Charlie laughed. "He'd think he had discovered freedom, loose in the theater." He finished his drink and shook his head at Sandy, who reached for his glass. "Mr. Cavanaugh, when you saw Gray Wilmot leave the high-school auditorium, did you notice the time?"

"Not really. I know I started to leave at nine, but it was raining too hard. I growled at it a minute or so, then went back to the auditorium. I was on the opposite side from him. By the time I realized he was leaving and I got back out to the front hall, he was already outside, out of sight. The rain was coming down harder than ever. Five after nine, maybe ten after. Not later than that."

"Maybe the people you had to disturb to get out noticed the time. Did you know any of them?"

"I always take an aisle seat," he said almost apologetically. "I can't stand being a captive audience if the play's really bad. Besides, I didn't sit down again after that. I stood in the back of the auditorium. I was looking for almost anyone I could get a ride with." He fingered his suede jacket and said ruefully, "I wasn't dressed for rain any more than I am right now. I have an aversion to getting wet."

"Don't blame you," Charlie said, and looked at Constance. "We'd better be on our way. Thanks for letting us see the birds, and for the drinks."

In the car Constance asked, "Why do you want to talk to Shannon?"

"Oh, I thought she might know the times that William was in and out both those nights. I noticed that Sunshine doesn't wear a watch. More than that, though. I'm curious about her, about all of them the way they were thirty years ago. Did you know Ginnie would remember what happened the day of the fire?"

"I thought she might. She was reacting to that day, not Peter Ellis's death. I think she wandered into her kitchen that day and saw her father on the floor. Seeing Peter Ellis dead stimulated that memory that had been repressed all these years. She became the three-year-old who had to close the door so no one would see her father like that. So, of course, she had to repress that action, too."

"And if she's lucky, maybe she'll never remember," Charlie said, and started to drive.

TWENTY

Rain was pouring down when Charlie and Constance finished dinner and stood in the doorway contemplating the block between them and their Buick.

"An umbrella's in the car," she said morosely. A gust of wind drove rain their way.

"You want to wait while I get the car and come around for you?"

"I think I'd get wet just standing here," she said, drawing her coat collar up. "Let's do it."

They ran to the corner and turned, then Charlie stopped, the rain streaming down his back and off his bare head. He gazed down the street; she realized he was looking at the back of the theater complex, at the shop and sidewalk in front of it. A streetlight on that corner seemed to dance in the driving rain. He took her arm and they walked the rest of the way to the lot where they had parked. They could not get much wetter.

There were few people out on foot, and those who were out were obscured by umbrellas. When they got in the car, the wind drove the rain hard against the windshield. Charlie started the engine, humming softly to himself.

"Aren't you freezing?" she asked, wishing the heater would warm up faster.

"Nope. Rain I can take. It's snow that gets to me. I wonder if Mrs. Shiveley knows about hot rum toddies."

When they got to the inn, it turned out that she knew all about such things, and finally they were back in their rooms, in robes, sipping the steaming drinks and listening to the wind in the trees, the rain pelting the windows. For a long time they sat quietly, glad to be warm and dry again, until finally Charlie opened Ginnie's sketchbook and began to study the sketch Constance had ordered from her. He thought of it that way.

She had been doing the hospital scene, with Big Nurse's desk, the files, but she had drawn over everything as if she had been unaware of it. Now there was the man on the floor, a back door partially open behind him, a cabinet with a large pot of flowers before a window, through which a ray of light spilled into the room; on the other side of the door, a sink, more cabinets that turned the corner, a refrigerator. The table was wooden with matching chairs. A tablecloth had been pulled partly off the table, by the man's fall apparently. One end of it trailed on the floor in the spilled brandy. The bottle had the distinctive shape of a brandy bottle.

He turned his attention to the objects on the table. A loaf of bread, uncut, with a knife stuck in it. Not the way anyone would start to cut bread, he thought. It had been plunged deeply into the loaf. A wedge of cheese was on a plate. A wineglass had been overturned; the spilled wine? brandy? had been drawn in carefully. And that damn candle, he thought in irritation. A stub of a candle burning on another plate, or shallow bowl, a soup bowl? It didn't look like a soup bowl, or like the other plate with the cheese, either. And the candle flame was taller than the candle itself. It was on the dish surrounded with . . . waves? He looked closer and sighed. Waves. What the hell did that mean?

Constance was almost through reading *Troilus and Cressida*; she glanced at Charlie, but he was absorbed in the sketch and she did not interrupt him. She made a note of the page she wanted to read to him and returned to the play. When she looked up again, he was regarding her absently.

"Let me read you this one little speech," she said. "It's Pandarus talking." She found the passage and read: " 'If ever you prove false one to another, since I have taken such pains to bring you together, let all pitiful goers-between be called to the world's end after my name; call them all Pandars; let all constant men be Troiluses, all false women Cressids, and all brokers-between Pandars!' "

"That's pretty strong stuff," he said after she closed the book.

"It's a strong play. Full of lechery and betrayals and war weariness. It's the most cynical thing Shakespeare ever wrote, I bet."

Charlie drained the last drops from his mug and stood up. "Speaking of lechery," he said with an evil leer.

She laughed softly.

It was still raining the next morning when they drove out to talk to Shannon Tessler. The rain simply made everything greener than ever, but across the valley the hills and mountains had been swallowed by clouds. The small town seemed cut off from the entire world now.

"I thought you might come back," Shannon said to Constance when she opened the door for them. She nodded at Charlie when Constance made the introductions. "Leave your umbrella in the stand," she said, "and you can hang your coats on the tree where they can drip." The coat tree was shaped like a rack of a mammoth buck.

"Thank you for letting us come," Charlie said when she led them into the living room and motioned them to chairs.

"I expected another visit," she said again.

"Yes, I guess you did. Who started the rumor that Ginnie was unstable, Mrs. Tessler?"

"Not me," she said with a faint smile. "Is that what you're thinking? That I did it?"

"Did your husband?"

"No. He never would have thought of such a thing."

"Were you and your husband already living here when Ro first came?"

"Yes. William had a temporary job with the Shakespearean Festival that year. We had a small orchard that was our livelihood, but he was interested in the theater and wanted to work there when he could. Then Ro came with Lucy and Vic. The first year we stayed on the orchard and he was at the beck and call of Ro so much that we never even saw him. We had to get a tenant to run everything finally and we moved to this house. A few years later we sold the orchard."

"What were they like, Lucy, Vic, and Ro?"

"Ro was possessed, as he still is, by the theater. Lucy and Vic were like children. We were older than they were, of course. They were like children, squabbling, fighting, loving, leaving each other, running back. Like children playing at being grown-up, playing house. When they fought, she went home to Ro."

"And then Ginnie was born. Did things change then?"

"For a time. They were children with a living doll for a time."

"And Ro? How was he after Ginnie was born?"

She looked at Charlie, then averted her gaze and looked at the rain in her yard. "He adored her."

"Was Lucy a good actress?"

"She was quite good."

"Did she ever act in the Shakespearean playhouse?"

Again she looked at him with a curious expression, as if she wanted to ask him questions. "He wouldn't let her," she said flatly.

"But she tried? She wanted to play Shakespeare? How did he stop her?"

"I don't know. She never told me. But he stopped her, and after that . . . After that I think she fell in love with Vic. I think she grew up then. And Vic grew up. They were going to leave, go to

182

Europe, but not until the baby was born. She wanted her child born here, in the States."

Charlie regarded her soberly for several moments. "Maybe she didn't tell you, but sometimes we don't have to be told, do we? Roman Cavanaugh came here and rearranged your life, your husband's life; he controlled his sister for years, and her husband. Is he still running everyone's life, Mrs. Tessler?"

"Of course," she said. "He has to. He can't help himself."

"Why don't you tell us why you wanted us to come here again," Charlie said very gently.

When she did not respond, he said, "He started that rumor about Ginnie himself, didn't he?"

"Yes." Her voice was low, hardly audible. "That's how he controls her. She believes she has this instability, this latent insanity. She isn't even aware of how he twists her, how subtly he makes her accept his truths that are lies. She won't let herself fall in love, swears she'll never have children of her own, that her work is all she can handle, all she wants. She's afraid. He has made her afraid to trust herself."

"She seems to love him very honestly," Charlie said when she stopped.

"We all loved him very honestly," she said with great bitterness.

"And he only loved Lucy, his sister," Charlie said.

She became rigid, then shifted in her chair as if it had become uncomfortable. "He loved no one but Lucy," she said harshly.

"Did anyone else know?"

"I don't think so. Not William. I didn't until we moved into this house. Ro used to pass on his way to visit them. The day she drove him out, he came in here, so pale I was afraid he was having a heart attack. And all at once, I knew. That's the day I realized how blind we all were, how stupid. That's the day it ended with them, that Lucy discovered she had a husband who loved her fiercely, a child, money, everything in the world. The day she realized that she no longer needed Ro." Abruptly she stood up. "William knows nothing of any of this. He knew there was someone I cared for, but he

183

thought it was Vic. I let him believe that. It seemed simpler at the time. Now if you'll excuse me . . ."

Silently she led them to the door, watched them put on their coats and retrieve the umbrella. With her hand on the doorknob, she said, "You said he rearranged our lives. That's wrong. He took our lives. He took my husband, took my life. He takes what he wants. Please, don't come back."

She opened the door and let them out. The door closed quietly behind them.

"Well, Christ on a mountain," Charlie muttered, back in the Buick, not starting yet.

"That poor woman," Constance said. "Poor Lucy. Poor Shannon."

"Poor Ginnie," he added. "All this surfaces because we had to find out why Ginnie was trying to close that office door, why she forgot doing it. You were right about this mess. It's a goddamn can of worms stretching back for twenty-six years. Try to look at current events and history smacks you in the face. Try looking at the past, and yesterday, last week is all you can see. I wish to hell Ginnie had left that goddamn door alone."

He turned the key then and they drove back the winding road to the highway where he made a left turn instead of driving back to Ashland. She did not ask why, but gazed at the green countryside being drowned in the steady rain. He was scowling at the world.

They drove north to the town of Medford, twelve miles from Ashland, and he slowed down, made a turn at a shopping center. "I want to try something," he muttered. "Let's go shopping."

He bought a baking pan, paper plates, and candles. When they were through there, he drove to a liquor store where he bought brandy.

"I'm done," he said then. "You want anything?"

She shook her head. "Let's go home." For years Charlie had been on the arson squad in New York City, until fire had invaded his dreams, his life at home, his daydreams. He had started to inspect every building they entered, looking for the way out, the hazardous conditions that might lead to a holocaust. He had come awake cursing and shouting from deep sleep, fighting fire. Rags in a corner had become suspect; paper blown against a wall, suspect; faulty wiring, too many plugs in a single socket, suspect; a gas can in the sunlight . . . Everywhere arson was suspected, fire imminent. Finally she had forced him to admit that he had to transfer out of arson, into anything else; he had resisted at first, then agreed, and had gone into homicide.

It had helped, but it wasn't the final answer. The final answer had been his resignation after twenty-five years, his resignation, and enough time to start the healing process that had not yet been finished. She had known he had to resign when the realization hit her with shocking intensity that he no longer distinguished between criminal and victim, when everyone had become a potential murderer or arsonist in his eyes, everyone a potential victim inviting violence.

He had grown up in New York. He said that one day he had turned east instead of west, otherwise he might have been on the other side. It was that simple. She issued the ultimatum when he shot and killed a drug dealer who had gunned down a pimp, his live-in girlfriend, her two children, and a neighbor child. When Charlie received his last citation for meritorious duty, he had said coldly to the gathered media, "They were just sacrifices, all of them. We need sacrifices, don't we? The kids are better off dead."

"We are leaving the City," she had said. "You're retiring, and so am I. We're getting the hell out before you get killed."

"You're off your rocker!"

"Not me. You're slipping faster and faster and I won't have it! Do you even remember that kid you were? That idealistic kid who thought an honest cop would set an example? Who thought a change here, a little change there, and the whole goddamn system would slowly turn around? Where the hell is he now, Charlie? You're pretending that kid is a casualty, dead, gone, forgotten! I don't believe it. But you don't dare remember him every day, or even once a year, or you'd break down in tears. Admit it, dammit!"

185

He had stormed out to get drunk, and she had sat with a pencil and notebook and worked with figures. He had walked from their Ninety-eighth Street apartment to the Village and back, and she had figured exactly how much money their two pensions would bring in, how much the royalties from her moderately successful books on popular psychology would continue to bring in, how much money they needed to finish their one daughter's education.

When he returned at three in the morning, she had met him stony-faced and exhausted. He was equally exhausted. Slowly he had nodded, and then she had wept.

And now, she thought miserably, he had that same hard look on his face that he used to get, that same bitter expression. She had known this was a bad case from the start, messy, dark, with a history of evil and meanness to plague the present, to distort the present. That damn fire, she thought. That goddamn fire!

He drove to the theater, although it was at the beginning of the lunch break. Inside, Eric Hendrickson said that Ro and Ginnie had gone out together; Gray was in his office with orders not to be disturbed. Only Juanita Margolis was around. Another superb reading, Eric said on his way out. Actually, to Charlie's eyes it appeared that a mob was in the theater—the morning cast for the reading had not yet dispersed; the cast for the afternoon read-through by the actors had started to assemble; stagehands were doing something to the overhead grid; an electrician was snaking wire through the backstage area. . . . Anna Kaminsky's voice floated over the subdued hubbub. Before they could move away, she appeared with an angry expression.

"They want me to take their word that next month they'll change. Five pounds thinner, ten pounds heavier! Two inches off the waist . . . Hah!" She stamped out.

"Let's take Juanita to lunch," Charlie said, and led the way to her office.

She was eating a sandwich at her desk. A coffeepot on a warming tray was on a table. A cigarette sent smoke curling upward from an overflowing ashtray.

"Sorry," she said when Charlie invited her out with them. "I have to be here for a call from New York. You know, with the three-hour difference, it's a problem. If I leave, by the time I get back, they're off for the day."

What an attractive woman she was, Charlie thought. She had knowing dark eyes, lustrous dark hair, a trim figure, complexion that suggested Chicano, but most of all she was intelligent-looking.

"May we ask you a couple of questions here?"

A look of amusement flashed over her face and she nodded. "I'll even answer between bites."

"Fine. Are you married?"

"Divorced."

"How long have you worked for Ro?"

"About twenty years. And I've been divorced about twenty years." The amusement played with her features, softening her mouth, crinkling the skin at her eyes, making her appear years younger than she looked when she was not smiling.

"That was one of the questions," Charlie admitted. "Another one is, can you prove that you were in Medford the night Ellis was killed? I mean really prove it with witnesses?"

She nodded. "The police are satisfied."

"That's a problem," Charlie said with a sigh. "As soon as they think they know who their culprit is, they stop seeing things that don't fit in. Human nature makes them do it, it's not a conspiracy. We all see what we expect to, and we're all blind to what doesn't fit our scheme of reality."

"I was with a group all evening," she said, still good-naturedly. "One of them held my hand during most of the movie."

"That's nice," Charlie said, pleased with her.

"No, not really. You see, he wants me to move to Medford and I won't do that."

"It's only twelve miles."

"I know." Her tone said that subject was closed now.

"The morning Gray Wilmot announced he had picked Sunshine's play, I understand there was a fight. Will you tell us about it?"

She shrugged slightly. "It wasn't a fight. A disagreement about the play. Gray was furious at first, but it blew over quite fast. He defended the play and Ro accepted it. That was that."

"And were you furious?"

Her eyes lost their sparkle of amusement; she picked up her sandwich and took a large bite and disposed of it before she answered. "I was furious."

"Do Ro and Ginnie fight often?"

For the first time she looked surprised. "Never, as far as I know."

"She had a fight with Gray over Sunshine, didn't she? Wasn't Ro in on that?"

"No. And Ginnie didn't yell at Sunshine until she caught her eavesdropping. She went straight to Gray because everyone thought, still thinks, that Sunshine is his problem. I can't even imagine her going to Ro with something like that."

Before Charlie could go on to something else, Constance asked, "Why not? Isn't the hierarchy such that he's the final authority?"

"Absolutely. He makes all decisions ultimately, and once he's laid down the law, that's it. But Ginnie's been trying so hard to make people accept her as an adult. That's the last thing she'd be likely to do, go running to him like a child when things weren't going right."

Charlie stood up. "Did you drive over to Medford that night?"

"Yes. Do you want the names of the people I was with? I'll happily supply them." A snap had come to her voice, although she did not raise it. She would do, Charlie thought; she would not go running to anyone with her problems, either. He shook his head. "I would like to see the original play of Sunshine's. I understand you had to retype it before you could even copy it. Do you still have the original?"

She looked at Constance, who was equally surprised and bewildered. "Sure. We keep everything here." She went to one of the files and opened it, pulled out a folder, and took the manuscript from it. "I hope your eyes are good. It nearly blinded me." She handed it to Charlie.

"Tell me something about the procedure of making a play," Charlie said. "This is the original, Sunshine's draft. Then what?"

A look of infinite, if somewhat pained, patience crossed Juanita's face. "I retyped it and made copies and handed them out. We had our meeting the first of the following week. Gray defended it and Ro accepted that. The next step was for the rewriting to start. That was between Gray and Sunshine. They worked here, at the theater, for a time, then moved to Gray's house to finish. Gray must have typed the final version. Sunshine's such a poor typist, I don't think she could have done it. Then Gray did the promptbook." At Charlie's blank look, she added, "That's for the director, with his notes, his cues, whatever he feels important. It varies from director to director. At that point the play was finished, except for changes that rehearsals might suggest. You know, things like finding out that a certain actor can't say certain lines as written. That always happens with a new play. You can't know until the actors get their parts. And that's that."

Charlie regarded her for several seconds in thought, then asked, "Miss Margolis, what if the play had still been bad? Would Ro have refused to produce it?"

"Of course."

Her phone rang and she hurried back to the desk. "Hello, Steve? It's about time you called back!" She waved to Charlie and Constance, who went to the door and let themselves out.

"What about the promptbook?" Constance asked in the hall.

"Good question," he said. "The play was done at that time. Why did Laura tell Ro Sunshine was rewriting it again?"

"Or why did Ro say she told him that?" Constance asked.

"Another good question." He took her arm and they started to walk toward the rear of the theater.

TWENTY-ONE

A gravel truck had pulled up outside the stage door; two men were leveling a pile of gravel where the lake had re-formed under the hard rain. Charlie watched them for a moment, then closed that door and started for the back double doors. Ro and Ginnie were entering, Ro closing a large black umbrella. He gave it a shake or two. "They," he said darkly, nodding toward the stage door, "were supposed to be here last Friday. Charlie, Constance, can I have a word with you?" He patted Ginnie's shoulder, and she nodded at them all and vanished among the many people who were now returning, milling about.

"Won't take more than a minute," Ro said, motioning toward his office. Constance and Charlie followed him.

He let them in and closed the door, then went to his small closet and took off his coat, put the umbrella in the stand, and came back. He glanced curiously at the folder Charlie carried, but asked nothing about it.

190

"I won't even ask you to sit down," he said. "This is the busiest-possible time for everyone here. Readings, cast readings, rehearsals, conferences . . . It all comes together now or it never comes together. Everything from costume fabrics to upholstery materials, everything needs attention today, this morning, yesterday morning. . . ." He rubbed his eyes, then said more briskly, "I need information. How long does the police routine take? That Draker keeps hinting that he's ready for an arrest, the paper's full of it this morning. When is he likely to do anything?"

"I don't know," Charlie said honestly. "I'd guess not until he gets his lab reports back, and that could be another week, two weeks. It depends on how busy the lab is."

Ro turned to Constance. "I'm really frightened for Ginnie," he said. He sounded near desperation, and looked haggard. "I made her go to lunch with me, but she isn't eating anything. She's a ghost of herself, lost ten pounds at least, nothing to say . . . I'm afraid for her." He took a breath and exhaled the way someone does who is trying consciously to relax. "I want to get her away from here, abroad somewhere."

"What does she say to that?" Constance asked.

"I haven't mentioned it yet. I . . . Will you talk to her? She respects you. She borrowed a book from Jack and read it, your book. That's what she was willing to talk about at lunch," he said bitterly. "Not our problems here, not work, the plays, only your book."

"Ro," Charlie said firmly, "they won't let her leave now. And it would make it look even worse for her if she ducked out."

"For a weekend then! For God's sake, they can't object to just a weekend away. At the coast, down to San Francisco, someplace where people aren't looking at her, wondering, where she won't see it every time she picks up the paper!" His voice was harsh and ragged now. "You didn't know her before. You don't know how she's changed. It terrifies me, that much change in her that fast."

"If she could go away and have it all over when she got back, that might help," Constance said in her no-nonsense voice. "But it won't do her a bit of good to go away and brood about all this,

191

knowing that they might be waiting with a warrant for her on her return."

"You won't help her?" Ro asked in resignation.

"We didn't put her in harm's way," Constance said briskly. "The killer did. And until the killer is found and the police are satisfied, no one is likely to help her. I think she is hanging in there pretty well."

He shook his head. "You don't know how she was before, how she's changed." He moved toward the door. "I won't keep you."

At the door Charlie paused. "I forgot to ask before, but when you found Gray's promptbook for Sunshine's play, where was it?"

Ro looked at the redwood coffee table, then the round table in the middle of the room, and finally at his desk. "God, I don't know. I don't remember. Everything was . . . I can't remember."

"How about the portfolio with Ginnie's sketches?"

"Draker told me he found that on my desk. I had to identify it for him."

"Okay. Thanks. And, Ro, forget about sending her off somewhere. Believe us when we tell you it would do more harm than good."

Ro looked at his watch. "Christ, I've got to get to the cast reading. See you two later."

He opened the door and ushered them out and hurried off down the hallway. From on stage they could hear a concertina playing.

"Listen," Constance said. "It's 'Mack the Knife.' Let's have a look."

They watched from the wing as the musical director, Larry Stein, walked to a young man with the concertina and spoke in a low voice. The man nodded, and when Larry Stein had walked to the front of the stage, he started to play again, this time singing along "When the shark has had his dinner/ There is blood upon his fins. But Macheath he has his gloves on:/ They say nothing of his sins.'

Larry Stein approached him again and they walked backstage together. Ginnie appeared and all three stopped as she talked gesturing with sweeping motions.

"This place is a three-ring circus," Charlie said in wonderment.

"Five," Constance corrected. "They're getting five plays ready all at the same time." She continued to watch Ginnie for another minute. "I don't know how any of them stay sane. Are we leaving now?"

"Let's go home."

"Charlie, aren't you hungry? We haven't had any lunch yet, remember?"

He had forgotten, she knew. She had learned over the years that there were times when she had to put food in front of him, that he then ate with a good appetite, but, without help, might not have anything for days. On their way to the car, when he asked if she had brought any cards in the suitcase, she nodded, and this, too, was part of his system of thinking. He would play solitaire for hours.

That afternoon she watched in fascination as he began to assemble the items he had bought earlier. First he cleared their table and spread newspapers on it. The baking pan went down on them. It was a sheet cake pan, nine by twelve inches. In the center of it he placed a paper plate and surveyed it all. Satisfied, he opened the package of candles, took out one, and laid it down on the paper. He cut off the end of it, a piece about an inch long, and then carved some wax away from the wick. He stood this up in the middle of the paper plate. And, last, he opened the brandy and took a drink from the bottle.

"Good stuff," he said. "Shame to waste it. But here goes." He poured some carefully around the candle on the paper plate. Constance caught her breath sharply, drew back when he struck a match and lighted the candle. "And now we wait," he said. He sounded very tired. She took his hand and held it; his eyes were distant, a stranger's eyes.

They watched the flame in silence. After a moment or two Charlie raised her hand and kissed it, withdrew his hand and pulled out a chair, sat down, his gaze riveted on the steady flame.

Constance sat down opposite him. The flame was hypnotic,

burning so steadily, without a waver. In her mind's eye she saw a small child awakening in her room, getting up, thirsty? wanting to go to the bathroom? wanting company? She had been ill, feverish, probably she was thirsty. She called out and no one answered. She looked in the living room, other rooms, finally the kitchen, and saw her father on the floor, sleeping on the floor. And on the table a candle flame that was dancing in the draft the open door suddenly created.

The back door was open, she remembered from the sketch. Opening the other door must have made a draft, made the flame twist and turn, and the child remembered the fire in Shannon's yard, the terror. She backed out, closed the door behind her, frightened. Constance knew this because Ginnie had done the same thing when she found Peter Ellis on the floor. The child had taken over, repeated her other actions, crying out in the only way she could for someone to see, to do something, to understand. She must have got her own drink in the bathroom, used the toilet, gone back to bed, even to sleep again. Ro found her in bed, wrapped her in a blanket, and carried her out with his own hair burning, the blanket smoldering.

Suddenly the candle flame changed, began to twist to one side, sputter a little. She looked quickly at Charlie; his expression did not alter. Nothing was happening that he did not expect, she knew, and watched the flame. It leaned over, straightened, leaned over farther and fell, and in that instant the brandy ignited in a pale blue flame that covered the whole paper plate. In another moment the plate was burning with a yellowish flame. Silently Charlie smothered it with another plate. He looked remote and rigid.

She got up and went to the bar, came back with two glasses. She poured brandy into them and handed one to him.

"Cheers," he said, and drank it down.

"Vic was murdered," she said soberly, "and no one suspected, no one knew."

"Murder," he agreed. "Why else the candle in the middle of the afternoon? But someone knew." He looked at Ginnie's sketchbook, open to the kitchen scene.

He began to clean up the mess he had made and Constance tried to bring something to consciousness, something someone had said. . . . She sipped her brandy, her eyes narrowed in thought. And suddenly she set her glass down hard and sat straight. "Charlie, she thinks Ro did it!"

He waited.

"Remember the argument Gray told us about between Ginnie and Ro, about the name of the trapdoor on stage? She insisted it was the Macbeth trap and he was insistent that it was the Hamlet trap. She became upset, denied it vehemently, according to Gray. Don't you see?" she cried when Charlie showed no sign of understanding. "In *Hamlet*, the uncle kills the father. That's what she was avoiding that night."

He sat down heavily and stared at her. "I was coming at it from a different direction," he said, "but yours works just fine."

She went on. "He told us he thought Lucy had taken Ginnie to the doctor. He went over there prepared to kill Vic because Vic and Lucy were going to leave. He forced them together, forced her to marry Vic, but never planned on her falling in love with him. He did it for Vic's money. He must have needed much more than he had been able to save, more than he could borrow, and Vic had plenty. He must have been horrified when he realized that Ginnie was in the house. . . ."

"Is Ginnie likely to remember this? Really remember it?"

"I don't know. They keep saying how different she is. Maybe all this is struggling to get through to her. Maybe she should remember."

"Maybe, but not right now. That's ancient history. It's a damn shame she's reacting to what happened when she was a baby. That's what bugs Draker; she's not reacting the way she should." He went to the window and stood looking out for several minutes, then cursed fluently and turned back to her. "I knew it! It just had to happen! It's snowing!"

* * *

The snow did not last long, and it did not stick; in fact, the sun came out for a few minutes before nightfall, but there had been enough snow to act as a goad, Constance knew. She could almost see his yearning for wide scorching beaches and hot sun, palm trees, and tall sweating drinks.

That night they ate an excellent dinner prepared by Mrs. Shiveley at the inn. Afterward Constance read Sunshine's play while Charlie laid out game after game of solitaire. He never won.

"How was it?" he asked when she put the play down with a sigh.

"Dreadful. I don't blame them all for being upset that he chose it. I wonder what the losers were like."

Charlie gathered up his cards and reached for the play.

"Why did you want it?" she asked.

"Curious. What is there about it that made Gray risk his job right off the bat? The play he read was pretty good, I thought."

"It's as if she planted an acorn and he brought up a wonderful oak tree from it. Magic. Only the kernel is there, nothing else. And the kernel is pretty trite, at that. How an ambitious person can use everyone in sight without a qualm of conscience. But read it. Have fun."

When he finished, he put it down without comment and started to shuffle the cards. Constance got out her notebook and pen. He played solitaire; she asked questions on paper, or doodled, or made lists. . . .

Did Lucy suspect him? she wrote, and studied the question as if someone else had put it there. And, she asked herself and did not write this down, what difference did it make now? Why did Ro start the rumor that Ginnie had caused the fire? To protect himself, obviously, but . . . From what? she added. Who would have suspected him, except Lucy, and Lucy knew that Ginnie had not played with matches. Did Ginnie see or hear him that day? she wrote, and now she put her pen down and left her chair, paced slowly. Charlie looked at her with sympathy and asked nothing. He saw that he had played a red eight on a red nine, and gathered the cards together.

After a few more minutes Constance sat down again. "Charlie? Let me tell you what I think happened."

He put down the cards.

"Ginnie heard Ro and Vic that day. They must have argued violently and one of them stuck the knife in the bread hard, probably Vic, since Ro had other plans. When Ro realized that Ginnie was home, saved her life even, he knew that she was a threat to him. What if she babbled about Uncle Ro fighting with Daddy? He covered himself by suggesting she played with matches. The police accepted that, they always do, don't they."

He started to protest, but he realized she was not looking at him, was not asking him a question.

"Ginnie was so traumatized that she couldn't talk, but it was too late, the rumor was there. And by doing that to her twenty-six years ago, he's responsible for the danger she's in now."

"You think he's as crazy about her as everyone keeps telling us?"

"Oh, yes. He did save her, and he did leave everything here and take her abroad when Lucy died. The way he looks at her, his eyes really do light up, his whole face lights up. That's not a cliché, it actually happens with him. I don't think he's putting on an act. That's why he's so desperate for her safety, I think. He knows he's responsible."

"Let's leave it for tonight. Is it a decent hour for two middle-aged people to go to bed?" He held out his hand for her.

Half an hour later he exclaimed, "My God, where did you learn that?"

"I read a book once," she answered.

"Thank God for literate women," he said fervently.

TWENTY-TWO

Ginnie carried a model into Ro's office and placed it on the table. It was the set for Sunshine's play: part of a living room on the right, cut-away flats of walls and a window, mountains in the background, and a café table with a red-and-white-striped umbrella over it on the left. The rock they called a practical rock rose up steeply against the mountains. She backed away from the model and sighed.

"One down, four to go," she said.

Ro walked around it and studied it intently. "It's good, honey. Better than the play deserves. You look awfully tired, though. Knock off for the weekend, will you?"

"I'd better not," she said. "With any luck I can finish *Cuckoo's Nest,* and get a good start on *Witness.* And I have clay drying out for the fireplace for the *Inspector General.* They're coming along. Maybe I'll be able to finish them all before they arrest me."

"For God's sake! No one's going to arrest you!"

She made a hopeless gesture. "Charlie says they're just waiting for the lab reports. They're trying to prove that dirt from the inside of my car came from the banks of the river. Maybe some did. I haven't cleaned it in months, and I go there sometimes. I could have tracked dirt back with me."

"Ginnie, go up to Mount Ashland for the weekend. Do a little skiing, will you? Please. You have to get some rest, honey. Damn the models. William doesn't need them."

"Gray ordered them. He needs them."

"Well, I can fix that. You don't have to finish them. Take a day or two off. That's an order."

She shrugged. "I'm better off working."

There was a knock on the door. Ro snapped, "Come on in," and Gray entered with Constance and Charlie.

"Another great reading," Charlie said. "I don't understand how you can do it. Go from one play to another like that, as if each one is the only one on your mind."

Gray had gone to the table and was kneeling before the model, not touching it. "Wonderful," he said. "It's really fine, Ginnie. Just right. Good colors . . . Can you get those colors in fabrics?"

"I'm sure we can. William and I will go scouting Monday. Or he will."

"I'm on the track of file cabinets we can rent," Ro said. "I think there are six of them I can lay my hands on."

Charlie and Constance exchanged glances and hung back listening. Ro, Ginnie, and Gray discussed the different sets, the problems they anticipated, when Ginnie would have the others done. . . .

"Can you come back around three?" Gray asked Ginnie. "Valerie and I want to block off the sets for *The Threepenny Opera*. You could help."

Valerie was the choreographer, and she, like all the others, seemed to be under Gray's direct orders.

Charlie had been watching closely, listening to how everyone responded to Gray, took his suggestions, which he supposed were really orders even if they didn't sound like it. It was impressive. Gray was impressive. He looked hungry, always dressed in jeans and plaid shirts, sweaters, boots. Too pale and haggard-looking. And very impressive.

Ginnie nodded. "I'll come back."

Ro seemed about to speak, but clamped his lips together and looked at his watch.

"Oh, Mr. Cavanaugh," Charlie said, "could you spare us just one minute? Alone," he added, grinning at Ginnie and Gray. They both looked startled, then almost indignant.

"See you later," Ginnie said, and quickly left the office. Gray hesitated only a moment longer, then also left with a vague wave to no one in particular.

"What I'd like," Charlie said, drawing a sketch from his jacket pocket, "is for you to show me about where you think Gray Wilmot was sitting that night in the high-school auditorium. This is a generic high-school auditorium," he said apologetically. "We're on our way over there in a few minutes, but meanwhile maybe this will do." The auditorium he had drawn was idealized past the point of reality. There was a rectangle with a block labeled "stage" at one end, and a few curved lines at the other. "You see, I'm not sure where the doors are, the clock, anything."

Ro examined it with a frown. "The whole end here is made up of doors," he said finally. "I was about here, at the extreme left, and I guess Gray was at the far right. No clock. There's a clock in the hall outside the office. If there's one in the auditorium, it doesn't matter, since it's all dark anyway when they have a production."

Charlie was looking at the drawing thoughtfully; at last he started to fold it again. "How did you know when Gray left? If it was dark, no clock . . ."

"I said before that I didn't know for sure," Ro said patiently. "Just after nine, maybe five minutes, ten. I'm not sure. And I was bored with the play, not paying much attention by then. I was more interested in a ride than the play, I'm afraid." He looked at his watch, pointedly this time.

"Mr. Cavanaugh, if they have you on the witness stand and ask if you can say with any certainty when Gray Wilmot left, what will you answer?" Charlie asked quietly, apparently engrossed in the meticulous folds of the sketch.

Ro hesitated, then said helplessly, "I don't know. I just know it was raining. And that started at ten before nine. It didn't seem important that night to check the time."

Constance was studying the model Ginnie had delivered. "This is lovely," she said. "So detailed. Right down to fabrics. I suppose it's a great help to William Tessler when he starts actually building the sets."

"He's good enough to get by without them," Ro said. "But it's a help in knowing how much room people have to move around in. Gray can visualize all the action much better with models, I'm sure. I always could, I know. It helps the costumers, the lighting crew, everyone."

"I had forgotten that you have been a director," Constance said.

"And a painter, lighting technician, choreographer, prompter, actor . . ." He laughed. "In the early days everyone had to do everything now and then. They still make drama students do it all, just so they know what each job entails."

"We won't keep you," Charlie said then. "Thanks for your help. Actually, I was looking for Sunshine. Has she been around this morning?"

Ro's mouth tightened. "Probably. I haven't seen her, though. She's scared to death of me, I guess. And I like it that way."

"Well, she's a strange woman," Charlie said, "but sometimes people like her notice things. I don't have an idea of what she wants with us this time. If you do see her, will you tell her we're going away for the weekend? We'll catch up with her Monday or Tuesday."

Ro shrugged. "She isn't likely to come to me for information, but I'll pass the word." He opened the door to the hall, then looked at Charlie and Constance worriedly. "You're really going to take off for the weekend? Isn't there something you could be doing, some line you could be following?"

"Sorry," Charlie said lightly. "I guess we're all waiting for the lab reports right now."

Holding the doorknob, poised to leave, Ro asked, "What if they find the same kind of dirt that's in the riverbank in the samples from her car? Then what?"

"I expect they'll arrest her," Charlie said. "As far as circumstantial evidence goes, that's pretty good. People have been arrested and found guilty on less."

Ro's face was the color of putty. He closed his eyes briefly, then nodded. "I have to go," he said in a heavy voice. "Do what you can for her. I think she needs a lawyer. Not Wedekind. God only knows who hired him and why. She needs her own lawyer. I'm making some calls this afternoon."

Charlie looked at Constance. "Let's see if Sunshine is around anywhere, and if she isn't, let's go to the high school and have a look, and then off to Mount Ashland and skiing. Okay?"

Dejectedly Ro said, "I tried to get Ginnie to go skiing this weekend. Anything. She really needs to relax away from here. But she wouldn't."

"Well, the play's the thing, the show must go on," Charlie said. "I guess she got a good dose of that philosophy from her mother and from you."

"Lucy was a pro," he said. "The best Peter Pan I've ever seen. She had those long slender legs, like Ginnie's, and a young freshness in her attitude, the way she moved. . . ." He stopped walking with them and seemed to be looking through the floor to another time, some other place. Abruptly he started to move again. "We've never done *Peter Pan* since that one time," he said. "Never."

When they parted at the door, he waved absently to them and walked away in deep thought. Constance watched him, then turned to Charlie. "And where are we going for the weekend?"

"Home," he said happily. "To the inn, I mean. First, to the high school."

They drove to the school and entered the main door to the office, where they got permission to look at the auditorium. On the way Charlie eyed the lockers with distaste. There were students in the halls, opening, closing lockers, talking, watching the two outsiders with frank curiosity. "Best days of my life," Charlie said, "were not spent in high school. That last year was pure torture. I wasn't sure I'd graduate right up to the last week. God, those lockers! Trying to get all your stuff in that tiny space! Knowing anything of value would be stolen the minute you left it."

There were a few lockers without combination locks. He pulled one open, empty, and examined it, shaking his head.

Constance was thinking: What secrets were in those lockers? Pot, cigarettes, pilfered change or even bills, illicit makeup, not allowed at home, kept in secret in a locker with a combination lock. Pornographic pictures, books, love letters, stolen test answers . . .

"And here we are," Charlie said, and pulled open a door to the auditorium. It was like high-school auditoriums all over the country, they both thought, not very good acoustics, probably, uncomfortable seats that were not raked enough for those in the back to see the stage well. There were four sets of double doors that could be opened but were now closed. And if Ro had sat over there, and Gray over there, Ro could have seen him leave, Constance thought; and there was no clock visible from the back of the room. It was on the back wall, out of sight of the audience unless they turned around to look at it.

They did not linger long. Back in the main hall, they both were startled suddenly by a loud bell and the instant swarm of students that seemed to materialize magically. Charlie took Constance's arm and pushed her toward the nearest exit, two double doors at the front of the building. The auditorium was at the end of the corridor and there were two more doors that led to the parking lot at the side of the building, but that way was blocked almost totally by students in a solid mass.

Charlie was whistling softly when they reached the Buick and got in. He put the key in the ignition, then looked at her. "There's not enough money in the world to pay me to go back to my good old high-school days," he said. "I think every other year or so we should make a pilgrimage to a school just to keep the memory alive."

"I liked high school," she protested. "A lot of people do."

He nodded. "And people like being sick with a cold, or having poison ivy, or freezing their buns at football games. I know. It takes some of us sane folks to keep you crazy folks from hurting yourselves. Let's go to Medford to shop."

"I can't believe what you want isn't in Ashland," she said tartly.

"But if you sneeze in Ashland, good old Dr. Jack comes bustling around before you've had a chance to throw away the Kleenex," he said cheerfully and started to drive.

In Medford he bought an old electric typewriter. The K did not print and the B lost the upper curve of the letter, and the O was out of alignment. "Perfect," he exclaimed to the incredulous shopkeeper. He did not haggle over the price. They went to a stationery store where he bought a ribbon and a ream of sixteen-pound paper that was grayish and slick.

"All through?" he asked her.

She sighed. "What are you up to?"

"I've had my creative impulses awakened," he said earnestly. "I feel a great restlessness in me, an uneasy feeling of something that needs to be expressed. I have an irresistible urge to write."

They had dinner in the inn that night and immediately afterward returned to their room, where Charlie had already worked for over an hour at the cranky typewriter. He went to the desk where sheets of paper were face down, and read them. There were only two.

"When do I get to read it?" Constance asked.

"Right now, if you want. I think I'm bogging down just a little bit with the plot." He handed her the pages.

She suppressed a smile. They looked worse than Sunshine's, with X-ed out words, type-overs, misspellings. The spacing was atrocious, with hardly any margins, and the speakers' names typed in what seemed a random manner. Now and then they were even centered.

She glanced at him; he was watching her closely, feigning an aloof air. "I am a creative artist, not a typist," he said. "You know?"

She grinned and read the beginning of his play. By the time she finished the second page she could no longer stifle her giggle, and once started, it turned into helpless laughter.

"It is not a comedy," he said coldly.

"I know. It's just that . . . that . . ." Her laughter overcame her again and she put the pages down and staggered to the bedroom for tissue.

"You're hysterical," he said when she returned. "After you pull yourself together, maybe you'll show me what's so funny."

She nodded, wiping her eyes. She groped for the play and took several deep breaths, then read: " 'I will render you all asunder just like the butcher's knife rents the bread.' " She could not continue.

He took the play from her and studied it intently.

"Darling, I'm sorry," she began, but it was hopeless. "Where in the name of God does that 'you all' come from? And how can a knife rent bread? Why a butcher's knife? And—"

"I can see that you're not my natural audience," he said stiffly. "Wayne is talking to Virgil about Virgil and Florrie, the woman they both love. I believe 'you all' is quite appropriate in that context."

"Yes, dear," she said. "And 'render asunder' is fine, really fine. Poetic even. And I sort of like renting the bread with a butcher knife. It grows on you, doesn't it?"

"Why don't you just watch a sitcom while I work at my art," he said huffily.

Her mirth was gone now. Somberly she asked, "What are you up to?"

"Making cheese."

"Oh, Lord, I was afraid of that."

"A mousetrap without cheese is like a drama without characters. It won't play in Peoria."

"Have you ever written a play before?"

"Nope. Have you?"

She shook her head.

"Well, we won't worry about that. I doubt if Sunshine ever did either, and she won first place."

"How much do you think you need?"

"Eight pages—ten, if I can get them out. And a synopsis or whatever it is."

"Okay. Let's examine Sunshine's play. Yours is moving too fast. It would all be over in ten minutes at that speed. I'm afraid we've got a lousy weekend coming up."

"But we may discover unplumbed depths of creativity just itching to be set free. We may start a whole new school of play-writing, Hollywood, television, Broadway! There's no limit!"

She did not look up at him. She was making notes, Sunshine's play open on the table before her. "Charlie," she said absently, "shut up, please."

He grinned and went to the bar to mix them both a drink. It was going to be a long weekend, a hard weekend, but a lousy weekend? He did not believe that for a minute.

TWENTY-THREE

All week Ginnie had worked hard, into the late hours of the night, the early hours of the morning. She was in no mood for a party when Ro called Sunday afternoon asking her over for drinks. Reluctantly she agreed to come when he said that Constance and Charlie were back in town and they would be there. By the time she arrived, Brenda, Bobby, Jack Warnecke and Sandy, half a dozen others were already on hand. Gray was in a corner looking sullen and tired. She nodded to Eric, spoke briefly to William, and then collapsed onto a chair next to Gray.

"He always does this," she said unhappily. "Last party before the final rehearsals start, with no more fun or games until the first opening night."

Gray nodded and sipped his drink, something in a tall glass, not very strong-looking. He glanced at his watch. She knew the signs. As soon as it was polite to leave, he would be gone, back to work.

Only at work was it possible not to think, not to worry, not to grieve. She looked at her own glass, mostly tonic water and ice cubes.

In the first half hour there it seemed that everyone in the room drifted over to ask how she was doing, how she felt. Jack Warnecke's glance was piercing, a thorough examination with one swift look, she felt. And Brenda wanted to hover. She watched Constance move about the room easily, speaking pleasantly to one, then another of the guests, as if she were the hostess. She envied Constance, she realized suddenly. She was so self-assured, so calm and poised, so elegant in her high heels and lovely pale blue silk dress with a jacket, discreet pearls. She looked past her to Charlie and found herself nodding. Perfect for Constance; he was strong and capable, with just enough cynicism, just enough idealism to make him intriguing. He had two faces, one for the world, one for his wife. She liked that. And she liked the way Constance looked back at him. That, she imagined, was what it meant to be in love. Would she ever have found that with Peter? Unanswerable. She looked down at her glass to hide the sudden welling of tears. This was what happened when she wasn't working, she thought angrily, and decided she had put in an obligatory appearance, that she could leave now.

Some of the cast members entered the apartment with Larry Stein; they were giddy and loud. When two of the women started to move toward Gray, Ginnie stood up. "Oh, Lord," Gray said. "Here they come. See you later."

She looked at him in surprise. Most men would love to have two lovely women descend at once. He looked grim.

She looked around for her uncle to tell him she was leaving. Constance was on the balcony with Sandy Warnecke, examining the paintings. Charlie and William were in a discussion that seemed to need a lot of arm-waving. Eric and Anna Kaminsky and Bobby were drawing pictures on an envelope, arguing. She saw Constance open the door to the spare bedroom and close it hastily, move on to the last of the paintings. Ginnie suddenly had one of those intense memories that seemed so silly to keep intact. She had come home

208

from school one afternoon to find Uncle Ro and someone unknown hanging a painting up there on the balcony. The sunlight had been at a low angle, but was bright and golden, and for a moment she had been seized with terror. It was as if she had come awake in a strange house, with strangers all around, speaking an unknown language, doing unfathomable things. The same feeling of terror gripped her lower stomach now, caused it to spasm.

"Honey, are you all right?" Ro asked at her elbow, and she started and knocked over her glass, which she had put down on an end table.

"Sorry," she said, near tears. "I was . . . daydreaming, I guess."

Ro picked up ice cubes and wiped up a few wet spots with a napkin. "No harm done," he said easily. "Look, I want to talk to you and Gray tonight. Will you have dinner with me, both of you? Sevenish?"

She started to say no and he caught her arm. "Please, Ginnie. It's important to me. It's about next year's lineup. I want to do *Peter Pan*, and I want to send you off into the world to do some research on flying, but we need to talk."

"Uncle Ro," she said helplessly, "don't you understand I might not even be here? What if they arrest me?"

His face darkened and his grip on her arm was almost painful. "At seven," he said. "Kelly's. I made a reservation, hoping you'd agree. I'll speak to Gray about it. Can you give him a ride? I might be held up a few minutes. I have to wait for Sunshine to bring over the new play she's been working on. That damn woman," he added sourly, shaking his head. "She called and said she'd drop it off a little before seven, but God only knows if she'll be on time. Anyway, I'll get there as soon as I can."

"Ro," Sara Lytton called, "do you mind if I put on the music for *The Threepenny Opera?*" She was holding up an unopened album. She was to be Polly in the production.

"Put it on," he said. "Haven't heard that album myself yet." He looked back at Ginnie. "Seven. I'll tell Gray you'll pick him up at about a quarter to. Okay?"

She nodded, thinking what the hell difference did it make? Uncle Ro wanted this dinner and would have it. She looked around for Gray and found that he had been backed halfway across the room by Amanda White.

"You can tell Gray to give me a call if he isn't going or doesn't want a ride. I'm leaving now. See you in a couple of hours." The Moritat began and she heard herself singing the words silently: "And the shark he has his teeth and . . ." Ro kissed her cheek and she left the party, the music alive in her head.

"Of course I believe in all kinds of psychic powers," Constance was saying to Jack Warnecke a few moments later when Ro joined them. "It's the organization of them that charlatans use that I don't believe in. What if you can have prophetic dreams, say once a year, and your scientist demands that you have them on schedule in order to prove they exist? That leads to real problems, and, I'm afraid, fraudulent reports."

"I thought scientists all dismissed that sort of thing," William said, studying her curiously.

"You dismiss it if you're willing to discount the evidence of your own eyes and ears and expunge your own memory periodically."

Jack Warnecke was smiling at her indulgently; he looked as if he might pat her on the head.

"Take Sunshine," Constance said, including Ro in the conversation now. "She's highly intuitive. She sees things, knows things that escape most people. Where do you draw the line between well-developed sensory abilities and psychic phenomena? I think she crosses the line."

Charlie joined the small group and put his arm around her shoulders. "Tune in tomorrow," he said cheerfully, "and we'll tell you more. Sunshine's going to read her cards tonight for Constance. We'll see if there's a tall dark man in the future, or inherited wealth, or something. And I," he added, suddenly somber, "intend to grill her thoroughly. She was with Laura all afternoon the day she was killed. But Sunshine doesn't talk to cops." He mimicked her slurred, soft speech. "I'm hoping she'll talk to Constance, after we win her confidence by letting her read the damned cards."

Ro grimaced. "She drives me nuts," he muttered. "She's as crazy as they come."

"Not really," William started and was interrupted by Gray, who said he was leaving now.

"See you at Kelly's," Ro said, and Gray nodded and left. Ro watched until the door closed after him. He turned to Charlie. "If they don't try to pin all this on Ginnie, they'll go after him, won't they?"

"Sure. He had plenty of time to get from the high school to the theater that night, and if Laura saw something, or guessed something, why didn't she tell? Who else would she have wanted to protect? From everything I've heard, she hated the theater and everyone connected to it."

"Blackmail," William said brusquely. "She was trying to blackmail someone."

Constance shook her head emphatically. "She just wasn't the type, from everything we've heard about her. Evidently she didn't think much about money. All she worried about was losing Gray, either to the theater, or to Ginnie."

"But there hasn't been anything between him and Ginnie," Ro said.

"All I'm telling you is what Sunshine told us," Constance said with a shrug. "And she said that Laura told her. Maybe she was looking into the future, anticipating what might happen."

"God, I'll be glad when that woman crawls back into her cave," Ro said bitterly. "She's done nothing but cause trouble from the day she came here."

"Well, we're off," Charlie said, taking Constance's arm. "See you at rehearsals."

Ro walked out with them to the back of the apartment complex where they had parked the rented Buick next to his Fiat.

"Get it running?" Charlie asked.

"Just needed the battery charged. They say that happens if you leave them parked."

"Use it or lose it," Charlie said, and opened the door for Constance.

"You know Gray couldn't have got down to the river the night Laura was killed there," Ro said, frowning. "How do you suppose they'll account for that if they begin to suspect him?"

"They'll say they walked to the edge of the cliff over the park and he hit her there and followed her body down. I looked; it could work like that."

"Bullshit!"

Charlie shrugged. "They really need a suspect with motive and opportunity. They'll cling to the ones they have."

He got in the driver's side and closed the door. Ro waved to them and went back inside his apartment. When Charlie released the hand brake, the car began to roll down the slight grade to the street. He turned the wheel hard at the street and headed down the hill and did not turn on the key until they approached the cross street.

Constance reached out and put her hand on his thigh. He glanced toward her with a small grin, but he was not really seeing her. She could always tell.

"Where is this restaurant?" Gray asked as Ginnie drove out of town.

"Just past Medford. It's good. Or Uncle Ro wouldn't go there," she added.

"He never eats at home?"

She shook her head, then realized that he was not looking at her, but staring moodily out the window. "He won't cook, and hates to have anyone in the house long enough to do it for him. He wants Mrs. Jensen to get in and clean while he's out, and to do the theater cleaning before he gets there. But why he had to pick one this far beats me."

Gray laughed. "Back East we didn't think anything of going miles away, taking an hour to get to a decent restaurant. What's this one, fifteen minutes?"

"Yeah. I think he wanted to go where people won't give us those looks while we're eating. You know what I mean?"

"I know," he said in a low voice.

Neither spoke again until she had parked in the lot behind the restaurant. Ro had reserved a corner table; the dining room, lighted by candles in red holders, was agreeably dark. No one would stare, Ginnie thought; they couldn't even see them. Ro had said for them to go ahead with drinks. Gray asked for a Gibson, and she ordered white wine.

"You don't drink much, do you?" she asked idly.

"Nope, and I don't do drugs, or sky-dive, or anything else exciting."

"Me too. People think what an exciting life I must have, and really all I want to do is work."

"Laura called it an obsession," he said. "She was probably right."

At Harley's Theater, backstage was almost as dim as the restaurant. Two twenty-five-watt bulbs yielded feeble light and made deep caves of shadows here and there.

The stage door opened and Ro Cavanaugh slipped inside, closed the door softly. He went to his office, not hurrying. In the office he turned on the lights, put down a paper bag, and took off his coat, tossed it over a chair back, and went to the desk, where he sat down and put a tape player on a pile of papers. He turned it on. The music was the Moritat from *The Threepenny Opera*. It was turned high. He picked up the telephone and dialed a number that was written on a slip of paper; when there was an answer he asked to speak to Miss Braden.

Ginnie watched with curiosity when a waiter brought a phone to their table and plugged it in. "Miss Braden? A call for you."

She looked about self-consciously and lifted the receiver, said hello. She moved the earpiece away from her head a little. "I can't hear you," she said. "The music's too loud." Uncle Ro, she mouthed to Gray, as she waited for her uncle to turn down the

213

music. When he came back, his voice was clear. She listened, said okay, and hung up. The waiter removed the phone and she frowned at the spot where it had been. "What the hell was that all about?" she muttered.

"What did he want?"

"He's still at home. He said he's waiting ten more minutes for Sunshine and if she doesn't show up, he'll leave. We're supposed to go ahead and order. It'll be half an hour before he can get here."

"Let's get an appetizer or something," he said and reached for a menu.

She moved her own menu and it hit her wineglass, knocked it over. She made a strangled sound and jumped to her feet, staring at it. Again the feeling of terror wrenched her, but this time everything was swirling out of control. Sunlight, candlelight, her father on the floor, Peter . . ." She clutched her chair back for support and would have fallen without it. She shook her head violently, trying to clear the merging images.

"No," she moaned. "Oh, God, no!" She snatched her purse and ran from the restaurant.

TWENTY-FOUR

Ro hung up the phone and turned off the tape player and put it in his pocket. He took from his pocket the small container of sleeping pills Jack Warnecke had given him and stared at it for a minute. Then he opened the bag he had been carrying and withdrew a quart bottle of orange juice. It was half full. He opened it and dumped in all the pills and shook the bottle. He put it on the round table, went to the bar and brought out a glass and put that on the table also. He poured Scotch into a second glass but did not touch it again. He looked at his watch, glanced at the table, and left the office, went to the back door and waited. A few seconds later there was a tap; he opened the door and admitted Sunshine.

"Hello, Ro," she said in her soft voice.

"Come to the office. We have to talk." He turned his back on her and she followed him through the dimly lighted hall to the office. They entered and he closed the door.

215

"How much do you want?" he demanded, standing with his back to the door, watching her move about the room.

"I don't know what you mean," she said.

He went to the table and picked up the glass with Scotch. "I brought juice for you. Help yourself. Sunshine, what exactly do you want now?"

"But I already told you, Ro, you know? Just to be produced, to have Gray be my director, maybe have Amanda in my next play." She poured juice into the glass and lifted it. "We already agreed to all that, you know?" She put the glass to her lips.

"I wouldn't, if I were you," Charlie said then, rising from behind the chair where he had been crouching. Sunshine screamed and dropped the glass. Ro looked stunned. "Come on out, Gus," Charlie said. Gus Chisolm emerged from the closet, and the door to the hall opened, admitting Constance. "The show's over, folks," Charlie said.

Sunshine was staring in horror at the orange-juice bottle. "He was going to kill me? Like the others?"

"I don't know," Charlie said. "What did you intend, Ro?"

Roman Cavanaugh had not yet moved or made a sound.

"I made a case against you almost immediately," Charlie said. "You left the auditorium the night Ellis was killed. You walked over here and let yourself in and he appeared and said he was taking Ginnie away. You hit him over the head and grabbed an umbrella and hightailed it back to the school. But Laura saw you. No one had missed you and you were covered for the rest of the time. Easy. It explained why the sketches weren't on the table where they should have been. Ellis walked over and handed them to you. Back at the school, you stashed the umbrella in a locker and some kid found it and claimed it. Easy."

Ro was shaking his head in disbelief.

"Laura's death was just as easy," Charlie continued. No one had moved. Constance stood near the door, Gus at the end of the desk, Sunshine by the round table. A tableau, well staged, Charlie thought distantly. "She was blackmailing you, not for money, but to get rid of Gray so he would go home again with her. At the restaurant you agreed to meet at your place as soon as you could leave. You got home and hit her with one of those good solid blunt objects, wrapped her in a sheet or something, and stashed her body in the bedroom until you could make your phone calls, have your meeting, and get rid of your guests. Then you used Jack Warnecke's car to dispose of her body in the river. Again, easy. Problem is I could have done the same kind of thing with almost everyone. And I kept coming up against the same reason not to. Motive. Why?"

"He was afraid Ginnie would leave with her lover, you know? He'd kill to keep Ginnie. I read his cards, you know?"

Charlie shook his head. "He knew Ginnie was obsessed with theater every bit as much as he was. All you have to do is look at William and Shannon to see what happens with a union between one who's obsessed and one who isn't. Or, from what I hear, Gray and Laura. I think he just didn't want Ginnie to suffer too much. Is that right, Ro? In fact, you're apart much of the time as it is, aren't you? One or the other gone for months at a time."

Ro nodded.

"But if he put something in the orange juice and wanted to kill me tonight, it must mean that you were right about him, how he did the other ones. I understand that he doesn't like me, you know? His aura's dark green, you know? I promised I wouldn't read Ginnie's cards or bug her or scare her or anything. There's no reason to try to poison me." She sounded plaintive and hurt, near tears. "I wouldn't have drunk enough to die anyway. I can taste pollution. I would have tasted it and stopped drinking."

Charlie nodded agreement. "What would you have done then, Ro? You made sure Ginnie and Gray were covered. You called Sunshine to meet you here; you must have had something on your mind. He would have done something, Sunshine," he said to her. "You see, he didn't have a motive for Ellis or Laura. He didn't have to kill to keep Ginnie, but he thought he had to kill to protect her."

"From me?" Sunshine asked softly. "I promised not to read for her or hurt her or anything."

"From you," Charlie said. His voice was as soft and easy as hers, as if they were discussing a new herbal brew that was only mildly interesting to him. "You were blackmailing him, Sunshine; Laura wasn't, you see." He looked at Ro again and said kindly, "It's really over, Ro. Today, tomorrow, next week. It'll all be out in the open. You can't hide history."

Finally Ro spoke. "I don't know what you're talking about."

"You do. Did you plan to hang all the killings on her? Make it appear she had gone by way of an overdose, out of remorse, maybe? A tidy way to get rid of the entire problem all at once, get on with the good life? Was that your plan?"

Ro shook his head silently.

"When I smelled blackmail, I thought she must have linked you to the killings, but it just wouldn't work that way. Oh, you'd kill to keep what you loved, but Ginnie wasn't at risk, at least not because of Ellis." Charlie shook his head, went on. "Imagine Sunshine holed up with Shannon for a few days," he mused. "She would have ferreted out every secret Shannon had by the end of day one. I kept thinking how strange it was that Sunshine really had been afraid of you, by all reports, and then she wasn't afraid anymore. The day Laura died you bawled her out in public and she ran, terrified apparently. But after that she came and went freely, and you glowered, but she stayed. No way to account for that change except by looking for blackmail, and if not for murder, then what? It must have been something she picked up from Shannon, and Shannon's been a recluse for years, so it must have been something from the past. The only way I can see that you're vulnerable is through Ginnie. It didn't have to be hard facts; hints, innuendos, rumors, suggestions, that would have been enough. And Shannon's been hurting to tell someone about the past. All Sunshine needed to do was mention that she had read the cards for Ginnie, that she had seen a terrible catastrophic fire. That would have been plenty."

Ro made a hoarse sound deep in his throat and Charlie went on more briskly. "You made a deal. She could roam the theater if she stayed away from Ginnie, and you would read her plays, produce one now and then. But deals get undone, don't they, Ro? How far can you really trust a blackmailer? She'd tell one way or another, wring you dry, keep you on tenterhooks. You had a taste of it when Laura said she was rewriting the play again. Sunshine told her deliberately, lied about it, knowing Laura would tell you; she was needling you, waiting for you to come to her, knowing this time she would be able to silence you with a word. You had to protect Ginnie or she might go crazy again. Isn't that what you were most afraid of? That she would become insane, catatonic even, maybe not recover? Weren't you willing to pay any price Sunshine demanded to prevent that?"

Ro stared at him dumbly and finally nodded. "But that's all past history. It has nothing to do with what's happening now, with Ellis, or Laura. It doesn't have to be brought into this situation."

Charlie drew in a deep breath. "I hope not. She was blackmailing you, wasn't she?"

"Yes. Just as you said. About something that's very ancient history. Not about now."

Charlie looked at Sunshine and shook his head. "Like I said before, Sunshine, the show's over."

She looked away from him to Constance, then swiftly to Gus Chisolm, who had not made a sound; he was leaning against the desk with his arms folded. "They're trying to frame me or something," she said in a frightened voice. "You heard him. Charlie made him admit something that's a lie. You're a policeman, aren't you? How can they do this?"

"Has she ever been in your office before tonight, Ro?" Charlie asked.

"Never!"

"I thought not. And tonight she's just been in this section, hasn't she? I was behind the chair the whole time, you know."

Ro nodded. He moistened his lips. "What are you getting at? She's been in the center of the room all this time."

"Just wanted to establish that. So if we find her prints in the bathroom, or the closet, or on any of the objects on the shelves, they had to have been put there sometime in the past. Right?"

"I've been in here lots of times!" Sunshine cried. "In the bathroom and everywhere. What are you trying to do?"

"You weren't afraid to come in, right into the lion's den?" Charlie murmured. He regarded her. "How can you account for your fingerprints in the promptbook, Sunshine?"

"Gray showed me," she said in a near whisper.

"Uh-uh. He didn't. And even if he had shown you the original, the book he brought here was a Xerox copy. Fingerprints were on that copy."

Ro made a deep sobbing sound. Charlie turned to him with a bleak look. "You were dealing with a blackmailer who just happened to be a killer, Ro, and a killer who didn't give a damn if Ginnie got pegged for it. Didn't you even wonder why she wasn't afraid to come here tonight, to the scene of the first murder?"

"No," Sunshine whispered. "It's a lie. I never hurt anyone, you know? I never told them bad things from the cards, or gave them bad things to eat or drink. I don't hurt people. I didn't even know Peter Ellis. And Laura was my friend. I gave her rose-hip tea for her cold."

"You knew that Gray was bringing the promptbook over here that night and you had to see it for yourself, didn't you? You knew that if he hadn't fixed it sufficiently, Ro would have tossed you out the door. You didn't have anything on him yet and you were desperate. Walking into the theater changed your life. Your genius suddenly had an outlet, didn't it? First-prize money, and a production, people who would finally give you the recognition you deserved. You couldn't bear to lose it after coming so close. You used William's key, didn't you? Slipped it from his pocket, slipped it back the next morning when you saw him. He didn't need it to get in. By the time he got here the place was humming, doors unlocked. He never even missed it. You came over here after he dropped you off. You went to Ro's office to read the promptbook, and Ellis walked in on you. You didn't have to know him; he knew you. And you knew he'd tell he had found you here. You didn't have a motive to kill Ellis. You would have killed anyone who walked in that door that night. It just happened to be him. Everything would be taken away from you again, wouldn't it? You knew damn well that Ro wouldn't tolerate having you in the theater at night, in his office. You hit Ellis and ran out the back door. and Laura saw you. A rainy night, strange town, she didn't even know what she had seen until days later when she saw Ginnie and Gray leave the theater, and suddenly she remembered the other figure she had seen that night. You. Did she actually tell you? Was she that stupid?"

Sunshine was staring wide-eyed at him.

He barely paused for an answer, continued. "It doesn't make much difference now. Poor Laura. A or B. Tell Ro, go to the police with what she had seen, what? Offer to trade with Ro? Save Ginnie in exchange for Gray? The point is that she couldn't do any of those things. She wasn't a blackmailer. And she couldn't bear to go to the police yet, to throw away what she saw as a ticket out of here. You lied about her, told us she had come to a decision the last afternoon that you spent with her. She couldn't decide. A or B. Did she ask for advice? That would have been pitiful, a little ordinary mind like hers trying to manipulate a genius like you. Ro saw her as sick that night, but you knew better. You could read her without even trying, the way you can read all the others. You could see she was ready to break. During the afternoon when you were together, did she try to pump you, hint that she knew? It never even occurred to her, did it, that she might be in danger? All she could think of was getting out of here, taking Gray with her. Obsessed. She couldn't see your pain and humiliation at the public display Ro had put on at your expense, treating you like a bum, a nobody. You told her you were rewriting again, knowing it would get back to Ro, planning the scene when he screamed at you the next time, how you'd slip the knife into him ever so gently, give it a twist, a turn, how you would shame him. Her obsession blinded her to anyone else's pain, blinded her to her danger. They're all obsessed, aren't they? Like children to be read and manipulated and used. Somehow you got her to take a walk with you. Another stroke of genius. You couldn't go to your

221

rooming house, or to her house, or to a bar, or anyplace, really. Just out in the open, in the good clean air. Onto the first foot bridge where you hit her and pushed her into the river. Then you had all the time in the world to go up the river farther and pick out a spot to mess up, make it look like she had gone in there. Make it look like someone had driven her there. That was a very good stroke; it really fooled them all."

He stopped, as if waiting for her to comment. She continued to stare, almost unblinking in her fixity of gaze.

"You remember when we met? You called me the Emperor, but you were wrong, weren't you?"

Slowly she nodded. "You're the Magician," she whispered.

"That's right," Charlie said gently. "I'm the Magician who knows all and can do all. I've told you the true story, haven't I?"

"You got some of it wrong."

"Just small details. You write autobiography, don't you? You play *The Climber* is your story, that's why it's so powerful. It speaks the truth. Gray recognized it. The others did too and were afraid and tried to reject it."

"Yes, they tried that," she agreed. "People are afraid of the truth, you know?"

"I know they are. What did I get wrong in the story?"

"Laura asked me to go walking. She still didn't know who she saw that night, you know? Just a poncho. But I knew they'd make her remember. They can do that. Focus on one detail and everything around it, and then on another, and pretty soon you have the whole picture, you know? Or she would have seen me run sometime and that would have given her another piece of the picture, or something else, you know?"

Constance felt faint from the abrupt release of tension. It had grown almost tangible in that office over the past fifteen minutes or so. Now it vanished. She could sense Gus Chisolm folding mentally, and before her eyes Ro seemed to shrink a little, to relax pose that had grown unnatural. At the same moment, she became aware of harsh breathing behind her, on the other side of the office

222

door that was still open a few inches. She moved away from it and pulled it open wider. Ginnie and Gray stood there. Ginnie was ashen, and Gray only slightly less pallid.

Ro took a step toward Ginnie, his hand outstretched. She flinched away from his touch.

"I'm calling Draker," Gus Chisolm said hoarsely. As he dialed, he watched Ro Cavanaugh walk from the office out of sight. No one made a motion to stop him.

"Let's all sit down," Constance said wearily. "Sunshine, are you all right?"

"Oh yes. But she—" She nodded toward Ginnie. "She'd better get a drink of water or something, you know?"

Constance glanced at Ginnie and nodded. She was wide-eyed, ghastly pale, staring as if in shock. Constance took her by the arm and moved her to a chair. Ginnie made no resistance.

"Will you tell us about it all?" Charlie asked Sunshine easily. "Starting with Peter Ellis, that night?"

Sunshine gave him a close look and protested gently. "It started with my play, you know? Gray and I produced a masterpiece, you know? I just wanted to look at it that night, read it again. That's when Peter comes into it. He said, 'What are you doing in here alone? Is Ro here?' And he handed me Ginnie's sketchbook." She paused and smiled. "But you'll have to wait and read it in my new play. They'll let me write a play, won't they?"

"I'm sure they will," Constance said, and she released Ginnie's arm. It was going to be a long night, she thought, after leaving Ginnie. She had better put on some coffee or something.

Gus spoke briefly on the phone and hung it up, scowling at Ginnie. "How long were you out there?"

"They just arrived," Charlie said lazily. "I heard them come in. Isn't that right, Gray?"

After a moment Gray nodded. His color was coming back; it seemed almost as if his face had been that of a sleeper and only now he was awakening. He went to stand by Ginnie's chair and put his hand on her shoulder. "That's right. We became alarmed when Ro didn't show up at the restaurant. I thought his battery might be dead again. We checked his apartment and then came over here. Didn't we, Ginnie?"

Ginnie looked at Constance, who was watching her with great kindness and warmth. Her gaze traveled to Charlie, who looked relaxed and even sleepy. He nodded very slightly, or, she wondered, had she imagined a nod? She could feel Gray's hand on her shoulder squeezing too hard, hurting her. She remembered dashing from the restaurant, finding Gray beside her, Gray driving over here. She felt distant, far away from this whole scene, numb. Watching Charlie, as if seeking a clue about what she should do next, she nodded, then moistened her lips and tried to speak. When nothing came out, she nodded again, and lowered her gaze to her hands in her lap. It started with the new play, she told herself. That's when the nightmare began, with Sunshine's new play.

Then people started to move again. Constance began to make coffee. Gus Chisolm muttered something about too damn much coaching. Gray drew the other straight chair close to Ginnie's and sat down. He did not touch her. Charlie relaxed in one of the easy chairs and Sunshine on the couch, where she sat gazing at the ceiling with a dreamy expression. They waited for Draker to arrive. No one spoke until Sunshine said softly, "Amanda White will play the part of the brilliant young playwright."

TWENTY-FIVE

Draker was as furious as Charlie had expected him to be. His thin face was livid; a tic jumped in his cheek, and his hands clenched and sprang open spasmodically. Wired too tight, Charlie decided judiciously. He said, "I borrowed a key from William and asked Gus to come along just to keep it clean. I wanted another look at the layout of the office here. When I heard someone coming, naturally I ducked out of sight."

Draker snapped at Gus. "Where were you? Why'd you get mixed up in it?"

Gus sighed mournfully. "Just like he said. He asked me to come along just in case he stumbled over something, to make it legitimate, so you wouldn't claim he salted the mine while your back was turned. I was in Juanita's office with Constance when we heard the stage door open and close. We waited until Ro came into the office here. When he left again to let Sunshine in, I ducked in here and Constance waited outside the door."

Draker examined Constance's bright-eyed face and turned away in disgust. "And how'd you just happen to be here?" he demanded, trying to pierce Gray with his hard stare.

"Ginnie and I were supposed to meet Ro for dinner. When he didn't show up, I thought his battery had died again. We came back to pick him up."

All according to plan, Constance thought, when Draker sent his deputies to pick up Ro and finally turned to Sunshine. Charlie was the best director yet, she knew. Together they had worked on this particular play all weekend. Now he had given them all their cues and was content to let them take it from there, improvise as much as they had to, as long as they stayed within his guidelines.

"What happened here tonight?" Draker snapped at Sunshine. "Why did you come?"

Sunshine was still looking at nothing in particular with a dreamy air. "To tell Ro about my new play," she said almost inaudibly. "I'll show you." She got up and moved toward the door. A deputy also moved to block her exit. She ignored him, turned to gaze about the room with a rapt expression. Slowly she walked to the bookshelves, trailed her fingers over some of the books, then went on to the desk. Gus moved out of her way, as he might have done for a sleepwalker.

Sunshine began to speak in her soft, gentle voice. "She knows her books will be there among the others soon. She has reached the first rung and the rest of the steps will be easy now. She sits down to read her own work one more time, and he, the angel of death, enters. He is dressed in black, a black cape, black to the floor, the Shadow of Death. Always there is the Shadow that would drag her back down, but this time she has the courage and the resolve to confront him and to defeat him." She had picked up a sheaf of papers, and put them down again to reach out for an imaginary object. She pantomimed picking it up.

"Lieutenant," Constance said then very firmly, "I think Gray should take Ginnie home."

"By God, so do I!" Gus said heavily.

Brusquely Draker made a motion to his deputy. He did not shift his gaze from Sunshine as Gray and Ginnie left together. Ginnie walked steadily, her back very rigid.

After they were gone, Sunshine acted out the rest of that night when Peter Ellis caught her in Ro's office. She needed little prompting as she went directly to the scene with Laura. "She is looking for the final release, the final freedom. The cards told her: Death in water. Danger in water. Dreams and illusions, fantasies lead to danger in water. Still she seeks her angel of destruction to walk with by the water. 'Ro will make a deal,' she says, feverish, hysterical, wanting only release, the release her angel can offer, no one else. 'I'll tell him I'll swear I saw someone else leave the theater,' she says, throwing little stones into the water. 'He'll have to fire Gray. Not right now, next month. He'll make a deal like that, won't he? Won't he?' Throwing stones into the water, the roar of the water all around, white water racing away with its secrets. 'If he won't,' she says, throwing the stones, 'I'll leave tomorrow. I won't come back. He'll understand the risk to Ginnie, won't he?' Throwing stones, not looking at her angel of destruction. Her finest scene, pale face, drawn, Camille seeking release."

Sunshine had left the desk, was standing at the end of it, gazing down at the floor as if watching the tumbling, swirling water. She bent down and picked up an invisible rock, raised it over her head, brought it down, and then let it drop.

"And the water takes away the ultimate secret, hissing, roaring, hiding all things."

She stood with her head bowed, as if waiting for applause. She was an incongruous figure in a long skirt, her slip showing beneath it, her hiking boots, the many layers of shirts, sweatshirts.

For a long time no one moved or spoke. Finally Draker said in a voice thick with anger and disbelief, "You killed her because she saw you leave the theater the night Ellis was killed? You killed him because he found you in here?"

She looked at him with a sad, sweet smile and shook her head. "I am the conduit for the light of truth, you know? A lens that magnifies the truth for others to understand and grasp. Gray understood my play. If she took him away, no one would have

defended it, you know? He"—she nodded toward Charlie—
"understands a little bit. But not like Gray does. Gray will always be
my director, you know?"

Soon after that, Draker sent his deputies away with her, and then
he turned on Charlie. "You won't get away with it! This is a setup
from beginning to end! You stage-managed this whole charade and
you know it and so do I! And you helped him!" He turned on Gus
with a furious look.

"All's I know is that that woman just confessed to two murders,"
Gus said quietly. "Two people threatened her and she killed them
both. That's enough for me."

"And you," Draker snarled at Constance, "gave her a couple of
lessons in the nut department. It won't work!"

She did not look away, did not make any response, and suddenly
he was again reminded of his Aunt Corinne, who also had regarded
him as if he were a curious specimen. He broke the gaze.

"Lieutenant," Charlie said, not unkindly, "shut up and I'll tell
you what I have. Okay?" Abruptly Draker sat down on one of the
straight chairs. "I smelled blackmail from day one," Charlie said.
"And Sunshine lied about a number of things. She said Laura had
made up her mind about something when Laura was still
undecided. She said she was rewriting her play again after it had
gone into the promptbook. She said she never told people bad
things, when, by God, she was a vulture, a harbinger of evil. She
would have killed anyone who walked through that door the night
Ellis caught her in here. But there's no proof. And Laura's death.
No proof. So I got her over here with Ro just to get them talking. I
lured Ro over with a play he believed she had written, and I waited
to see if he would call her for a meeting. He did. I wanted to force
Ro to admit she was blackmailing him. From blackmail to murder,
that's not such a great step, but without that admission from Ro,
there was nothing. No place to get a wedge in. And she had to
believe I had proof, just to get her talking. She thinks you lifted
fingerprints in the bathroom, off the promptbook, here and there
around this room. And Ro thinks she wrote the play that was
delivered to him this afternoon."

"And not a shred of proof," Draker muttered with bitterness.

"She isn't likely to renege," Constance said. "She's the star of her own play now."

"What does she have on Ro?"

"You'll have to ask him," Charlie said blandly, and they all became silent, thinking, considering. No one made a motion to leave. Not yet, Charlie thought. They were still waiting for Ro.

When Ro walked out of the theater, he paused only a second to look back at the building, then went home. Inside his apartment he took the play from his pocket and began to burn it one page at a time. Now he understood that Sunshine had not written it; Charlie had. Bait, he thought, watching the paper char, the edges curl, then erupt into flames. Bait for him? Or for Sunshine? He was not certain; it no longer mattered.

He waited until the ashes were cold to scatter them; he mounted the stairs and walked the length of the hall, examining each painting in turn. He lingered before the Kandinsky, even touched it lightly, then moved on, making a circuit of his apartment, touching an object here and there, shifting something now and then. Finished, he stood in the doorway and surveyed the living room and nodded. Then he went outside and got in his Fiat. The motor came to life instantly at his touch. Good little car, he thought, in spite of his neglect. He drove slowly through the town, past the Elizabethan Theater which he admired and did not covet, past the wooden bridges in the park, up to Park Drive on the ridge, down past Ginnie's funny little house, and then he headed out of town.

He drove on a dirt road. This was where they used to come for fresh eggs, back a mile or two. Ashland was to his left, perfectly raked up the mountainside, all the lighted eyes watching his performance, center stage, alone on stage. He opened his window all the way, crediting the cold air with the burning in his eyes.

He saw her again, flinching away from his touch, the way Lucy had flinched away. Just like her mother, he thought, just like Lucy. Don't let them bring it all up again, Charlie, he said under his breath. Please let it start with Sunshine and her damn play, with

Peter's death. "Please!" For a moment he thought it had started to rain, but then he knew he was weeping. The way she had jerked away from his hand, just like Lucy.

Ashland was almost behind him; soon the road would curve, go under the interstate, loop back to enter it. "Exit right," he said. "Show's over, folks. I gave you your money's worth. I'm sorry," he added in a whisper, and heard Ginnie's voice from the distant past when he carried her from the burning house. "I'm sorry, I'm sorry," she had cried over and over, and then said nothing. Nothing. And now she knew what she had refused to say then, knew what it was she had forgotten all those good years. And flinched away from his hand. He saw her flying down the hill on her bike, her cheeks flushed red, her eyes sparkling, and he smiled. She should put her models on display, they were so very good. People should see them.

There was only a quarter tank of gas. Enough. Enough. He squealed the tires making the turn for the interstate, and again when he entered it, and now the wind was a hurricane carrying him away faster and faster and faster.

The word came a few minutes after the deputies left with Sunshine. Draker talked to another man in the hall outside the office door and then returned with a venomous expression. Icily he said, "Ro Cavanaugh's dead. His car left the interstate doing over hundred an hour. Are you satisfied? Is that how you planned the grand finale to your show here tonight?"

Charlie looked very tired. "Do you have any more questions for us?"

Draker turned away and shook his head. "Tomorrow. Get out. I want a statement tomorrow."

Gus left with them. On the street beside the Buick Gus said, "I was on the phone when Ro walked out, but you could have stopped him." To his surprise it was Constance who replied.

"He knew, I imagine, that one of them had to leave, either he or Ginnie, and perhaps he felt it was his turn this time."

Gus nodded, unhappy with it, but accepting. "See you tomorrow," he said and left them.

230

*　*　*

Gray watched Ginnie with a growing feeling of hopelessness. She sat at the table in the kitchen in silence, staring ahead, paying no attention to him or anything he said. He had put a sandwich down before her; she had taken a bite and then forgotten about it. He could not tell from observing her how hard she was working.

She remembered the sun slanting through the window, and how, all through her life, now and then a sudden glimpse of sunlight aslant like that had filled her with inexplicable terror. She saw the image of the spilled wine, and tried to remember how many times spilled wine, water, coffee, anything that flowed over a tabletop like that had filled her with the same terror. And the guttering candle. She did not even own a candle, hated candles, in fact. She saw Peter sprawled on the floor and in another lifetime her father sprawled, and now she began to separate the two images, to put them in their own times. They kept merging, and she had to start over with minute details, like the water drops on Peter's raincoat. Gray's raincoat, she corrected. There was nothing that went with the early snapshot image, just her father on the floor, the spilled wine, the curtain blowing in the slanting sunlight. "I'm sorry," she whispered. "I'm sorry." Then she put her head down on her arms on the tabletop and she wept.

When Charlie and Constance arrived, Ginnie was wan, her eyes puffy, and that was how she should look, Constance thought with satisfaction. Completely normal.

"I'm all right," Ginnie said. "Brenda's coming over to stay a day or two. Poor Brenda." She almost smiled.

"I made us sandwiches," Gray said. "We've both eaten. Is there anything else I can do?"

"Sit down," Charlie said. "It's not over yet. Ginnie, your uncle was in a car wreck. He's dead."

"Christ!" Gray muttered. "Jesus Christ!"

Charlie continued speaking to Gray in a practical tone, well aware that Constance was watching over Ginnie, who had gone even whiter than before. "You'll want to see William tonight, and

Eric, I suppose, line up a chain of command to keep things moving." Gray nodded as if dazed. "Snap out of it," Charlie said more brusquely. "All hell's going to break out at the theater if there isn't someone on hand to keep them in line. Who's it going to be?"

"Yeah," Gray said weakly; then he drew himself up straighter, a distant look on his face. "Yeah," he said again, this time without uncertainty. "God, the rehearsals tomorrow! I'd better go." He looked at Ginnie. "Don't worry about things, okay? We'll see to everything for the time being. Just don't worry."

She forced herself to look at him, to hear what he was saying, to return from the great distance she had fled to at Charlie's words. She looked at him, and heard her own voice say, "Yes. But no changes. Everything exactly the way we have it planned. A meeting the day after . . ."

Gray was at the door. He stopped and looked back at her sharply, then shrugged. "Whatever you say." He left.

When he had gone Ginnie turned to Charlie. "It all started with Sunshine and her play, didn't it?"

"I'm almost sure they'll accept that," Charlie answered carefully.

"Before Brenda gets here," Constance said, "we want to tell you who hired us to help you. Let's all sit down a minute or two."

Ginnie looked from Constance to Charlie in disbelief when Constance finished telling about the visit from Dr. Braden and his wife.

"They were right," she said slowly. "I don't want anything from them. My mother didn't and neither do I."

"Your decision," Charlie said. "They'll show up one day and you can run them off or not, as you choose."

"It's another piece of my past," she said. "You've given me back a past I never had. We should know our own pasts, shouldn't we?"

"As much as we can bear," Constance said. "Not all, not always. Ginnie, you had nothing to do with the fire that killed your father. Nothing."

"I know," she said in a whisper. "Now I know. I didn't. For many years I had bad dreams about fires, about running and screaming trying to escape. I woke up sweating and crying. But couldn't have helped my father. He was dead already. There wasn't anything I could have done. You let me remember all that. I don't know how, but you did it for me. I owe you a lot." She breathed deeply. "It's better to remember. It really is."

"It isn't all the way over," Constance said gently. "They'll have more questions, of course. Whatever comes up, remember that Ro loved you very, very much, more than he could say."

Ginnie looked at her hands clenched together on the table. After a moment she nodded. "Yes. I know he did. But no one's going to dig up any more of the past now. Sunshine did it, and it started with her play. The nightmare started with her play, we all know that."

Constance nodded. "I don't think Sunshine will want to share billing with you, Ro, anyone else. It's her new production, written, directed, starred in, produced by Sunshine. I think that's how she'll play it, but just in case, be warned."

Constance and Charlie did not linger after Brenda arrived. Charlie drove down the steep hill carefully. He was getting a headache; it was after eleven, and they had not eaten dinner, he realized.

"She doesn't know it all," Constance said sadly. "I hope she never does."

He looked at her hard. "What else is there? She knows damn well that Ro killed Vic and blamed the fire on her to save his skin."

"She doesn't know that Ro was her father."

"Good God!"

"Didn't you guess? Shannon suspects, but I don't think she really is sure. She won't tell. And it explains why Lucy punished him so severely, not even telling him indirectly for three years that Ginnie had recovered. And it explains his terrible feeling of guilt over Ginnie, knowing he was responsible for the trauma of the fire, seeing her relapse when Lucy died, watching it overwhelm her again recently. He knew he was responsible for so much of it, and he loved her more than he could say. He probably believed the theory about children born of incestuous relationships. He watched for signs of instability, saw them over and over. Poor Ro. Poor Ginnie."

"You're guessing, aren't you?"

"Of course. The way we both guessed that he took that missing sketchbook. It must have given him a terrible start when he saw that figure on the floor, but she obviously didn't remember, so he returned it, tried to dismiss it, and watched her more closely than ever. I'm guessing, but if I were doing therapy with her, I'd act on all this as if I knew it for a fact."

He grunted, remembering being at the inn, Constance's protests about the trap he was preparing. "We both know Sunshine did it," he had maintained. "I know it for a fact and I don't have a scrap of evidence. Probably there isn't any to be had. If she doesn't confess, they'll nail Ginnie for sure. If she's convinced that I do know it for a fact, I think she'll talk, go all the way. I've seen that happen more times than I want to think about. But I need strong bait for Ro to snap at." He had returned to the end of the synopsis of the play he was writing in Sunshine's name.

What he had written was: "When you start unraveling the past, it doesn't stop until it's all out, back to day one. You can't stop it, all you can do is keep it from starting. If you don't follow my orders, do exactly what I want, I'll tell her who her father really is, tell her why she's so crazy."

He shook his head; the headache was gaining ground. He had not consciously thought about Ro and Ginnie, that he was her father. It had been enough to know that Ro had taken his little sister as lover, enough to know that Ro had killed Vic. He had simply wanted to make the stupid play a compelling reason to make Ro jump. And he had. He had.

Now all he wanted was dinner, a quiet evening with Constance and two airline tickets for Hawaii. Hot beaches, brilliant sunlight, mai tais in the shade of a palm tree. Constance put her hand on his leg, the way she did when he drove, and he covered it with his hand, the way he did. The fact that she was now feeding ideas directly into his brain did not bother him at all.